WAKING JOE WHITE

Sarah Prince had come out West six months ago, seeking adventure. She secretly dreamed of daring escapades and passion, but she still hadn't even been kissed. She supposed there would be time and opportunity for that later. She studied Joe's finely shaped lips. Or maybe now, perhaps she might steal a kiss while he slept.

Why was this man so intriguing? she wondered as she lowered her head toward his. He was rough, and fresh, and an outrageous liar to boot. He had pawed her this morning, placing his hand in her hair and laying a finger on her throat and resting his large hand at her waist in an almost proprietary manner. Strangely enough, she could still feel the very places where he'd touched her; a line from the base of her throat to just below her chin. She tingled there, the skin unexpectedly warm and alive. At her waist, if she imagined hard enough, she could still feel the weight and warmth of his hand.

She hesitated, stopping her downward progress when her mouth was an inch or two from his. What if she kissed Joe as she wished, a brief touch of her lips to his, and he woke? What if she laid her mouth on his and he opened his eyes and found her out? Oh, she would be positively mortified.

One Day, My Prince

LINDA JONES

LOVE SPELL BOOKS   ◆   NEW YORK CITY

A LOVE SPELL BOOK®

July 2000

Published by

Dorchester Publishing Co., Inc.
276 Fifth Avenue
New York, NY 10001

ISBN 0-505-52388-4

This book is lovingly dedicated to my new daughter-in-law,
April. Here's to many happy years to come.

One Day, My Prince

Prologue

1888

Deacon studied the reflection in the mirror before him, liking what he saw. He didn't consider himself a vain man, not by any means, but he couldn't deny that he'd been blessed with good looks; he had his mother's fair hair and the green eyes of a traveling preacher, a strong jaw and full lips the ladies seemed to like well enough. A thick, well-groomed mustache he'd recently cultivated only made his face more masculine and striking.

But Deacon Moss was more than a pretty face. Much more. He was a fast gun. The fastest. Feared by many and loved by many more, he lived a good life. The best. At the age of twenty-three he enjoyed a reputation that had been as carefully cultivated as his mustache. What more could he possibly ask for?

In addition to his handsome face, the mirror reflected a woman sitting on the bed they'd just shared. He watched as she slowly pulled one of her stockings up over a shapely leg, and then straightened her blouse so that the nipple he'd been admiring was tucked, once again, beneath green satin.

Deacon took a long breath, inhaling and exhaling slowly. By God, he loved women. Each and every one of them. Well, as long as they minded their manners and stayed in their place he loved them. Rosie was a sweet girl, and his favorite lady in at least three states.

She probably wasn't even twenty years old, but at times her eyes looked much older. Just her eyes, though, and only on rare occasions that came and went quickly. Sometimes he wondered why, what haunted her, but he never asked. It didn't matter. What mattered was today, that he could count on her to be pretty and lively and honest, and she was always happy to see him. She never gave him any bullshit, not Honest Rosie.

Strangely enough, he was always happy to see her, too, though he wrote his happiness off to too many weeks without a woman.

Deacon smiled as Rosie looked up and caught his eye in the looking glass. She smiled back.

"Who's the best, sweetcakes?" he asked,

knowing what the answer would be. *You, Deacon. You're the best.*

But the answer didn't come. Her smile faded a little, and she resumed her lazy efforts at straightening the clothes they'd mussed. She'd undressed him completely, starting at his buttons before he'd even kicked the door closed. By the time she'd finished, he'd been so anxious to get at her he hadn't even bothered to take all her clothes off; he'd removed just what was necessary.

"Who's the best?" he asked again.

Her clothes straightened, her pale hair spilling over her shoulders and down to the mattress, she sat cross-legged on the bed and looked him square in his reflected eye. "You're a good man, Deacon," she said, *still* not answering his question. "I'm always glad to see you come back to Silver Creek. You're so much fun."

In the past, she'd invariably told him *he* was the best. The best looking, the best lover . . . the fastest gun she'd ever seen. "Fun?" It was time to get specific. "Rosie, darlin', who's the best-lookin' man in town?"

She fidgeted, twiddling her thumbs in her lap. "Right this very minute, you mean?"

He caught and held the reflection of her eyes. "Yep."

She squirmed, but didn't avert her eyes. "Why, that would be Joe White."

Who the hell was Joe White? Deacon took a

deep breath and comforted himself by studying his fine profile. "Joe White," he said flatly.

"Yeah." She sighed.

He caught Rosie's eye again. "Well, sugar lips, who's the best lover you've ever had?" He was confident that *this* time she would answer correctly.

"Joe White," she answered in a whisper.

Deacon ignored the fact that his cheeks turned red and a muscle near his eye twitched. "Is that so? I may just have to meet up with this Joe White fella." His nostrils flared, quite dramatically. And then a deep dread settled in his heart.

"Rosie, honey?" he asked softly. "Who's the fastest gun in town?"

She fidgeted, but then she locked her eyes to his and answered, "That would be Joe White."

Deacon jumped up out of the chair and spun to face the whore on the bed, Honest Rosie, who never told a lie, who prided herself on always, *always* speaking the truth no matter how much it hurt.

"Who the hell is this Joe White fella?" Still naked, he stood beside the bed and glared down at Rosie.

But the girl wasn't just honest, she was fearless. Even though his hands were fisted at his sides, even though he was furious at this new development, Rosie stared up at him clear-eyed and unflinching. "I don't rightly know. He came into town a few days back. Came in on his own, not on the train or nothing. He's been asking a lot of questions, about Eddie and Charlie Lockhart and some other fella named Butler." She lifted her eyes bravely. "Eddie got spooked and called Joe out."

"Fast Eddie?" Suddenly, Deacon felt vaguely ill. Eddie was *almost* as fast as he was.

"Joe, he beat Eddie's draw by a mile." Her face positively glowed, damn her.

"Eddie's dead?"

Rosie nodded. "After that, I kinda got to know Joe a little better," she admitted.

"You mean"—Deacon spat—"he came up here to celebrate by buying himself a whore."

She didn't flinch at *that*, either. "Not exactly. I mean, he didn't exactly buy me."

It took Deacon a second to catch her meaning. "You mean to tell me you *gave* it away? You just . . . you just . . ."

Rosie nodded and tried to leave the bed. Deacon gave her a tender shove and she sat back down with a gentle bounce.

He paced beside the bed, thinking. This was not a situation he could ignore. Joe White and all his questions were bound to be trouble. Big trouble. Deacon wasn't above bending the law here and there, and he'd broken it on occasion. A stagecoach robbery here, a small-town bank there. No one got hurt, though. And usually no shots were fired, but for occasional warnings.

Deacon didn't see anything wrong with relieving those who had plenty to fill his pockets when he had nothing.

Right now, even, he was flush with the takings from his most recent heist. Shoot, the woman whose jewelry and cash he'd taken had been so darn pretty, he'd given her a quick kiss before he made his escape. And she hadn't seemed to mind, though the men she traveled with had blustered irately.

If this Joe White fella was asking after Lockhart and Butler he probably was an outlaw himself, looking for employment or revenge. Deacon had considered hooking up with them himself, a while back. Lockhart didn't waste his time on stagecoach robberies. He and his gang hit banks and trains; they went after the big hauls. Problem was, the people who worked for Charlie Lockhart had a tendency to wind up dead or missing.

Deacon Moss prided himself on being a man of action, not a whiner. What he really should do was call this Joe White out and get it over with. But if White could beat Fast Eddie by a mile, that might not be too smart.

Then an idea came to him, and he knew it was the right thing to do.

"Sugarplum, what does this Joe White look like?" he asked calmly.

Rosie smiled, showing him her dimples. "He has black hair, and the bluest eyes you've ever seen, and the face of an angel."

"How tall is he?"

"About six-three, I'd guess."

A good two inches taller than Deacon. "What does he wear?"

"Oh, he wears this real nice black hat, and a fine black leather vest, and denims and tall boots with square toes. He's partial to plain white shirts, but I did see him in a lovely check yesterday, and—"

"Yep, you noted all the pertinent details," Deacon interrupted sharply. "What kinda horse does he ride?"

Rosie's expression went all dreamy and soft. "A pure white mare, the whitest horse I ever did see."

He threw open the door and gave a shout. "Leonard! Isaac! Get your sorry butts up here!"

A door down the hall opened, and a half-dressed woman stepped into view. Naked as the day he was born, Deacon stared her down until she slipped back inside and closed her door. He heard the bolt slam home.

Leonard and Isaac scrambled up the stairs, all but tripping over one another to get to the top quickly. Deacon shook his head. Good help was *so* hard to find.

When they came to a halt in front of him, they looked him squarely and pointedly in the eye. "Whatchu want, boss?"

Deacon felt a momentary sliver of doubt work its way into what remained of his conscience. Some might call his plan cowardly.

17

And then he remembered the way Rosie had looked when she'd spoken the newcomer's name, the way she'd *given* herself away. For some reason that bothered him mightily. Being a reasonable man, he also remembered that this Joe White was a nosy bastard who had killed Fast Eddie.

Deacon placed one hand against the doorjamb and leaned into it casually. "I want you to find some new gun in town by the name of Joe White. Tall fella, black hair and hat, pretty face. Rides a white horse. He's a fast gun, I hear, so you'd best sneak up on him and take him by surprise."

"Deacon!" Rosie hissed from her seat in the middle of the bed. "What are you—"

He turned to glare at her. "You'll shush, woman, if you know what's good for you."

He returned his attention to Isaac and Leonard. Neither of the brothers was too smart, but they were always eager to please.

"Take him to the edge of town," he instructed, "where there won't be any witnesses, and get rid of him." Dammit, he couldn't rest easy until the son of a bitch was dead.

Leonard looked up expectantly. "Then what, boss?"

"Come back to town and I'll buy you a drink."

He closed the door and turned to face Rosie, who had come to her feet and acted like she thought she might leave the room. Probably to warn that pretty boy Joe White.

With a smile, he grabbed her around the waist and tumbled her to the bed. "You ain't goin' anywhere, sweetness. Why, we've just barely got started."

She slapped him lightly on the shoulder. "I can't believe you'd actually send your dimwitted thugs after Joe just because I said he was better than you."

"At every damn thing," he added in a low voice, so she'd be certain to note his perfectly valid reasoning.

Rosie stopped struggling, softened in his arms, and Deacon felt a jolt of pleasant surprise when she tilted her head back and smiled. The pleasant sensation didn't last long.

"Do you really think those two dunderheads can take on Joe White and win? Why, by tomorrow morning you'll be looking for a couple of new morons to run with."

"You think so?" The idea didn't particularly worry him. Leonard and Isaac easily could be replaced, if it came to that.

"I'm sure of it. And then Joe will come after *you*."

He didn't like that idea quite as much. "We'll see." To distract her, he reached beneath her skirt and rolled down one stocking, and then he expertly flicked open a few buttons of her blouse. Yeah, he liked Rosie, he liked her a lot.

He maybe liked her more than any other woman he'd ever met. "Right now, I got other things on my mind."

She smiled and wrapped her arms around his neck. "Deacon?" she whispered. "We can do whatever you want, but it ain't gonna be *free*."

She might've been trying to rile him; he couldn't be sure. He didn't let her little reminder that she'd favored Joe White over him stop him from doing exactly what he wanted. This time he peeled off every stitch of Rosie's clothing, and they didn't leave the bed for hours—and by God, she didn't mention that damn Joe White one time.

The saloon below had quieted somewhat and Rosie had dozed off when a soft knock sounded on the door. Just to be safe, Deacon grabbed his Colt before slowly opening the door.

He stepped back to let Leonard and Isaac step into the room, where they were bathed in soft lamplight. Leonard's lip was swollen and seeping blood, and Isaac limped and grumbled. Dirty, ragged and bleeding, they both looked like they'd been to hell and back.

"Well?" Deacon prompted.

The mattress squeaked, and he glanced over his shoulder to watch Rosie wake and pull the sheet up to cover her breasts. She yawned and stretched one arm over her head.

Leonard smiled crookedly. Isaac said, "How 'bout that drink, boss?"

He congratulated Leonard and Isaac on a job

well done, and ushered them from the room with a promise to be down shortly to celebrate Joe White's demise. When he turned around, he was caught off guard when he saw that Rosie was crying. Not sobbing, all hysterical, but leaking slow, fat tears from her big blue eyes.

Deacon sat before the mirror and grabbed Rosie's comb to fix his hair before dressing and joining the boys. He could see her reflection, there in the glass, as if she reclined just above his shoulder. She sat up and gathered the sheet to her breasts, and a few more tears fell slowly and silently.

He'd never seen Rosie cry before. Ever. She was a tough broad, his kind of woman. He wouldn't let her see that those big, sloppy tears bothered him. He didn't dare.

He smiled widely. "Who's the best, sugar lips?"

This time she didn't hesitate. "You are, Deacon Moss. You are."

Chapter One

Cold. Joe wished, for a long, painful moment, that he could just go back to sleep. There was no pain there, in sleep, no relentless wind. The chill breeze kept him from drifting off again, slipping over and around his prone body like icy fingers until he forced himself to lift his head from the grit that pillowed his cheek.

In a heartbeat he remembered what had happened.

"Sonofabitch," he muttered hoarsely as he rolled himself, slowly and carefully, onto his back to stare up at the stars. Those two weasels had come out of nowhere, jumping him from behind in the dark alley beside the boarding house where he'd been staying. He'd put up a good fight, getting in more than his share of solid licks and heading toward victory, until one of the bastards had hit him over the head with something solid and heavy, and then everything had gone black.

He lifted a hand—it was more of an effort than he wanted to admit—and touched the tender knot on the side of his head.

The night's events came back to him in bits and pieces; slow and gradual as he stared at the black sky sprinkled with countless stars. He'd come awake on the back of his horse, slung over the saddle like a dead man. They were already far from town when he awoke, lost in darkness and silence. As soon as the horse came to a halt, one of the ruffians tossed him to the ground, and then the other . . . Joe wracked his brain to remember . . . and then the other one shot him.

He put a hand to his side, where his flesh ached and throbbed and burned like hell. "Damn," he whispered when his exploring fingers fell on damp, sticky fabric.

Well, this was no fine end for a respected lawman and fast gun. Jumped from behind, taken by two strangers who had appeared, in Joe's estimation, to be less than ingenious. He moved a hand to his thigh, feeling instinctively for his gun, and cursed again when he found it gone. They'd left him alive—which was most likely a mistake—but they'd taken his weapon and left him out in the middle of nowhere without a horse.

A soft whicker belied that last supposition, and Joe actually managed to smile. They might've tried to scare Snowdrop off, but by God that horse was too well-trained to run far or long.

"Come here, girl," he whispered, and she did, lowering her nose to nuzzle his chin. "If I could move, I'd climb up there right now and we'd head back to town and take care of those varmints, wouldn't we?"

Snowdrop whickered again in response, and Joe reached up to stroke her nose.

"Unfortunately I'm not sure I can move at all, much less make it into the saddle."

That was the sad truth, but Joe ground his teeth and tried to sit up anyway. Lying here in the dirt and doing nothing but admiring the stars was a sure way to die. Every muscle in his body hurt, and the pain in his side was excruciating. When he had almost reached a sitting position, the world swam and tilted and he was sure he'd pass out. Well, he'd pass out if he was lucky. There were worse possibilities at the moment.

No one would miss him. No one would look for him. He'd ridden into Silver Creek on his own, not even notifying the sheriff that he was on assignment in the man's county. No, the locals didn't always appreciate federal assistance, and they usually ended up doing more harm than good. Webb wouldn't miss him for weeks, and then . . . by then Joe White would just be another name added to the list of law-men who'd disappeared while searching for Charlie Lockhart.

"You know, Snowdrop," he said as he sat very still and tried to regain his strength. "I knew this was a dangerous business when I decided to deputy for Marshal Webb, and I knew full well that coming after Charlie Lockhart would have dangers all its own. But I figured I'd go down in a gunfight; take a few bad guys with me; die quick. Leave sobbing, brokenhearted women on the boardwalk." He grinned at his ridiculous words, and even Snowdrop snorted. "I never figured on dying like this; slow, in the middle of nowhere, all alone."

The mare protested, shaking her head and snorting loudly.

"Sorry about that," Joe apologized as he worked awkwardly up and onto his knees. "Of course I'm not alone."

He didn't speak again as he came to his feet; he didn't have the strength. Snowdrop's sturdy leather gear and stirrup made a good handle as he made the slow rise, and the mare didn't seem to mind the weight Joe burdened her with as he used her strength to supplement his own.

His hands shook, his eyes refused to focus properly, and his legs were unsteady, rubbery and uncooperative. It would be easiest to drop to the ground, here and now, and drift back into that restful sleep. . . . He fought that urge and kept trying.

Standing at last, he leaned against the mare and took a few shallow breaths. Deep ones, he was certain, would send him tumbling to the ground again, and he was pretty sure that if that happened he wouldn't be able to get up.

Joe turned and placed one hand on the saddle horn and another on the cantle. He stepped into the stirrup. The simple act of raising his leg made him feel like he was going to pass out again. *No*, he thought with the first real touch of panic, *not pass out. Die*.

He didn't want to die here. Not like this. So, with an effort he knew would be his last, he hauled himself into the saddle. If he fell this would be finished, done; he didn't have the strength to try again. He almost went too far over, almost slid clear to the other side and onto the ground, but he caught himself in time. Barely.

The effort of getting into Snowdrop's saddle started his wound to bleeding again. He felt fresh blood, warm and wet, seep over his cool skin. It would be so easy to just lean over and go back to sleep, to rest on Snowdrop's neck and bleed to death.

Slipping off the vest was an effort. Removing his shirt almost sent him tumbling to the ground. Twice. But eventually he did get the shirt off, and with what felt like the last bit of strength he'd ever have, he wrapped the shirt around his midsection, covering the wound with the thickest folded portion, tying the sleeves to make a nice, tight bandage. The vest was draped across his thighs, and he considered putting it back on as a small amount of protection against the cold. Looking down at the vest, it seemed way too much effort.

"Back to town, Snowdrop," he whispered, and then he let his head fall to the mare's neck. His eyes drifted closed.

"By God I'll heal up, find the sonsofbitches who did this to me, and tear out their hearts. You hear me?" Thinking of revenge gave him strength. For a moment.

He opened his eyes and barely lifted his head. "Snowdrop," he whispered hoarsely, trying to give the reins a tug and finding he didn't have the strength for even that. "Dammit, you're going the wrong way."

And then Joe lowered his head and closed his eyes. The cold wind whipped him one time, then the world went black.

Alice lifted her chin and put on a tight smile. "We'll be fine, Miss Prince," she said, as the schoolteacher wiped a smudge of oatmeal from Glory's cheek. "Really."

"I hate for you to miss any more school than you absolutely have to," Miss Prince insisted, straightening Faith's collar absently. "You're such a smart girl. You and Becky and Clara can't spend every day running this farm and neglecting your studies completely."

Alice wanted to scream at the well-meaning

woman. *We have no choice!* Since their mother's death and the desertion of their one hired man more than six weeks ago, the affairs of this farm and the lives of the seven Shorter sisters had fallen squarely on Alice's shoulders. The fine townspeople of Jacob's Crossing wanted to split them up, to send the sisters in seven different directions. All but Miss Prince, that was, who seemed as determined as Alice to keep the family together.

"We'll study after lunch," Alice said calmly. *If there's time.* "And we always read before bed." *If we're not too tired.* "I appreciate you helping out with the younger girls, I really do."

Miss Prince had moved into the house after the death of Alice's mother, Elizabeth Shorter, over the objections of the mayor who had hired her almost six months ago. She'd done her very best to help, though she was oddly lacking in everyday household skills.

Miss Prince had been a great help, but Alice knew *she* was head of the family now. At fifteen years of age, she had responsibilities many adults would be reluctant to take on.

She watched as Miss Prince herded the four younger girls to the wagon her sister Becky had already hitched up. The rising sun made the schoolteacher's red hair turn to flame before the woman covered her head with a plain straw bonnet and set out for town.

Alice headed for the barn and the first of the chores that would fill her long day. Clara worked in the kitchen, and Becky was no doubt already taking care of the animals in the barn and wondering where Alice was.

In this time of crisis everyone had learned to do more of what they did best. Clara, who was barely thirteen, was a wonder at running the household. She was a fair cook, liked everything clean and neat, and did more than her share when it came to dealing with the younger girls. Becky, the second-oldest and less than a year younger than Alice, could be a grump when she didn't get her way, but she was patient and caring with animals of all kinds; especially horses. The barn had become her second home. In the moments when Alice felt panicked and certain this new situation was too much for her, she thought of her sisters and how hard they were working, too.

She had almost reached the barn when something caught her eye. A flash of white in the west, a hint of movement. A moment later she recognized the approaching figure.

"Clara!" she shouted. "Get the gun!" She didn't take her eyes from the horse and the man on its back, afraid if she did she'd lose sight of the stranger . . . giving him a chance to sneak up on the house.

He approached slowly, giving Clara plenty of time to deliver the gun to Alice. The three sisters were waiting, the weapon steady and pointed in his direction, when the white horse and silent rider came upon them.

Alice lowered the pistol slowly, sensing no threat from the large, bare-chested man in the saddle. As far as she could tell he was unarmed, and his eyes remained closed. A crude bandage of some sort was wrapped around his waist, she saw as he came closer. The man slumped forward, and bounced loose-limbed with every step the horse took.

"Is he dead?" Clara whispered.

Alice took a step forward and cocked her head to get a good look at the man's face. Goodness, he was pale! His face was almost as white as the horse he sat upon. "I don't know."

About that time he moaned, low and indistinct.

"Not dead," Becky said curtly. "But not far from it, by the looks of him."

They didn't have time for this! But then again, they couldn't very well ignore the fact that a very ill man had found his way to their door.

"Becky, take the reins," Alice instructed. "Clara, you'll have to help me get this man off his horse."

They both balked, but only momentarily. Clara led the horse to the house, where she and Alice climbed onto the raised porch. From there, they could better get a grip on the rider; and he had a shorter distance to fall when his weight turned out to be too much for them.

The man landed on the porch with a thud and a moan. Clara stepped quickly back, squealing childishly as she wrinkled her nose at the wounded man. Becky snorted once, then ignored her sisters and the unseated rider to lead the white horse to the barn. Before they'd gone far, Alice heard her sister's soothing voice; her kind words directed at the fine animal.

With the man lying prostrate on the porch, he looked impossibly big, long and solid. From here it was easy to see that his bandage had once been a shirt, and that it was stained with dried blood and a small spot of fresh blood, as well.

"Should I ride to town and get the sheriff?" Clara asked, her voice small and a little scared. She never offered to run errands to town, but seemed anxious to get away from the stranger.

Alice shook her head. The others had their chores but her responsibilities were greater, more burdensome. She had to take care of everything, to make the decisions, to see that the Shorter sisters stayed together and well and safe.

"No," she said without hesitation. "He's too badly hurt to be carried to town, so it would just be a waste of time. If he's still alive tomorrow, I'll have Miss Prince deliver a message to Sheriff Potter."

She doubted the man would be alive at sunset, much less tomorrow. They'd have to bury him, she thought with a sad sigh. Goodness, she hated burying people. She had lain to rest her father five years ago, her uncle four months ago, her mother. . . . She still couldn't think about her mother without tears threatening, so she dismissed the memory as quickly as possible.

"Let's get him into the house," she said pragmatically. "You take the feet end," she said, slipping her hands under the stranger's armpits and dragging him toward the front door.

There were hands everywhere; little, warm hands on his face and his hands and his legs, fingers that poked at the wound in his side. He should have protested, but he didn't have the strength.

Joe barely opened one eye, and in spite of the pain he was quite sure, for a moment anyway, that he'd died and gone to heaven. Three fair-haired angelic little women, dressed in calico, hovered over the soft bed he lay upon. One of them was examining his wound; one checked for fever with a soft hand on his forehead, and another straightened the blanket that covered his legs.

"Dammit, Alice," the one at the foot of the bed whispered. "I can't believe you brought him inside."

It was not heaven, after all, unless angels were given to cursing.

"Watch your mouth, Becky Lee Shorter. That's no kind of language for a lady."

Becky Lee Shorter snorted.

The little one who continued to feel his forehead, as if a blazing fever might erupt at any moment, kept her eyes on the one doing the doctoring. "Is it bad?"

"Yes," the one called Alice answered softly. "But the bullet went straight through, so I won't have to go in and dig anything out."

The idea of that child performing surgery on him brought Joe fully awake. "What the hell do you think you're doing?" he growled, his voice much softer than he'd intended for it to be.

The hand at his forehead was finally removed, as that little caretaker jumped back with a squeal. The child at the end of the bed, the one with the smart mouth, backed toward the door. Only the one who'd been examining his wound, the one they called Alice, seemed unaffected.

"Trying to save your life," she said, looking him square in the eye. "Would you like us to stop?"

He had a feeling that if he said yes she'd do just that. Drag him from this nice, soft bed, drape him over Snowdrop, and send him on his way.

"My horse—" he said.

"She's in the barn," Becky said, her voice and her eyes softening a little. "As soon as she's cooled down I'll feed and water her. She's beautiful."

Joe actually smiled. "Yes, she is. Will you take care of her for me?" *Until I'm healed. If I don't make it.*

"Sure. What's her name?"

"Snowdrop."

Becky smiled. "What a wonderful name."

The name had been, on occasion, more than a little embarrassing. It was hard to strike terror into the hearts of bad men while riding a horse named Snowdrop. "My sister named her, years ago."

It was some sort of delirium, surely, that made him remember so clearly the day his sister had given Snowdrop to him. The day he'd ridden away from home without looking back. It was delirium, surely, that made him ache for the only family he'd ever known. That was stupid. A waste of time. Those days were gone.

Alice appeared to be in charge, and she cleared her throat to silence the room and interrupt Joe's oddly sentimental memories. "Your wound looks pretty bad, but you might make it."

"Thanks for the encouragement," Joe drawled.

Even though Alice looked to be little more than a child, she had a take-charge gleam in her eye, a no-nonsense severity in her posture. When she told the other girls to get back to their chores, they didn't argue with her.

As the two girls left the room, Alice turned her eyes to him. She took a deep breath, and seemed to be pondering the situation. Hard and long.

"What's your name?" she finally asked.

"Joe White."

"My name is Alice Shorter," she said primly. "Nice to meet you."

He nodded, as best he could.

"Mr. White," she said, and the hairs on the back of his neck stood up at the honeyed tones coming from her mouth. This was the voice of a female who wanted something and wanted it bad; he recognized the sound too well. "I think I can save your life. If I do, will you do me a tremendous favor?"

Chapter Two

Her day was long enough, Sarah thought as the Shorter house came into view, without adding the long trip to and from the farm on the outskirts of town. But what choice did she have? Alice might think differently, but it simply wasn't safe or proper for the girls to be living on their own.

The house she approached was large and well-built. It wasn't grand, not by any stretch of the imagination, but was a sturdy, spacious home, a testament to the prosperous ranch Willem Sheridan had once built here. The stock and much of the land was gone, now, sold off over the past few years, but the fine home remained untouched by the illness and bad fortune that had befallen the family who lived in it.

If only the judge would agree to give her custody of the girls. Unfortunately, it was unlikely he would agree, especially since Mayor Drake had promised to vehemently oppose any efforts she might make in that direction. Oh, that man infuriated her! He'd proposed marriage half a dozen times, and had merely smiled when she'd turned him down; as if her refusal was part of a game. In truth, she despised the man who'd given her the job as schoolteacher for Jacob's Crossing. He was unctuous and beady-eyed, overbearing and much too persistent, and he insisted on treating her with condescension, as if she did not know her own mind; not exactly qualities she had in mind for her future husband.

In the back of the wagon, Faith and Glory talked with great enthusiasm about the story they were reading at school. At five years of age, Glory was the youngest of the Shorter girls, but she was a quick learner and could read almost as well as Faith, who was one year older. Evie had curled up on a blanket at the rear of the wagon bed and was taking a nap as she did every afternoon on the ride home, the sleepyhead. Even though her sisters teased her about an eight-year-old still taking an afternoon nap, she continued the practice. Dory, who, at eleven years old, was mortified that she'd been sent to school with the little ones instead of asked to stay home and help her older sisters with the chores, rode silently in the seat beside Sarah.

Elizabeth's death had been hard on all the girls, but they'd stood strong together, as a family, as sisters. If the judge split them up and sent them in all directions, it would be a true miscarriage of justice. Still, with no family to take them in, it seemed a forgone conclusion that when the judge made his next scheduled stop in Jacob's Crossing that's exactly what would happen.

Sarah tried not to be discouraged. She had at least three weeks to come up with a solution of some sort. There had to be a way to keep the girls together.

"Here we are," she called loudly, for Evie's benefit. The little girl stirred and lifted her head as Sarah brought the wagon to a stop near the steps to the front porch. Becky would be out shortly to care for the animals, and with Dory's help she would put the wagon away.

Alice insisted that the Shorter sisters didn't need a guardian, and in a way she was right. The girls kept the small farm running smoothly, though the older sisters worked much too hard. By now, Clara would have supper cooking, and Becky would have the animals taken care of, and Alice would've seen to the small garden—all they could manage without the help of the hired man who'd quit after Elizabeth's death. Since it was Thursday, the laundry would be done. The house would be clean, the lamps would be filled, the meal would be plentiful and delicious. And not one of the girls would utter a word of complaint.

This afternoon, though, something was different about their arrival. Usually everyone was hard at work, and barely noted the return of the younger girls and their teacher. But today the three older girls stood in the front parlor, hands clasped, eyes wide, faces toward the door as if they'd been standing there waiting.

"Good afternoon, Miss Prince," Alice said with a wavering smile.

Becky headed toward the door, grabbing Dory's arm as she passed. "Let's take care of the horses, shall we?" she said, shifting her eyes in Sarah's direction as she passed. "Evie, you too," she added.

"Come along," Clara said sweetly, stepping from her eldest sister's side to herd the two youngest girls to the kitchen. "I have something important to tell you."

Sarah started to follow the little ones into the kitchen, curious about this important news, but Alice stopped her with a soft voice.

"Miss Prince, if I may have a moment."

Something about the tone of Alice's voice disturbed Sarah. It was so formal, so distant. She wished that Alice would act like a child again; smile, scream, cry. She'd turned into a perfectly composed little lady overnight, and it simply wasn't natural.

"Certainly," Sarah said, setting her books on the table by the sofa. "Is something wrong?"

"Of course not," Alice said primly. "As a matter of fact, we've had a bit of unexpected good fortune today." She tried that wavering smile again. Something about it was not right. "It's difficult to explain. Why don't you come with me?"

The interior of the Shorter house was plain but comfortable, with big rooms and plenty of them. Elizabeth's brother had once planned on having a large family, but when his wife died giving birth, twenty years ago, Willem Sheridan had given up on that hope and settled in this big house as a lonely widower. Over the years he'd prospered as a rancher, building his empire and then watching it fall apart. When his widowed sister and her seven daughters had moved in more than two years ago, his big house had been filled at last.

What had once been an empire was now a small farm—nothing fancy, but sufficient for a woman and her seven girls. It had been a secure home for life, and they'd had a few dollars hidden away for the hard times that always came, sooner or later. Everything would've been fine, if only the hard times hadn't been Elizabeth's death.

Alice led Sarah to Willem's room, the only bedchamber on the ground floor. It was positioned on the other side of the foyer, directly across from the parlor. No one had slept there since Willem's death a few months earlier. The girls preferred their two shared rooms above stairs, and Sarah had settled into the third bedroom upstairs—Elizabeth's old chamber—for the duration. She wanted to be near the girls at night, in case they woke and needed her.

When Alice stopped before the downstairs bedroom she took a deep breath, as if to calm herself. She opened the door slowly and peeked inside before swinging it wide open.

Sarah hadn't known what to expect, but she certainly hadn't expected *this*. A man filled the big bed. A long, wide, dangerous-looking man. His eyes were closed, his face was unnaturally pale, and a wide white bandage had been wrapped around his midsection.

And still he looked dangerous. It was the size of him, she supposed, or his bare, hairy chest, or the stubbled jaw he clenched even in sleep. Black hair, neatly trimmed and slightly mussed by his pillow, contrasted sharply against his pale face.

Without warning he opened his eyes, and the bluest, hardest, most penetrating gaze she had ever seen, set on Sarah in a very disturbing way.

"Miss Prince," Alice said almost nervously. "I'd like you to meet my father, Joe Shorter."

* * *

Joe took shallow breaths. Every bit of air that entered his lungs hurt, but by God at least he could breathe. He could thank Alice and her fine doctoring for that.

"You must be the schoolteacher that's been helping out with my girls," he said, every word an effort.

Frowning sourly, the red-haired woman took a single step toward the bed. "Alice," she said, addressing the child while she kept her eyes pinned on him. "Your father is dead. He's been gone five years."

"Well, you see, he's not really dead. Mama just told everyone that because she was so embarrassed about him deserting us. Once she figured he wasn't coming back, it was just easier to tell everyone he was dead."

Fire flashed in Miss Prince's dark brown eyes. Well, the story certainly didn't make him out to be a hero, but it would buy the girls some time.

"Why did he come back?"

"He heard about Mama, and came home to take care of us, isn't that right, Poppy?"

Joe watched as Miss Prince's eyes and lips narrowed. She didn't believe this story, not for one minute.

"That's right, sweetheart." He kept his eyes pinned on the prissy schoolteacher Alice had told him so much about.

Sarah Prince was the kind of woman he'd

never liked; prim and proper, looking down her nose at those she considered beneath her. Like him. Her prudish dress was buttoned so high and so tight she likely couldn't breathe any easier than he could. Still, the severity of her attire couldn't possibly disguise the fact that beneath the plain green muslin she possessed nicely rounded hips, a tiny waist, and a world-class pair of tits.

His eyes lingered there, only for a moment, and then he looked her in the eye. He saw disgust there, real holier-than-thou loathing. He couldn't allow her to see his own distaste. Not now. He could do this for Alice. "Unfortunately, I was bushwhacked on my way here, and some sonofa—" he caught himself just in time. "Some son of a gun shot me."

Miss Prince's eyes lit on the bandage that circled his waist. "Perhaps we should send for the doctor—"

"No!" Alice said, her voice rising sharply. "That sorry drunken sawbones couldn't save my mother, and he is *not* touching my father!" Her lower lip trembled and she lowered her voice. "Even *I'd* make a better doctor."

For the first time since he'd met Alice Shorter, just hours ago, Joe saw a spark of fear in her eyes. She hadn't been afraid of him, she hadn't so much as flinched as she'd cleaned and bandaged his wound, but the very mention of the doctor terrified her.

"I don't need a doctor," he agreed. "Alice has

been taking good care of me. She's all the doctor I need."

Miss Prince stood at the foot of the bed and looked down at him. Disbelief and disdain were evident on her prissy face. It must be hard to look so all-fired dignified with those freckles sprinkled across a pert little nose, he found himself thinking. She managed, though. "Elizabeth told me her deceased husband's name was Albert."

Joe shot a quick glance at Alice. They'd decided to stick with his own first name, something he'd be sure to answer to, since no one in Jacob's Crossing had actually known Albert Shorter. The real man had died long before the girls' journey from Georgia to Texas. Apparently, Elizabeth Shorter and this prim schoolmarm had been better friends than Alice had known.

He planted his eyes unflinchingly on Miss high-and-mighty Prince. "Albert Joseph Shorter," he said. "For the past five years I've been going by Joe."

She didn't so much as blink. "Elizabeth said her husband was a plain man, with a pot belly and a round face."

"Riding the range will take the fat off of you, that's for sure," he said with a half-smile. "And are you saying, Miss Prince, that my face isn't plain?"

She simply pursed her lips and stood straighter and taller. "She said Albert stood no taller than she, and Elizabeth was about five-foot-six. As you are injured I will not ask you to stand, Mr. . . . Shorter," she almost snorted his pretended name, "but it is quite clear to me that you are much taller than five-foot-six."

"I had a late growth spurt," he said, without a smile this time.

"Elizabeth also said—"

"Miss Prince," Joe interrupted, his patience with the irritating woman gone. "I don't have to prove myself to you. My girls know who I am, and that's enough."

"But—"

"That's enough," he said softly.

He heard the others coming. They'd been told by now about the ruse. Miss Prince was about to be in the minority. Eight to one.

They streamed through the door, one small, beribboned girl after another. They all had hair some shade of blonde, from the palest pale to a hue the color of wheat, and they were all dressed in colorful calico. Their voices rose and fell with excitement as they streamed into the room and to the bed.

"Poppy!" One little fair-haired child cried with a bit too much enthusiasm. A budding actress, he supposed. "You're home!"

The two littlest ones came to the side of the bed and stared at him wide-eyed. Their cheeks, still plump with baby fat, were pink and pale and perfect. "Hello, Poppy," the smallest one said softly. "You probably don't remember me, but I'm Glory." Her hair was so pale it was almost white, and it shimmered in the sunlight that streamed through the window. "I was just a baby when you left, so I don't remember you, either."

He laid a hand on her shimmering hair and returned her smile. It was hard not to. "Of course I remember you, Glory," he said for Miss Prince's benefit. Then he turned his eyes to the honey-haired child who stood beside Glory. Alice and Clara had filled him in on the basics. "And you're my Faith."

Miss Prince backed away, and the bed was surrounded by seven pretty little ladies.

Alice turned to Miss Prince. "It was so kind of you to help out, but now that our father's returned, there's no reason for you to continue to live all the way out here. I know it's been an inconvenience for you to stay so far from town."

The prissy schoolteacher looked like she still had her suspicions. "Well, it's too late to pack my things and return to town tonight. I'll move back to the boardinghouse tomorrow," she said. The girls were so excited that Joe was certain he was the only one who heard Miss Prince's softly spoken "maybe."

Sarah sat in a parlor rocker that gave her full view of the door to the room where Joe Shorter—or whoever he was—slept.

Well, he hadn't gotten much sleep this

evening, that's for sure. The girls had been streaming in and out of that bedroom for the past several hours, giggling, laughing, talking. The little ones were asleep now, and only Alice, Becky, and Clara remained awake. They were, all three of them, in with their long-lost *father*.

She didn't know who this impostor was, but she was quite certain the wounded man was no relation to the Shorter girls. All her earlier arguments stood, but there was one she'd never had the chance to present.

Elizabeth's husband, Albert, had been fifteen years older than she. When he'd died five years ago he'd been nearly fifty years of age. The man in that bed *might* be thirty; he was certainly nowhere close to the fifty-five he'd have to be to be the girls' father.

It was likely that no one in Jacob's Crossing knew as much about the late Albert Shorter as Sarah did. She and Elizabeth had become friends quickly after Sarah's arrival in town. They'd shared tea on many occasions, visited often, and talked about the girls and the city and everything else in their lives. Elizabeth was the only person around who knew how and why Sarah had found her way to Jacob's Crossing, and Sarah was quite sure Elizabeth hadn't shared her memories of her beloved late husband with anyone else. She'd been such a private person, so shy and quiet.

Clara and Becky left the room together, and spotting Sarah in the parlor they said a bright goodnight. A moment later, Alice left the room as well, closing the door softly behind her.

When the girls were all safely upstairs, Sarah rose from her chair and headed for the closed door. Yes, there was something about the man in that room that frightened her, and it was highly improper for her to go into his bedroom unescorted. But she hadn't come so far in life by being timid.

Without knocking, she opened the door. The man on the bed opened his eyes, barely, and glared at her.

"What do you want?" he muttered, so exhausted she could see the weariness in his eyes, in the deliberate way he moved and spoke.

All she had to do was look at him to know he and Elizabeth had never been together. Elizabeth Shorter had been a fine, gentle, sweet woman. This ruffian didn't know what the words fine or gentle meant.

"I want you to listen to me, just for a moment, Mr. . . . Mr. . . ."

"Why don't you call me Joe?"

She stopped at the end of the bed and looked down at him, trying to make her own glare as disturbing as his. "All right, *Joe*. Let me begin by saying that I don't know who you are, but I do know, to my very bones, that you are not Albert Joseph Shorter."

"We've been over this—"

"However," she interrupted. "I see no reason

to share my misgivings with the rest of the town, or with the judge when he comes to town in three weeks to decide who will be guardian to the girls."

She had his attention. My goodness, the full effect of his glare warmed her to the bones, and chilled her at the same time. It was quite disturbing.

She refused to be daunted by something as simple as cold blue eyes. "I imagine this is a scheme either you or Alice cooked up, and given the circumstances I can't in good conscience share what I know to be the truth with the judge."

"And why is that?"

"What has Alice told you?" she asked. "Not much, I'd wager. She seems determined to handle every crisis alone. It's bad enough that they would consider splitting the family up, but the people who have offered to take the girls in . . ." she shuddered at the thought. "It's unthinkable. The saloon owner and his wife have *magnanimously* offered to take Alice and Becky. Can you imagine what that life would be like for them? Working in a saloon? I've led a sheltered life, Mr. . . . Joe, but even I can imagine."

It was clear, from the tightening of his jaw, that he could imagine, too.

"The hotel owner and his wife have offered to take in Clara and Dory, stating that they'll be able to work off the debt for their room and board by cleaning and cooking." Her anger came through in her voice. "And the mayor has located an orphanage in Dallas that will take in Evie and Faith. An orphanage! They'd send them away from their sisters to an orphanage!"

On the bed, Joe worked slowly and steadily into a sitting position, though it obviously pained him. She tried to ignore the way the muscles in his arms and his chest bunched and hardened, a fascinating play such as she'd never seen before. Goodness, until she'd come West she'd never seen a man's chest at all, and the few she had seen since her arrival had been less than magnificent. Scrawny, pale, hairless. As she watched, she found herself fascinated, only for a moment, by a pair of tiny, tight, flat nipples on that utterly masculine chest.

"And what about Glory?"

When he spoke, Sarah lifted her eyes and locked them on his, trying to shake off her improper thoughts and determined to make sure this man noted the severity of the situation. "Mr. and Mrs. Halberg own the adjoining ranch, and they've expressed interest in purchasing this farm. Whatever small amount he agrees to pay will be used to settle debts, and the rest would most likely go to the city council, even though they claim that if there's any money left it will be divided between the girls."

"Can't they make him pay what the land is worth so the girls will get some money?"

Sarah pursed her lips. "The mayor has a hand in this, and I swear he's. . . ." She took a deep breath. "But that's not the worst of it. You see, the Halbergs lost a daughter to pneumonia over a year ago," she said softly. "Glory apparently looks a bit like little Nancy Halberg did, and is about the same age Nancy would be. Mrs. Halberg wants to adopt Glory and change her name to Nancy."

"Well, that's right creepy," Joe said in a low, raspy voice.

"Yes, it is," Sarah agreed. "I tried to convince the town council and the mayor and the sheriff to recommend that I be guardian to the girls until they reach majority, but they have flatly refused. Without the recommendation of someone in authority, the judge won't hear of allowing a single woman to take charge of the girls. Not when the town council has its own plan."

"Thanks for filling me in, Sarah."

She raised her eyebrows at his improper use of her given name.

She let the impropriety slide, for the moment. She had to learn to accept that things were different out West. Here people were lazier, less formal, more open. That's why she was here, right?

"I just want to make sure you understand one thing," she said softly, setting her eyes on him in a way that guaranteed he'd take her seriously. "If you hurt these girls in any way, I will see that you pay dearly for it."

"Thanks for the warning," he said with a wan

smile that showed he didn't feel at all threatened by her.

She smiled back, and his grin faded. "Tomorrow morning, I want you to suggest to Alice that I stay on here a while longer, at least until you're fully healed."

"Why would I do that?"

"Because the girls need me."

He looked, for a second or two, as if he were thinking of arguing. His jaw clenched and his mouth thinned. And then he nodded his head. "Why not?" A leering grin worked its way across his face. "Sure. Stick around, Sarah darlin'. In a few days I'll have my strength back, and I have to admit it'll be real nice to have a woman living right here under my very own roof." He winked at her and patted the mattress at his side. "Why don't you come on over here and have a seat, and we'll talk about it a while longer?"

If she hadn't had her head about her she might have panicked, but Sarah was nothing if not pragmatic. Men who looked like this one didn't want women like her. Hard, handsome, full of life, men like Joe wanted pretty, funloving girls, not plain, conservative women.

He was just trying to scare her off. So unwell he looked almost as pale as the sheet he lay upon, he thought a few unpleasant advances might scare her away from this house and these girls.

One thing Sarah had learned in her months

in Texas was that subtlety was lost on its inhabitants. Civility and good manners were often wasted here, especially on the men. This place and its people were unlike anything she had ever known. Still, she'd never been one to back down from a challenge. She had learned well.

"Touch me," she said softly, "one time, and your friends will be calling you Stumpy for the rest of your days."

His blue eyes got wide for a second, and then he began to laugh hoarsely. He grabbed the wound at his side and stopped laughing suddenly, an expression of pain flitting across his handsome face.

"Oh God, you're trying to kill me," he whispered as he eased himself back down into the mattress. "Don't make me laugh. It hurts like hell."

Satisfied, Sarah turned to leave. It was long past her bedtime. She made sure her own amused smile didn't bloom until the door was firmly closed behind her.

She heard Joe chuckle one more time, but the laughter didn't last long. It was followed by a low curse.

Chapter Three

Dammit, it was cold again. There was no wind this time to whip his hair and dance around his body, but he felt a terrible coldness that cut to the bone. Joe shivered uncontrollably, and pulled the blanket that covered him to his chin. He didn't bother to try and open his eyes. That simple task seemed too much of an effort. His bones were icy but his skin was hot; he could feel it, as if his flesh was on fire.

A soft, feminine hand brushed away the hair at his forehead and settled lovingly there. There was comfort in that cool, tender hand, comfort that took away some of the chill.

"Tess?" he whispered, knowing that no one else would ever touch him this way; soft and gentle and sweet.

From above he heard a soft, feminine sigh, followed by a low whisper. "He has a fever," someone, not Tess, said.

He opened his eyes to watch the woman who hovered over him, and when he saw her it all came rushing back. The ambush, the gunshot, the Shorter sisters.

And Sarah Prince, who continued to press her hand to his forehead.

She looked different this morning, like she'd been interrupted in the process of getting dressed. Her white blouse was severe, but she'd left three buttons at her slender throat unfastened so he could see the soft skin and the beat of her heart there. Even more startling to his battered senses, her hair hung loose, a long, coppery mass of thick locks falling over her shoulders and down her back. He'd never seen hair like that before, he was quite sure. It was thick but silky, and wasn't curly or straight but wondrously wavy.

Her head was turned away from him, so that a long strand fell near his face. He reached out to touch it, just to see if that magnificence felt as soft and silky as it looked.

It did. He ran his fingers through the long strands and held on.

The schoolteacher's head snapped around, and she looked down at him. He didn't let go of her hair, but kept his fingers tangled in the tempting mass.

"Good morning, Miss Priss," he said, realizing as he spoke that his mouth and throat were bone-dry and achy.

"What do we do now?" another voice asked, and Joe turned his gaze to the end of the bed where Alice Shorter stood, twisting her hands and gnawing her lip.

Sarah didn't hesitate to answer. "I want you to drive the girls to school and take over my class today."

"But I can't. . . ." Alice began.

The prissy schoolteacher turned her eyes to Alice and smiled; it was a confident, reassuring smile. "Of course you can. You're so far ahead of the other students you'll have no problem teaching for one day. Tell everyone I'm ill, but it's nothing serious and I will be back in school on Monday morning." She looked down at him again, her dark eyes mysterious. "I don't think we should tell anyone about your . . . father, not just yet."

"Faith and Glory will want to tell everyone."

"Tell them it's a secret," Sarah said with a small shake of her head. "For now. There's no reason to tell everyone that your father's here until we're sure. . . ." she caught herself before saying more, but Joe was happy to finish her thought for her.

"In case I kick the bucket," he rasped.

"He can't die," Alice said softly, and so desperately that if he didn't know better, Joe himself might even have believed he was her long-lost father.

Alice did, eventually, leave the room to help her sisters prepare for the day ahead. Sarah disentangled her hair from his fingers and tossed the strands he'd caressed over her shoulder, and then she sat on the bed beside him—very near to where he'd patted the mattress in invitation last night.

He had to admit, she didn't look too prim and proper as she spooned water into his dry mouth, as she dampened a washcloth and very gently bathed his face. She looked damn good, in fact. Every move she made, every breath she took was graceful, temptingly feminine. And those freckles ... he'd never known freckles could be so enticing.

It was an effort, but Joe reached up and laid a single finger on her, there where the lace of her stark white blouse parted and revealed the elegant column of her throat. Just as he'd suspected, the schoolmarm felt wonderfully cool, deliciously soft.

She frowned, and then flinched when he dragged that finger up and then down again.

"Behave yourself," she said prudishly, lifting her chin and backing slightly away, but not leaving her place at his side.

"Couldn't help myself, Miss Priss," he whispered. "You just look so darn pretty this morning."

She harrumphed, in a very feminine and genteel way. "Now I know you're delirious."

"Does that mean I might get to keep all my

body parts?" he whispered. "I don't want to be called Stumpy. I mean, think about it. Stumpy Shorter. That's just a godawful name."

She smiled. "Since you're delirious, I might allow you to keep both your hands."

He lowered his hand; the effort of holding it up was more than he liked to admit. But he wasn't ready to break his contact with Miss Priss, he wasn't ready to let her go. Not just yet. He settled his fingers on her waist. "My hands? Whew, that's a relief. I thought you were threatening a much more precious body part last night."

He expected outrage, indignation, shock, but Sarah just sighed. "You're a terrible man, Mr. . . . whoever you are."

"Shorter," he said. "Albert Joseph Shorter." Sarah might think he was delirious, but he hadn't forgotten his promise to Alice.

"Of course," she said disbelievingly as she peeled away the blanket with which he protected himself. "And who is Tess, Mr. Shorter?"

Had he said Tess's name out loud? Of course he had. In their quick lesson, Alice had made it clear that there was no immediate family, no grandparents or aunts or uncles, so . . . "Just a woman I know. A friend. And I thought you were going to call me Joe, Miss Priss."

Sarah harrumphed again as she studied his bandage. "It's *Prince*," she said, enunciating her name clearly.

"Miss Priss," he whispered.

"I'm going to have to change this dressing," she said, choosing to ignore his barb. Her pert, freckled nose wrinkled momentarily, as if she found the prospect of doctoring him distasteful. Well, of course she did. She was a straight-laced schoolteacher, not a nurse.

"I can do it. . . ." he began, tensing every muscle in his body in an effort to prepare himself to move into a sitting position. Dammit, *moving* shouldn't be so damn difficult.

"You most certainly will not," she interrupted, using that bossy teacher tone he remembered from his own school days long ago, laying a stilling hand on his chest. He gratefully obeyed, relaxing once again, sinking into the mattress with relief.

She hovered over him, so close, so unintentionally inviting. Feeling brave, he lifted his hand again. By God, those extraordinary breasts hovered just inches above his chest, rounded, soft, tempting.

"Don't even think about it, Stumpy," Sarah said, without so much as turning her eyes to his face.

Sitting on the edge of the bed, Sarah fidgeted nervously. She'd never known this house to be so quiet. The uncustomary silence grated on her nerves, for some reason. Of course the house was quiet; the girls had all gone to town, and Joe slept soundly.

Sleeping was likely not the right word. His

fever had dropped, but he was not well. Fever and blood loss and the laudanum she'd administered a short while ago had taken their toll. The man who called himself Joe Shorter looked like death.

Though death was likely not so beautiful.

Men were not supposed to be beautiful, she knew that. They were supposed to be level-headed, and occasionally rugged, and strong when it was necessary. Stumpy did have a strong jaw, and his arms and chest hinted at extraordinary strength, and there was a masculine ruggedness about him, in his height and his wide shoulders and the size and roughness of his hands.

But his face was beautiful; perfectly proportioned, without a scar or a blemish or a line that was less than perfect from any angle. Even though he was quite pale at the moment, and a new beard roughened and darkened his jaw, there was still something extraordinarily *beautiful* about the man.

He had wonderful lips, Sarah thought with a sigh. Looking at them, admiring the shape and the softness and the color, she was reminded that she'd never been kissed. Twenty-four years old, and she'd *never* been kissed. Well, unless you counted Aunt Mabel's occasional feathery kiss on the cheek—which Sarah didn't.

That's why she was here in Jacob's Crossing, in a roundabout way. Because she'd never been kissed. Because she'd been raised in a sterile home with undemonstrative parents who'd scolded her for being emotional, and thought the best course of action for their only child was marriage to a man who would only perpetuate a life of coldness.

She was here because Sarah Prince had decided she'd had enough. Out West, in the places she read about in the newspapers and dime novels she sneaked into her room, people laughed and loved and lived life to the fullest. They danced and shouted and did outrageous things that would never be accepted in New York City.

And they kissed. She was quite sure of it.

In a moment of uncustomary contrariness, in the fever of a rare emotional outburst, she'd answered a newspaper advertisement for an educated woman willing to teach in a small Texas town. And when Mayor Drake replied by mail that she'd been selected, she'd sold some of her grandmother's jewelry and taken the next train west.

It was simply bad luck that the train had departed New York on the morning of the very day she was supposed to marry Hugh Towerson. Simply bad luck.

The West was not all she'd expected it to be, but she did not regret her decision. Perhaps her life in Jacob's Crossing was not exciting, but they needed her here, these children in the small school, Elizabeth Shorter, her seven daughters . . . and now Stumpy. Joe, she supposed she should call him, even if that wasn't his real name.

Sarah had left New York six months ago. She still hadn't been kissed, but she supposed there would be time and opportunity for that. Later. She studied Joe's finely shaped lips. Or now.

Why was he so intriguing? she wondered as she lowered her head toward his. He was rough, and fresh, and an outrageous liar to boot. He had pawed her this morning, placing his hand in her hair and laying a finger on her throat and resting his large hand at her waist in an almost proprietary manner. Strangely enough, she could still feel the very places where he'd touched her; a line from the base of her throat to just beneath her chin. She tingled there, the skin unexpectedly warm and alive. Her waist; if she imagined hard enough she could still feel the weight and warmth of his hand there.

She hesitated, stopping her downward progress when her mouth was an inch or two from his. What if she kissed Joe as she wished, a brief touch of her lips to his, and he woke? What if she laid her mouth on his and he opened his eyes and found her out? Oh, she would be positively mortified.

A coward, even though she was, for all intents and purposes, alone and unlikely to get caught realizing her fantasy, she laid her hand on his forehead and lifted her face away from his. He was feverish still, but not as bad as before.

Sarah sat up straight and tall, dismissing her brief and insane notions about stealing a kiss from a beautiful man who was practically dead.

And she wondered, not for the first time, about the woman he'd mentioned. Tess. What was she to him? A friend, as he'd said, or more? Was she a sweetheart, a lover, a wife—a woman who had surely kissed those tempting lips?

It was fully dark when Joe opened his eyes again. A lamp burned low, but outside the window all was black.

The lamplight illuminated a sleeping Sarah Prince. She sat up in a chair in the corner, her head lolling to one side, her breathing deep and even.

She'd rectified this morning's oversight; her hair was tightly restrained and her blouse was buttoned to the chin. Even in sleep she looked refined and proper.

In fact, she looked much too refined and proper. He wished, with a smile that proved to him that he was on the mend, that she would snore. Or twitch. Or talk in her sleep. But she slept on, as dignified as ever. That was too bad.

She knew that he was not Shorter, that he was not the girls' father. She couldn't prove it, though, and that's what counted. When it came time to face the judge Alice had talked about, the odds were with them. Eight to one.

Still, it might be best if they got Miss Priss out of the house. Less chance of her catching them in a mistake, more time for them to work on their stories. It might be a good idea for him to see less of her, too. Somehow she was prettier every time he looked at her, and that just wasn't right. A woman like this one was nothing but trouble, especially for a man like him.

Yes, they'd do best by just sending the well-meaning Miss Priss on her way.

Unfortunately, there were a couple of problems he could not ignore. If they forced her back to town, she might talk. She might mention how Albert Shorter was supposed to be short and round and plain. And dead. She might get the other townsfolk to wondering and asking questions.

But that wasn't the main reason she should stay on. He would repay his debt to Alice by making sure that these girls stayed in their home and together, but that was where his obligation ended. He certainly couldn't remain here indefinitely. Once he was well, he had to get word to Webb and continue the search for Charlie Lockhart and his gang. He didn't have much to go on, didn't know many of the robbers by name. There was Eddie Conrad—unfortunately now deceased, and the deadly Tristan Butler, who had been with Lockhart for years. No, he couldn't stay here, and like it or not the girls needed someone to watch over them in the coming years.

Sarah was that person. Dammit, he couldn't run her off, even though it would make his life much easier if he could.

Why did he already feel so damn responsible for the Shorter girls? Sure, they'd likely saved his life, but a man had to draw the line somewhere. Maybe he felt responsible because Alice reminded him of Tess twenty years or so ago: determined to take care of her family, willing to do anything to accomplish that mission.

Tess hadn't found a surrogate father or a prissy schoolteacher to help her out; at sixteen she'd married a man she didn't love in order to provide a home for the little brother she refused to give up. She'd married an older man, taking over the care of his house and his children. Almost overnight she'd changed from a bright, adventurous girl with dreams of a finer life to a somber woman with no dreams at all. As soon as Joe had figured out why, as soon as he'd understood what Tess had sacrificed for him, a heavy, relentless guilt had settled in his gut.

Sarah stirred, but in a delicate, reserved way. Her lips parted, her very fine breasts heaved, and she moaned low in her throat. And something in *him* stirred, something darker and baser and more primitive than the schoolmarm could ever dream of. Joe cursed beneath his breath.

He had a feeling Miss Priss could turn out to be a lot more trouble than he expected.

Chapter Four

While Clara was upstairs helping the younger girls change out of their school clothes, Sarah took over the kitchen. Stirring the pot of fragrant stew and then turning to the dish pan to rinse a utensil, she felt a moment of rare peace. It had been several days since she'd stayed home alone with Joe, and she found herself very glad, grateful even, for the moment of quiet after a long day in the schoolroom. Some days she loved her job. Other days she wondered what on earth had compelled her to travel halfway across the country simply to torture herself.

Inner peace had always been rare for Sarah. While her life had been peaceful—much too peaceful to suit her—she'd always felt restless inside; as if she were missing something, as if life passed her by while she stood aside and simply watched. Outwardly she was always composed and self-assured. Her mother had taught her well. But inside, turmoil occasionally overwhelmed her.

In recent days she'd experienced more inner turmoil than usual. With every passing day Joe's health improved, until she was quite sure he would recover completely from his injury. She felt great relief of course, that was the only charitable response. But she couldn't help but notice that the less helpless Joe was the more bothersome he became.

He'd been at the Shorter farm a week, and no longer felt compelled to remain confined to his bed. He was liable to pop up anywhere, at any moment, and frequently did. As if that weren't enough, he had the annoying habit of appearing without warning, when she least expected it. The man's movements were like a cat's, silent and downright sneaky.

Sarah had never liked cats much.

"Good afternoon, Miss Priss."

She nearly jumped out of her skin at the sound of his voice, and spun around to find Joe lounging in the kitchen doorway. "That's Miss *Prince*, Stumpy." It hadn't taken her long to realize that he was not lazily mispronouncing her name at all, but purposely insulted her by calling her Miss Priss. If she cared what he thought of her, her feelings might be wounded.

He grinned, a satisfied smile spreading slowly across his handsome face. Contented, cunning . . . like a detested, bothersome cat. And to think, she had once been tempted to kiss that smug mouth as he slept.

She no longer felt such foolish temptation. In fact, she didn't even like to get too close to this man who called himself Joe Shorter. Imagine, all that inner turmoil she'd felt!

Alice had unpacked some of her uncle's stored clothing for her "father." Willem Sheridan's shirts were satisfactory, if not ideal. They were a bit large, but the sleeves were too short. Joe's perfectly reasonable solution was to tuck the shirt tail into his waistband and roll the cuffs up, baring his forearms. Willem's leather vest was adequate, but the man's trousers were inches too wide and much more too short. Instead, Clara had laundered Joe's own denims, which he wore, though they fit him like a second skin. Such apparel was sinful, surely, but he refused to wear the baggy, too-short trousers Alice had offered. Sarah found it truly disconcerting.

Willem Sheridan's shaving kit had proved adequate, as Stumpy's smooth jaw attested.

"Shouldn't you be in bed?" she asked curtly, returning her attention to her chore so her eyes wouldn't be drawn to those sinfully snug denims.

"I feel a lot better," he said, stepping into the room. She felt his presence, as if the very air around him was as charged as a thunderstorm. "Seems to me I need to move around as much as I can, especially if I'm going to be in shape to go to town Saturday."

She turned to face him. "Oh, I don't think that's a good idea." Her heart gave a little leap in her chest. If the townspeople knew the girls' *father* had arrived, they'd insist that she return to her own room at the boarding house, wouldn't they? With Joe here, the girls had adult supervision. They didn't need her anymore.

And Sarah needed to be needed more than anything. The idea of returning to her lonely room at the boarding house was almost as disheartening as the prospect of returning to New York and her father's big, cold house.

"Why not?" Joe stepped closer, leaning over the stove to take a good long sniff of the stew, checking out the biscuits Clara had ready to go in the oven, and finally coming to a halt right in front of Sarah. And much too close; so close that she had to look up to see his face. The high work table and pan of cooling water were directly behind her, and she had no possible way to escape. None at all. "Sooner or later—"

"We have two more weeks before the judge arrives," she interrupted. "I can't . . . I don't want to return to town and leave the girls out here all alone, and if the townspeople learn that you're living here I'll have no other choice."

He raised his eyebrows slightly, and stared down at her with eyes that were amused, secretive, and deep—so deep she felt like she could fall into them and get lost. A long breath cleared her head of such ridiculous thoughts. Almost.

"First of all, they won't be out here *all alone*. They have me," he rumbled lowly.

"Well," she said, using her most disapproving schoolmarm tone of voice, a domineering mannerism she'd learned from her Aunt Mabel. "I'm not yet certain that you qualify as suitable adult supervision for anyone."

"Then stay," he said casually, not at all insulted. "What difference does it make?"

Sarah sighed and gave a delicate push against his chest. Obedient, he backed away and allowed her to move to the stove. The stew didn't really need stirring, but it couldn't hurt. And darn it, she felt a strange compulsion to do something with her hands.

"I teach the children of this town, Stumpy," she said, feeling much braver as she looked at the stew instead of him. "Their parents are not likely to approve of the current living arrangements."

He laughed, carefully as his side was not yet completely healed. "Jesus, Miss Priss, we have seven little chaperones. You sleep upstairs and I sleep downstairs. I can barely walk, much less—"

71

"Still," she interrupted, not at all interested in hearing what he was not yet capable of. "It's not proper."

Joe watched the back of Sarah's neck, and the thoughts that ran through his mind were anything but *proper*. How could a woman look so all-fired parsimonious and so temptingly *tasty* at the same time?

Her blouse covered her to her chin, as usual, but when she leaned over to look into the cook pot, a tiny bit of the back of her long neck was exposed. Damn, he was hard-up if the sight of such a tiny sliver of skin turned his crank.

He'd seen plenty of naked women in his twenty-seven years. Plenty. He'd bedded lots of women prettier than this one, ladies who would do anything and everything—and had. Not so long ago, in Silver Creek, a pretty little saloon girl had practically jumped him at the bar. If he hadn't had so much whisky in him at the time, he probably would've given her a smile and a *no thanks*, but at the time his head had been fuzzy from one glass too many, and he'd just wanted to drown out the memory of watching a man die. He'd always assumed a pretty woman was the way to accomplish that, right? A good memory to chase away the old one. A woman's softness to make him forget that he'd killed a man.

He wasn't exactly starved for a woman, so why did he want this one so bad? Hell, he didn't even *like* her. She was much too prissy for his tastes, much too skittish. She started every time he walked into a room. She watched him warily, like she expected him to sneak up on her and jump her bones.

But that one glimpse of exposed skin beneath coppery red hair looked so damn tasty.

If he had a lick of sense he'd call off the deal he'd made with Alice, saddle up Snowdrop, and head back to Silver Creek to take care of the varmints who'd bushwhacked him, then get back to the Lockhart business. He still hurt more than he liked to admit, but he could do it. All he needed was a gun.

But he wasn't about to go back on his word. Damn it, every time he looked at Alice he saw Tess—even though they looked nothing alike. At sixteen Tess's hair had been as black as his own, and she'd always been tall and willowy, almost skinny. But their eyes . . . there was a desperation in Alice's eyes he couldn't ignore. He remembered that look—too well.

Somehow he had to make sure the Shorter girls were cared for. He couldn't allow Alice to make the kind of sacrifice Tess had made, he couldn't allow her to give up her heart and soul to keep her family together.

But he couldn't stay here forever, either.

He continued to stare at the back of Sarah's neck. Okay, maybe he didn't like her much, but she seemed to be a good, reasonable woman. The girls could do worse. Much worse.

"I think we should all go to town Saturday," he said, an idea striking him that was audacious and brilliant. He ignored the notion that the solution was a little bit too familiar. "Everybody. The girls, and you, and me."

Sarah turned around and looked at him suspiciously. "Whatever for?"

"I think you and me should get hitched."

Her only visible response was a widening of her dark brown eyes. "You're insane."

He should grin and agree with her; but he didn't. If the Shorter girls had a chance of staying in their home, together and safe, this woman was their best shot. She wasn't Tess, he reminded himself. Sarah Prince was a grown woman who knew her own mind and didn't have to do anything she didn't want to do.

Joe didn't think of his sister often these days. She had her life in Tennessee, her own children to raise now that Harvey's kids by his first wife were grown and gone. The last time he'd seen her she'd said she was happy. She said she had accepted her life and had even learned to love her husband, Harvey. Still, even though she'd looked happy enough, he hadn't believed her. He'd never been able to forget the way she'd looked at sixteen . . . frightened, determined, desperate.

Since he'd come here, his sister had been on his mind too much. Best to get this situation under control and then get the hell out of town.

Alice might not agree, but Joe felt they could

trust Sarah Prince. She wanted what was best for the girls, and would most likely do anything to keep them safe and together.

"My name is not Joe Shorter," he said softly. "It's Joe White. I never saw these girls until a week ago."

She didn't look at all surprised. "I suspected as much," she said, somewhat snootily.

"But Alice saved my life, and I want to repay her," he explained. "When she asked if I'd pretend to be her father so she and her sisters wouldn't be split up, I said yes."

Sarah crossed her arms over her chest. Surely she didn't realize how the subtle move lifted and displayed her breasts. Yes, the woman did have world-class—

"What on earth does your subterfuge have to do with your ridiculous notion that you and I should. . . ." She swallowed hard and then wrinkled her nose. "Marry?"

A minute ago it had seemed like a good idea. Right now, he wasn't so sure. But what choice did he have? "Well, I can't stick around forever. I have business to take care of. Important business."

She raised two expressive eyebrows.

"But you seem to have the girls' best interests at heart, you seem to want to take care of them."

"Of course I do," she said softly.

A disturbing thought occurred to him. "You don't have marriage plans already, do you? A sweetheart?" *A Mr. Priss?*

75

"No," she said, and he could see that she gave the notion serious consideration at last.

Joe spread his hands, palms up. "We get hitched, the judge is satisfied, and when talk dies down I'll slip away. If the folks in town believe that I left the girls' mother years ago, they'll surely believe that I up and did it again. If in a few years you decide you want to get married for real, you can say I'm dead. In a way, it's true. Shorter's dead, and we'll be married using his name."

"Which means we won't *really* be married," she said thoughtfully. She seemed to like that part of the idea. In fact, a small, almost unnoticeable twinkle lit her eyes, and a smile tugged at the corners of her mouth. At that moment the prim and proper Miss Priss looked downright impish. "Well, that would solve a problem or two."

He was dying to know what kinds of problems Sarah had that could be solved by a pretended marriage; he didn't dare to ask.

He didn't get the chance, anyhow. Glory ran into the kitchen, her little legs pumping, cheeks rosy, eyes bright. She looked as if she had every intention of throwing herself at him, and he braced himself.

It was hardly necessary. Glory slowed down as she neared him, and when she wrapped her arms around one leg and gave it a squeeze her touch was gentle. The face she lifted to him positively glowed.

"I had a good day at school today," she said with a smile. "I read out loud, and did arithmetic, and at recess I played with Harriet Tidwell." Joe smiled back; Glory was a happy child in spite of the fact that her life to this point, all five years of it, had been filled with hardship and loss. She surely didn't remember her real father. Alice had said she'd been a baby, a few months old, when Albert Shorter died. After struggling for a few years to make it on their own, and failing, they'd eventually traveled here, Elizabeth Shorter and her seven daughters. Maybe they'd had a few good years here before things started to go wrong again with Willem's death, then Elizabeth's.

Something deep in Joe's heart was moved unexpectedly. There was no way he'd let some deranged woman get her hands on Glory and change her name and try to make her into a replacement for a child who was long dead.

He looked at Sarah again, and saw the same determination in her eyes, the same protective conviction. Something in his heart lurched again, and he didn't like it.

Deacon stared down at a dark place in the earth, a sign of disturbance and nothing more. No body, no grave, no bones. He raked a distracted hand through his hair and ground one heel of his boot into the gritty earth.

"You're sure he was dead?" he asked softly.

Leonard nodded his head viciously.

"O'course I'm sure. I shot him, and he fell, and we slapped his horse on the backside and run it off. If he wasn't dead when we left him here, he was soon after."

Deacon lifted his head and gave Leonard and Isaac his most chilling glare. Rosie was right. They were morons. "A bullet in the head would've finished it," he seethed.

Isaac spoke up nervously. "It was real dark, and we heard some coyotes—"

"Yeah!" Leonard's face lit up as the idea hit. "It was probably the coyotes what got him. That's how come there ain't no body."

Deacon wanted to believe the explanation, he really did. He wanted to believe that these two idiots had done their job and Joe White was truly dead.

But he didn't.

He lifted his head and looked out over the barren, hard landscape. There weren't many places a wounded man could go, especially on foot and bleeding. And he was bleeding, as the dark spot on the ground testified. Maybe White had stumbled a while and died a short distance away from here. Then again. . . .

With a low muttered curse, Deacon leapt into his saddle and headed back for Silver Creek. Leonard and Isaac rode hard to keep up, but they were clumsy and slow. For a few minutes they talked incessantly, trying their best to convince Deacon, and themselves, that they'd done their job well. After a while they lapsed into an eerie silence and fell back. Suddenly, Deacon felt sure that Joe White was *not* dead.

As he headed toward town, he accepted that notion. So what if the man wasn't dead? He was out of Silver Creek, and out of Rosie's bed. He smiled at the thought. Deacon himself had been in Rosie's bed all week, and she hadn't mentioned Joe White one time. She'd been a mite moody, but that would pass. He was sure of it.

Long before he reached the saloon, Deacon began to whistle. He forgot the morons behind him, the nuisance that had once gone by the name Joe White, and remembered only Rosie.

What was it about that particular woman that made him so dang crazy? He loved all women and they loved him. He loved the way they looked and the way they smelled and the way their bodies felt against his. He liked the way women laughed, and the way they smiled when they were happy. But lately, he'd just been thinking about *one* woman, and that was danged odd.

Deacon didn't worry about this new, odd development. Why should he waste time worrying when everything was going so well?

He tied his horse at the hitching post in front of the saloon, and pushed his way happily through the swinging batwing doors. The saloon did a modest business in the afternoon, a few slobbering drunks and a couple of professional gamblers waiting for the crowd of suckers to begin to arrive. Deacon ignored them all and climbed the stairs, two steps at a time, to Rosie's room. She might still be asleep, but he'd wake her if she was. And she wouldn't mind, neither. He knew how to wake her just right.

The first thing he noticed when he opened the door was the empty bed. Then he began to notice other, more ominous signs. Rosie's perfume and little jewelry box were not on the tall dresser where she always kept them. The wardrobe doors were flung open, and inside there was a dark emptiness instead of colorful silk and satin.

He turned his head slowly. The mirror over her vanity had been broken, shattered, the cracks working their way out from the center as if it had been punched hard right there. Suddenly he felt a little sick, ill deep in his stomach and high in his throat.

When he heard the rustle of silk behind him, he spun around quickly, hoping . . . no, Deacon Moss didn't hope, not for a *woman*.

Another of the girls stood there, framed by the doorway. She was a pretty girl with ordinary brown hair, dark eyes, and an hourglass figure. He'd seen her around, in the past week, but hadn't paid her much notice.

"Hi, Deacon," she said with a wide smile. "Rosie said you might stop by."

"Where did she go?" He didn't much like the harshness in his voice, the raspy croak.

The girl shrugged her shoulders and walked

into the room. "She wouldn't say. My name's Lola. Rosie said I could take care of you, since she's not working here anymore."

He didn't know what made him angrier; that Rosie was gone or that she'd just hand him over to another woman like he was . . . like he meant nothing to her. He wouldn't have handed her over without a fight. Dammit, he'd killed for her!

Well, he'd had a man killed for her, but that was almost the same. Only he wasn't so sure Joe White was truly dead. Maybe he'd come back to town and stolen Rosie away. Right from under his nose!

He stared at the whore before him. One woman was just as good as another, right? Rosie had been getting tiresome anyway, mooning over the fate of Joe White, daydreaming when she should've been giving him her full attention. And . . . and she was too darn skinny. Now *this* woman had some meat on her bones. Hell, once she was naked and in the bed he likely wouldn't know the difference, he wouldn't think of Rosie at all.

Lola licked her lips seductively, but Deacon barely noticed.

"If you know where she is," he said quietly, "You'd better tell me. Now."

Lola's seductive air vanished. "I told you, I don't have any idea where Rosie went. She wouldn't tell me or anyone else. She just packed her bags real quick and left."

She could have taken the train, a stage, or she might have hired a horse. Silver Creek was a crossroads of sorts; people moved in and out of town all day and all night. How the hell would he ever find her?

Deacon shoved Lola into the hall and slammed the door in her face. Never in his life, not once, had he treated a woman roughly. His mother had taught him better than that. But he couldn't stand to look at Lola for one more second, and he wasn't ready to walk down the stairs and face anyone, not just yet.

So he sat before the broken mirror and stared at his fractured reflection. He felt, for the span of a single heartbeat, like he was as cracked and broken inside as the looking glass.

"Who's the best?" he whispered.

No one answered.

Chapter Five

All the way to town, Sarah tried to convince herself that Joe's suggestion was a good, reasonable solution to a potentially disastrous problem.

She cast a surreptitious glance at the man who drove the wagon. While he didn't look happy, he didn't look particularly unhappy, either. He looked determined, resolved, and almost content. For some reason of his own, Joe wanted what was best for the Shorter sisters. How could she fault him for that?

All seven of the girls rode in the back of the wagon. They were unanimously in favor of the marriage, but Faith and Glory had been the most exuberant upon hearing the news. Of course, they had not been told about the part of the plan that included Joe's leaving. It was almost as if they expected him to stay. What an unreasonable and ridiculous notion. If he was thinking of staying on, he certainly wouldn't need to marry.

More than a few heads turned their way as they headed down the main thoroughfare. Sarah smiled and nodded to those she was well acquainted with, remembering her manners even though her heart raced and her mind was filled with reservations. The people they passed didn't stare at her, of course, they stared at Joe.

Because he was a stranger, because he drove the crowded wagon through town with his head high and his eyes straight ahead. Because he was a compelling man who commanded attention; Sarah constantly caught herself staring at him for no reason at all.

Alice leaned over the front seat and pointed to the turn that led to the Methodist church. As soon as Joe brought the wagon to a halt near the double front doors, Clara and Evie leapt from the wagon bed, shouting heartily that they'd be back shortly with the preacher. They disappeared around the white church and headed toward the Reverend Taylor's little house directly beyond.

Sarah stared at the white church, and her heart unexpectedly leapt into her throat. She'd imagined her wedding day a thousand times, as all girls do. A few years ago she'd pictured an elaborate, flowing wedding dress, a prince charming, a cathedral crowded with friends and relatives, candles and flowers. She'd even imagined love, though the concept had been as indistinct and elusive then as it was now.

Reality was always harsher than dreams, she reminded herself. So she wore a very nice mint-green day dress rather than a flowing white gown. And instead of a cathedral she'd be married in a small, clapboard church. And instead of a prince charming—she cast a furtive glance to Joe again—she would be marrying Stumpy, a man of little or no manners who insisted on being crude and difficult, who called her Miss Priss and often looked at her as if he were laughing at her on the inside. As if he found her *amusing*.

Yet, he was a man who would marry a virtual stranger in order to save seven little girls he'd known not much more than a week. For that, she told herself, she could love him a little.

The other girls clambered from the wagon and hurried after their quicker sisters, and Sarah set her eyes boldly on Joe White. Joe *Shorter*, she would have to remember. He looked at her, and she could almost imagine that she saw a glimmer of fear in his eyes.

"Having second thoughts?" she asked, her voice calm and soft.

He didn't shake his head and deny it. Instead, he gave her a small smile. "Maybe a few. What about you?"

"One or two," she admitted. "Are we doing the right thing? For the children, I mean."

The Reverend Taylor rounded the building, seven little girls in gingham and calico dancing around him, all of them trying to offer explanations at once.

Joe nodded once. "I can't think of any other solution. Can you?"

Sarah considered the question for a second before shaking her head.

Joe took a deep breath. "Then let's do it." He lowered himself, gently for the sake of his healing wound, from the wagon seat, then lifted his arms to assist her.

Let's do it was not exactly the most romantic proposal in the world, not even the most romantic she'd ever heard, but it was sensible and honest. Romance was highly overrated, anyway, Sarah decided, as a confused Reverend Taylor arrived to greet her and her groom.

"Your *what*?" the shopkeeper all but screeched, craning his neck as he leaned over the counter to stare bug-eyed at Sarah. A small crowd gathered around.

The scene didn't alter Sarah's composure. Joe wondered if anything ever ruffled her feathers.

"My husband," she said with a patient smile. "Joe Shorter."

The large man behind the counter turned his

eyes to Joe, and Joe answered with a wide smile and an overly friendly "howdy."

The questions came in a flood, from the shopkeeper and from the crowd that continued to grow, and Sarah handled them all with an unshakable composure. She told the story they'd concocted without so much as batting an eyelash or stumbling over a single word. He'd heard of Elizabeth's death and come to reclaim his daughters. His death had been highly exaggerated by Elizabeth in order to salvage her pride. For the sake of the children, who needed a mother, they had decided on this marriage.

That last detail had been Sarah's idea, not his. Joe had been more than ready to come to town and try to convince them all that he and Sarah had fallen in love at first sight, but she'd dismissed that idea quickly and insistently.

Which was too bad, he thought. He'd love to spend the afternoon trying to convince the onlookers that he and Sarah adored one another. He could touch her, hold her hand, maybe steal a kiss when only a dozen or so folks were watching. Not that she was his kind of woman or anything; he just wanted to ruffle her feathers once.

A grating, booming voice broke through all the rest, and Joe turned to watch a red-faced man work his way through the crowd. Dressed in an ill-fitting, checkered Eastern suit and a bowler hat, he looked out of place among the rough people of Jacob's Crossing. They parted for him, though, as if he were one of their own.

"Miss Prince," he said as he reached the front of the crowd. "I have heard the most disturbing rumor."

Joe took an immediate dislike to the man, to his small narrowed eyes and his thin lips and the condescending way he looked down at Sarah. So he leaned forward and placed himself squarely in the man's face. "That's Mrs. Shorter, partner. And who might you be?"

Impossibly, the man turned redder. "I am Mayor Lawrence Drake, and there has been a terrible mistake here. "Miss Prince is our—"

"Mrs. Shorter," Joe corrected again, softer and without the smile this time.

Mayor Drake took a deep breath that puffed out his puny chest. "Sarah is our schoolteacher. She's to remain single for one year. It's in the contract!"

Joe looked down at Sarah, who wasn't at all troubled by the mayor's outburst. "Honey," he said softly, but plenty loud enough for everyone to hear. "Is this true?"

She looked up at him with long-suffering eyes. "Well yes, I suppose it is. But the situation was rather urgent, wouldn't you agree? And certainly takes precedence over my contract with the township. After all, I'm more than willing to continue teaching until a replacement is found."

"Urgent?" the mayor repeated darkly.

Joe knew what the man was thinking, what a few of the others were thinking, as well. Most urgent marriages were helped along by the expected arrival of a baby. Sarah obviously had no clue.

"With seven daughters to raise I need all the help I can get," he said with a lazy smile. "And I need it now, not six months from now."

There were a few twittering "ohs" from the crowd.

"Shorter," the mayor said, planting his beady eyes on Joe. "Don't tell me you're—"

All of a sudden, Dory popped through the crowd. "This is my Poppy," she said brightly, standing beside him and reaching up to slip a thin arm around his waist. "He's come home at last," she sighed. She looked up at him with wide, expressive eyes, fluttering her long lashes. This was his little actress.

The mayor sputtered, for a moment, and then gathered his composure. "Nonsense. You're much too young to be these girls' father."

Joe just smiled. "Well, I'll admit I was rather young when I married Lizzy, not much older than Alice is today." Adding a few years to his age was no problem. He leaned forward and lowered his voice. "Lizzy was a few years older than me, that's true, and at first it wasn't a problem. Later on, though—" he shrugged.

"Are you saying," the Mayor seethed, "that your desertion of these girls and their mother was justified by your youthfulness?"

He withheld a grin, since the reaction would be inappropriate, but the mayor had just admitted, in front of all these people, that he was indeed the girls' father. "A body makes mistakes in his youth, Mayor. I'm a changed man."

In a few weeks or so he'd prove them wrong, but that wasn't important. Not now, anyway.

Sarah looked up at him and smiled, and the light in her eyes was real and touching. They'd just passed the first, most important hurdle. "I'm going to the boarding house to collect my things," she said sweetly. "If you'll help Alice and Clara with the shopping, I'll meet you here as soon as I possibly can."

"Sure, honey," he said agreeably. And then, on impulse, he lowered his head with every intention of stealing a quick kiss. After all, half the town was watching. It couldn't hurt.

She stopped him with a hand on his chest and a turn of her head. "Really, Joe," she said softly as he backed his head away, disappointed that he hadn't managed to steal even one little kiss on his wedding day.

He watched Sarah step from the general store and onto the boardwalk. The mayor turned to follow her.

"Mayor Drake," Joe called, catching up with the short-legged man in just a few long steps. Unhappily, the mayor stopped and turned to face him.

Joe gave Drake a wide grin. "I was just thinking that maybe we ought to get better acquainted, since I'm new to Jacob's Crossing and all. Sarah's the only person in this area I know, 'cept for my girls. Maybe you could show me around town a bit?"

Mayor Drake didn't like Joe any more than Joe liked him, but they pretended to be civilized. "This is not a good time."

"Oh, I hate to take you away from your official mayoral duties," Joe said. Over the man's shoulder he saw Sarah make a turn off the main way. She was headed to the boarding house, which is where Mayor Drake was going himself, if Joe knew men at all.

Sarah could handle herself, and she certainly wouldn't have any trouble with this citified fella, but Joe found he just didn't like the idea of the mayor trailing after her. It wasn't right. After all, she was a married woman, now. Sorta.

"Maybe you could just introduce me around," Joe suggested. "I haven't had a chance to get to town and meet the folks since I arrived."

The mayor was no longer quite so anxious to leave. "And how long *have* you been at the farm, Mr. Shorter?"

"Call me Joe, Larry. Can I call you Larry?" The man bristled. "And to answer your question, I've been home a few days. 'Bout a week," he added.

The mayor looked as if he'd just swallowed something large and bitter. "And Miss

Prince . . . Mrs. Shorter, has been out there all that time, also?"

"Yep." Joe felt the need to keep this man as far away from Sarah as possible. When he did leave, and when she did marry again, he sure as hell didn't want her to choose this blowhard. "She's something, my Sarah," he said dreamily. "All lady on the outside, so prim and proper, but that red hair of hers hints at what's on the inside."

Mayor Larry raised his eyebrows. "She has a temper?"

Joe smiled. "Nope. Not that I've seen, leastways. But she's got fire in her blood." He shook his head in appreciation. "I don't mind telling you," he said in a lowered, confidential voice. "I can't wait for tonight." When the mayor shot a shocked glance his way, Joe smiled and winked wickedly.

A man like this wouldn't know what to do with a fiery woman. He was taken with the prim and proper Sarah Prince, the lady, the Miss Priss.

Joe's smile faded as the mayor turned away. He suddenly realized that he was taking this charade too far, because all of a sudden he really did wish he and Sarah were going to have a proper wedding night.

"Oh, this is so exciting," Mrs. Brooke said as Sarah quickly packed her bag. "Married! And so quickly!"

Sarah gave her former landlady a small smile. "You needn't make it sound so romantic. I married Mr. Shorter because the girls need a mother as well as a father, and I did promise Elizabeth before she died that I would take care of them."

Lizzy! She would have to talk to Joe about that. No one had ever called Elizabeth Shorter *Lizzy!*

"Still," Mrs. Brooke persisted. "I hear he's a very handsome man."

Sarah sighed. Word traveled quickly in a small town. "Yes, Joe is very handsome." No doubt they wondered why a man who looked like Joe would marry a plain woman like herself. Now, if she looked like her mother . . . but she didn't. Hadn't her mother bemoaned that fact often enough in Sarah's days in her house?

Oh well, Joe's beauty and her plainness would only make it easier for the townspeople to believe that he'd abandon her when the time came.

It wouldn't be easy for her, when everyone in town believed her to be the unhappy, deserted wife. Sarah did not like to be pitied . . . but there had seemed no other way to keep the girls safe and together—especially not with the judge breathing down their necks.

Mrs. Brooke preceded Sarah down the stairs, talking the whole way about how lucky Sarah was to have caught herself a husband so quickly, as if Joe were a fish. Sarah actually felt the play of a smile on her face as she reached the foot of the stairs. Well, she'd wanted excitement in her life, and she'd certainly never done anything so audacious as pull off a pretend marriage in New York.

For a few seconds, as they'd spoken the proper words in front of the Reverend Taylor, the ceremony and the promises that came with it had seemed almost real. *Almost.* However, since there was no Joe Shorter . . .

"Good afternoon," Mrs. Brooke said heartily as the front door opened and a young woman stepped inside.

Sarah was stunned by the woman's beauty. Her fair hair, eyes almost as blue as Joe's, and an unblemished heart-shaped face were striking, indeed. If ever Sarah needed a face-to-face reminder that she was not pretty. . . .

The woman smiled. "I was hoping you might have a room," she said, setting her single, bulging bag on the floor at her side. "I've been staying at the hotel for a couple of days, but that place is downright nasty." She wrinkled her nose in distaste. "If I'm going to stay on in Jacob's Crossing I'll need a better place than that to live."

"You're in luck," Mrs. Brooke said. "A room just became available." She gestured to Sarah. "Our schoolteacher has married and is leaving my establishment."

Sarah stepped forward. "Sarah Pr . . . Sarah *Shorter*," she said. "Nice to meet you. Did I hear you say you planned to stay for a while? We will be looking for a new schoolteacher," she added hopefully.

She was answered with a dazzling smile. "No thanks. I'm thinking of staying on and opening my own café, but I'd like to meet the folks in town and learn my way around, first."

"Your own café," Sarah said. "How exciting."

"I've been saving up for a long time for a business of my own, and I want to make sure I locate in the right town. Oh, I didn't introduce myself," the newcomer said, nodding to Sarah and to Mrs. Brooke. "My name's Mary Rose Sheppard. My friends call me Rosie."

Chapter Six

When they reached home, Clara insisted that a special meal was called for, and the older girls agreed and made themselves busy in the kitchen. There was such joy in the house, such apparent relief. As Sarah watched Alice and Clara and Dory bustle about with pots and pans and plates in their hands, she had to smile. These children were better in the kitchen than she would ever be. *Much* better, if truth be told. Goodness, Sarah thought as she watched the well-organized activity; her mother would've swooned if she had ever expressed an interest in cooking. A daughter of Katherine Prince's doing domestic duty? Unthinkable.

Sarah's smile faded with the thought of her

mother. It was too soon, but one day she'd sit down and write a nice long letter explaining away her impulsive decision to leave New York. She dreaded the thought of trying to put her feelings, her reasons and excuses, into words. She doubted her mother would ever understand. Having a husband and seven step-daughters would surely squelch any ideas her parents had about her impossible return to New York and the staid lifestyle she'd escaped. She'd thought of that almost instantly, as Joe had put the proposition to her. And, of course, a husband and seven step-daughters would also keep Mayor Drake and his like at bay. Thank goodness.

Becky was as clumsy and useless in the kitchen as Sarah, so she'd set about another chore somewhere in the house. Footsteps clattered above, faint voices laughed and called out happily. It was the first time since Elizabeth's death that Sarah had heard the girls' laughter.

Sarah smiled. Any sacrifice, even a fake marriage to Stumpy, was worthwhile if it meant these girls could laugh again.

While the girls bustled about the house, Joe was in the barn with his horse, the aptly named Snowdrop. For such a crude man, he did seem to have a soft spot for that animal. And a soft spot for little girls, as well, she conceded. Which meant that he couldn't be all that bad, no matter how diligently he tried to shock and dismay her.

Dinner was almost ready when Becky and Glory came to fetch plates to set the long dining room table. "It's done," Becky said breathlessly, glancing over her shoulder to Sarah as she left the kitchen.

Puzzled, Sarah followed. Becky laid plates on the table with the quickness and surety of one who'd done this chore a thousand times. Glory, with the silverware, followed behind—not quite so quickly but efficiently enough.

"What's done?" Sarah asked from the doorway.

Becky looked at her and grinned. Goodness, she was a pretty girl when she smiled! At that moment Sarah realized how seldom Elizabeth's second born smiled. "We've moved your things into Poppy's room, and Clara's and Dory's things into your old room."

"Oh," Sarah said with a sinking heart. "You really shouldn't have."

"It was no trouble," Becky said gaily as she finished her chore.

That wasn't exactly what Sarah had meant, but she had no immediate response. They really and truly *shouldn't* have. She couldn't share a room with Joe!

"I've never slept in a room with just three people before," Glory said happily. "Maybe tonight Faith won't stick her elbow in my side."

"And I am *so* glad to get Clara out of my room," Becky added. "Sometimes she talks in her sleep."

"Yeah," Glory piped up. "And sometimes Dory sneezes when she first gets up in the morning. A lot, and really loud. Sometimes it makes my ears ache before they're awake good." Glory stood before Sarah, her smile wide, her eyes bright. "I'm so glad you married Poppy, Miss Prince."

Sarah's heart sank. Somehow, some way, Glory had begun to think this was real. The marriage, her Poppy. How would she feel when Joe left? Abandoned again, no doubt. And if Glory had convinced herself that Joe was here to stay and the marriage was a real one, then it was possible the other girls were suffering the same delusion. Some of them, anyway. Alice might know better, but if Becky had so joyfully moved Sarah's belongings into her new bedchamber . . . oh, this was not good.

"Since I'm"—she started to say *married*, but the word stuck in her throat—"going to be living here now, perhaps you should call me something other than Miss Prince. That's awfully formal for family." And she *was* family, she told herself firmly. Maybe Joe wasn't their father, and maybe he wasn't going to stay, but she would become family because it was best for the girls. "You can call me Sarah."

The girls agreed, and as they returned to the kitchen to help with the final preparations, Sarah stepped down the hallway to Joe's bedroom. Not content to study the room from the doorway, she stepped inside. Sure enough, the girls had moved her bags into the room and set her toiletries on the dresser. Her straw bonnet hung on the hat tree by the window, and her umbrella stood in the corner.

"Here, Miss Prince," Faith said softly as she walked into the room carrying a white and yellow porcelain vase that was much too large for her little hands. She made it to the dresser just in time, setting the unsteady vase full of carelessly arranged wildflowers before the mirror.

When Faith turned around and smiled, Sarah knew she couldn't be upset by this new development. Not yet. When it came time to tell the girls that Joe wasn't a permanent fixture in their lives, then it would be soon enough to give in to distress. Perhaps by then she'd be settled in the Shorter sisters' lives and they'd know they didn't need Joe White to get by.

"Thank you, Faith," she said. "They're lovely."

Faith's smile widened at the compliment, and she dashed from the room with the promise to wash her hands thoroughly before supper.

Sarah crossed the room and opened the tall wardrobe, knowing what she'd see. Sure enough, her dresses hung there neat as a pin. The girls had been quite efficient, as always.

"Well, well," a deep voice crooned softly.

Sarah spun around to see Joe standing in the open doorway with a perfectly sinful smile on his face. He stepped into the room and slammed the door with an easy swing of his booted foot.

"What have we here?"

One Day, My Prince

* * *

Joe hadn't expected this, wouldn't have dreamed it in a hundred years. While he'd been talking to Snowdrop, rubbing the mare's nose and making promises about how soon they'd get out of this place and back to Silver Creek, his *wife* had been moving into his room.

She was everywhere, as if she'd lived in this room for years. A scarf carelessly draped over the back of the chair, the womanly things on the dresser, a vase of flowers; the very *smell* of Sarah and her things.

And right now she stared at him wide-eyed and surprised and . . . not prissy at all.

"The girls moved my things in here without my permission," she said, only a slight tremble in her voice. "But when they told me about what they'd done they were so happy, and Becky smiled, and I just couldn't tell them to undo everything they'd done. I don't know why they thought it necessary to . . . to take such drastic measures."

He took a step closer, and she flinched so subtly he might not have noticed if he hadn't been watching her so hard.

A small frown wiped the surprise from Sarah's face and wrinkled her nose. "You did tell them this was a pretend marriage, didn't you?" she asked. "Alice, at the very least."

Joe took another step toward her, and this time she didn't flinch. Not at all.

"You *did* tell them," she repeated.

"Not exactly," he admitted. "Though I did think they'd have the smarts to figure it out for themselves. After all, they know I'm not staying."

Sarah took a deep breath, and after a moment's thought she placed her fingers at the bridge of her nose and closed her eyes. "I believe I feel a headache coming on."

"Do tell," Joe drawled.

She dropped that fragile looking hand from her face and stared at him, daggers in her eyes. "When you and Alice made your infernal deal you might have told her you wouldn't be staying, but I have come to suspect that she didn't tell the others. The younger girls seem to think. . . . They've taken to the notion. . . ." Even though her face reddened, she took a deep calming breath and looked him square in the eye. "The younger girls seem to think this is real," she said softly. "That you're going to stay and we're really . . . married."

Great. Just great. Every libidinous thought Joe had been enjoying earlier fled. *Really married?* No way. "I'll set 'em straight over supper." He turned away, no longer interested in studying Miss Priss's alluring assets.

"Wait," she called when Joe had his hand on the doorknob, her voice low and quick, hushed and unintentionally sensual. Wary, he glanced over his shoulder. Sarah clasped her hands together and took another of those interesting deep breaths. "Do you have to set them straight right away? Can't we . . . wait?"

"Why?"

She turned her head so she looked out the window, not at him. The sun was setting, the light that came through the curtained window soft. "They're happy tonight," she said, her voice as soft as the light that surrounded her. "I haven't seen them happy in a very long time. Not since before their mother died." Bravely, she turned her gaze from the window to him. "Becky smiled. Faith brought us flowers. Alice and Clara and Dory are preparing a special meal. A celebration. Glory has begun to call you Poppy as if . . . as if you really are her father."

Joe felt something inside him sink, heavy and foreboding. "What about Evie?"

Sarah smiled. God in heaven, she didn't look prissy at all when she smiled. Her mouth was wide and lush and expressive, her dark eyes sparkled. "Evie's sleeping, enjoying her usual afternoon nap. But I imagine she's as confused as the others."

"So, why shouldn't I *un*confuse them pronto?" Joe asked, his voice too low and harsh.

"They haven't had much happiness," she answered softly. "Maybe we should give them a few weeks free of worry about what tomorrow will bring, precious days of security and gaiety and a sense of family."

"We are not a *family*," Joe said defensively.

"I know that," Sarah said quickly, her voice soft. "But we can pretend for a while. For them." She swallowed hard. He could see the workings of her throat, the obvious shift of her stalwart shoulders. "I'll sleep on the floor."

Joe leaned back against the door, as casual as he could manage. "Ever slept in the same room with a man before?"

She shook her head.

"I snore," he said gruffly, hoping she would change her mind, that she'd dismiss this ridiculous notion. "And I sleep naked."

She was a tough woman to scare, he'd give her that. Sarah simply lifted her chin. "I've heard you snore, Stumpy. It's not so bad and you don't snore all night. And as for the . . . other, I'm sure you wouldn't mind altering your habits for the duration. I believe I saw a nightshirt in with Uncle Willem's clothing."

"I will not wear a nightshirt, Miss Priss," he hissed.

"Yes, you will," she said certainly.

Just like a woman. He smiled, a grin that should tell Sarah to back away. A grin that told her he saw through her Miss Priss routine, that if they were going to pretend, then by God no one would be sleeping on the floor. "No, I won't."

A sharp rap on the door interrupted their argument. "Supper's ready," a cheerful voice called.

"We'll be right there," Sarah answered. As she walked by she whispered. "Yes, you will."

It was the most ridiculous item of clothing he'd ever worn. No, it was the most ridiculous item of clothing he'd ever *seen*. The nightshirt hung, baggy and misshapen, to his knees. The worn, frayed collar had been embroidered with flowers. *Flowers*, for God's sake!

"Well?" Sarah called from the other side of the privacy screen she'd found in the attic and erected in the far corner of their bedroom. Faded silk over a tri-fold wooden frame, it might have once been a fine piece, but a few small tears and an odd cant to the warped frame detracted from its once elegant appearance. Yes, the screen had seen better days, but it served its purpose. "Does it fit?"

"How the hell am I supposed to tell if it fits or not?" he muttered.

"Come on out and let me have a look," she said in her prim schoolteacher voice.

Joe took a tentative step from behind the screen. Sarah, already dressed for bed in a nightgown that covered her from chin to toes and was every bit as concealing as any one of her dresses, stood at the foot of the bed, and when she caught sight of him she almost covered the smile that tugged at the corners of her mouth. Almost.

"See?" she said softly. "That nightshirt's not

so terrible. I think you look quite . . . quite . . ." the smile tugged at her mouth again.

"Ridiculous?" he offered as he stepped away from the screen. "Comical?"

"Dashing," she said, giving way to a full-blown smile. "If you're interested, I believe I saw a nightcap in the trunk, as well."

Joe lowered his eyes hoping to still the unexpected effect of that smile, but seeing her little toes peeking from beneath that stark white gown provided no relief at all.

Suddenly he felt like he'd been ambushed as completely and effectively as he'd been when those two varmints bushwhacked him. What the hell was he doing here? How had he gotten so completely sucked into this farce? He could see, with sickening clarity, his life stretching before him; he and Sarah would pretend to be married, but somewhere along the line it wouldn't be only the kids who thought it was real. He could get used to this, to her smile and her soft voice and her tiny toes.

Family had cost Tess too much; her youth, her hopes and dreams. He could never forget what she'd sacrificed for him, what she'd given up to keep her little brother close. Feeling safe anywhere, with anyone, was a mistake—just as surely as standing here admiring Sarah's toes was a mistake. By God, he couldn't let her suck him in like this.

She'd made a bed of blankets and pillows on

the floor at the foot of the bed. He'd slept in worse places.

"I'll take the floor," he said, careful not to look at her any longer than he had to. Currently she was an intriguing blur of white and cinnamon red out of the corner of his eye.

"Oh, no," she said, foolishly stepping into his path. "You're still recovering. You take the bed and I'll be quite comfortable here."

Her polite insistence stopped when he lifted his eyes to hers. "Fine. Sleep on the floor. But I'm sleeping there, too," he promised, his voice dark and low. "You lie down on the floor and I'll lie down right beside you. I'll snore in your ear all night and by morning we'll be cuddled up like any two newlyweds ought to be and my friends will no doubt end up calling me Stumpy for the rest of my days, just like you promised." He leaned down to place his face just a little bit closer to hers. "As tempting as the prospect is, I like *all* my appendages, Miss Priss."

"There's no need to be—" she began primly.

"And I am *not* wearing this," he insisted, grabbing at the nightshirt with both hands. As he whipped it over his head, Sarah jumped into the bed and pulled the covers up high. Over her head, in fact.

He tossed the detestable nightshirt to the floor and stood at the foot of the bed, near his place for the night, smiling at the lump in the bed. Silently he dared her to peel aside the coverlet and peek. Just once. "You didn't turn off the lamp," he said softly.

"I will," she said, her words muffled by the covers she hid behind. "As soon as you lie down and get under your own blanket."

With great care, since his side was still healing, he lowered himself to the floor and slipped between the blanket and the bedding on the floor. His head rested on a soft pillow. Yes, he'd slept in many places worse than this.

A moment later he heard the bed creak. The light was extinguished, leaving the room in darkness. There wasn't so much as a sound from the bed, not the rustle of the sheet or another soft creak. In fact, he couldn't even hear Sarah breathing.

In his mind he could still see her toes—toes which were, if his calculations were correct, a short distance above his head. He wondered if he reached up and snaked his hand onto the bed, if he slipped his hand beneath the covers and found her foot. . . .

He wanted her. Hellfire, he hated to admit it but it was the truth. Still, sorta married or not, he couldn't have her. She was a part of the trap, the sweetest, most tempting part of the trap. . . .

"You're an incredibly perverse man, Joe White," she suddenly whispered.

"Thank you."

"It wasn't meant as a compliment."

He decided to let the conversation die. If she said another word . . . another single, solitary word . . . he was going to climb up and into that bed with her and shut her prissy mouth the only way he knew how. With a kiss. A long, slow, deep kiss that would be just the beginning.

Unfortunately, she remained *perversely* silent.

"One day, Miss Priss," he whispered. "One day . . ."

She'd never spent a sleepless night. Never. No matter how uncertain her life was, how difficult her decisions, she was able to close her eyes at night and sleep.

But not tonight. How long had she been lying here with her eyes wide open? Hours, perhaps.

"Are you asleep?" a low voice from the floor at the end of the bed asked.

It would be safest to ignore the question and remain silent, of course. Much more prudent than responding to the impossible man she shared this room with.

"No," she answered in a whisper.

"I was just wondering," he said, his voice almost as low as hers in the dark room. "Where are you from? You don't have a Texas accent, that's for sure."

"New York."

"No kidding?" His voice was light and friendly, and not threatening . . . considering that he'd ripped that nightshirt off practically

109

right in front of her. If she hadn't been fast enough she would've seen much more than his bandages. "Yankee," he accused with a hint of humor in his soft voice.

"Are you decent?" she asked.

"Nope." His answer came quick and certain.

Instinctively, she smiled. "I mean, are you under the covers."

"Oh," he said. "Yep."

Moving slowly, Sarah twisted on the bed, lying on her stomach so that she looked over the foot of the bed to the man below. In the darkness she could see the white of his pillow, the outline of his head. Nothing more. "Where are you from?"

She saw the shift of his head, the eyes he pinned on her, the subtle shift of his body. "Tennessee."

"Rebel," she said, her voice as teasing as his had been. If she couldn't sleep, and he couldn't sleep, they might as well talk for a while. If they were going to pretend to be married, maybe she should know more about him. For some reason, she wanted to know more about him. She wanted to know everything. "What did you do? Before you were bushwhacked, that is."

He waited a while to answer, and she had almost convinced herself that he didn't intend to tell her anything. And then his voice drifted up to her.

"I hunt people."

There was no humor, no regret, no emotion at all in his voice.

"What?" she asked, unable to leave it alone.

"I'm a deputy U.S. marshal. Hunting outlaws is what I do best."

It seemed inconceivable, but then, in an instant, somehow right. He was a man compelled to do the right thing, to take care of others, to make the world a safe place for little girls. "Have you ever . . . killed anyone?"

"Yep. But I never killed anyone who didn't try to kill me first."

For some reason that bit of information comforted her. Many lawmen were no better than the criminals they chased, but Joe was different. Better.

"Why on earth did you leave New York for this hell hole?" he asked.

It seemed only fair that she answer, since he'd answered her questions so honestly. "I ran away from home."

"When?"

"A little more than six months ago."

Even in the dark she could see him smile. "Aren't you a little old for running away from home?"

Sarah leaned just slightly further over the end of the bed. "Perhaps I am a little old for running away, but I was desperate and could think of no other solution. My father had my life planned for me, planned down to the last detail." Goodness, on the night before the wedding that had never taken place, her mother had even told her how many children she should have before insisting on an end to marital relations. Two. "I don't mean to sound ungrateful. I had a good education and every *thing* a girl could want. I've traveled to London and Paris, had beautiful gowns I've never worn, jewelry and a fine house and a busy social calendar." She sighed, remembering her life.

"Sounds grand," Joe whispered.

"I felt like I was living in a box," she whispered. "A box that got smaller and smaller with every passing day. When Father told me I was to marry Hugh Towerson whether I wanted to or not, I couldn't breathe. I literally couldn't breathe. All of a sudden I could see my life stretching before me, every day exactly like the last. The box I lived inside getting smaller and smaller and smaller. . . ."

"What can you get in Texas that you can't get in New York?"

He sounded like he really cared, like he was truly interested. Perhaps it was her imagination, but Sarah decided to accept it. She needed someone to talk to, on occasion.

"Excitement. Adventure. Life," she whispered. "I want to help these girls, if I can." That was the easy part. Was she brave enough to reveal everything here in the dark? Perhaps.

"I want to learn to shoot a gun, and dance by the light of the moon, and walk in the rain," she said quickly and softly. It wasn't as difficult as she'd expected it to be. "I want to sing a bawdy song at the top of my lungs and wear a red dress. My mother would never let me have a red dress. She said it wouldn't suit my unfashionable and unfortunate coloring, that it would look vulgar on me. I always wanted a red dress, though." She sighed. *I want to kiss*, she thought. *And maybe even discover what love really is*. She wasn't brave enough to say *that* aloud.

For a long moment Joe was silent, his breathing so even and deep that Sarah began to wonder if he'd fallen asleep after all. Or worse—he'd found her confession silly, her dreams trite. Suddenly she wished she'd kept her thoughts to herself, that she'd pretended to be asleep when Joe had asked.

But finally he whispered, "Rebel, yourself."

Chapter Seven

Joe woke with bright light teasing his eyes, light from the sun that broke through the white curtains and touched his face and woke him in a less-than-pleasant way. He came awake slowly, reluctantly. Even though it was late in the morning, he hadn't had more than a few hours sleep.

He couldn't remember ever staying up half the night talking to a woman. Listening to her whisper about dancing in the moonlight or walking in the rain, wishing for something so simple as wearing a red dress and singing a bawdy song. He'd answered her questions about his life; most of them, anyway, and he'd asked a few questions of his own, simply

114

because he was curious and bored and looking for a way to pass the hours.

Some decent women would've been shocked by the revelation that he'd killed, but not Sarah. She'd taken the news in stride, seeming to take comfort in the fact that he'd never shot anyone who hadn't tried to shoot him first. It had to have been near dawn when she'd whispered, groggy and half-asleep, "Why?"

Why what? Why had he chosen his profession? Why was he here? Why the phony marriage? There were too many whys to consider, so he hadn't answered, allowing her to believe him asleep. A moment later he'd heard her deep, even breathing.

Glancing up now showed that she'd fallen asleep with her head at the foot of the bed. A long cinnamon-red braid fell over the end of the mattress, hanging so close to Joe that it was no effort at all to reach up and touch the end of that thick plait.

Last night she'd said he was perverse. Maybe she was right, because he had the oddest urge to teach her to shoot, to walk with her in the rain and dance with her by the light of the moon. He wanted to see her in that vulgar red dress. These were dangerous thoughts.

He sat up, being mindful of his healing wound, and glanced down the length of the bed. One of Sarah's small feet had escaped from beneath the coverlet and rested on the pillow that remained at the head of the bed. One tiny, pale foot attached to a delicate, shapely ankle and a fetching calf.

Sarah clutched the other pillow, and she pressed half of her face into it as if she were trying to hide from the intruding sunlight. In sleep, she didn't look prim at all. This close he could count the freckles on her nose, and he could study, much too closely, the shape of the lips that were relaxed in sleep.

Why did he want her? She wasn't his type, not at all. He could list a hundred reasons why he should steer clear of this woman, a thousand reasons he shouldn't be here at all.

His body wasn't listening.

With great care, he rose to his feet. It would be best to get dressed and get out of here. To the barn maybe. Surely there were chores to be done, animals to be cared for, some hard and physical labor that would exhaust him so he'd forget about the woman in his bed. If he could do it with his side the way it was.

He rolled up the bedding and slid it under the bed, since he'd need it again tonight. And tomorrow night. And the night after that. He cursed beneath his breath thinking of all the nights to come.

A brief knock was the only warning he had before the doorknob turned and the door began to swing slowly open. Since this was a house full of little girls, he had no doubt that one or more stood on the other side of that door. It wouldn't do for any one of them to see him in his present state; naked and semi-aroused.

He made use of the closest concealment available, jumping into the bed and yanking across his midsection some of the quilt that covered Sarah.

The door swung open, and he saw three little Shorter girls standing there; Clara, Evie and Faith. Clara carried a tray laden with two plates of breakfast food, and Evie and Faith each very carefully carried a cup of coffee. Rousing from her deep sleep, Sarah lifted the head that rested near Joe's feet. Sleepy and disoriented, she looked toward the door and the girls.

"What?" she mumbled groggily.

"Breakfast in bed," Clara said with a small smile.

Sarah arched up slowly, her head rising and her foot swaying to the side to land on his chest. When skin hit skin she squealed like she'd been shot and twisted around, wide-eyed. Her gaze raked slowly over him from foot to face.

"Mornin', honey," he said as her shocked eyes met his. He hung onto just enough of the quilt to keep himself decently covered.

The girls approached the bed with their offering; fragrant eggs, bacon, and coffee. "We're going to church," Clara said. "But we wanted to let you know where we'd be and make sure you got some breakfast."

"Wait," Sarah said, lifting one pale hand. "And I'll go with you." Her voice barely shook.

"You slept too long," Evie said as she set a cup of coffee on the dresser. Faith copied her older sister's move. "We have to leave right now or we'll be late for services."

"It won't take me long to get ready," Sarah said, very carefully scooting away from Joe, easing toward the edge of the bed. "Just a few minutes. . . ."

He reached out and grabbed her foot, keeping her in place on the bed. "Shucks, honey, we just got married yesterday. I'm sure the folks will understand if we don't make it to church just this one Sunday."

She gave him a fiery glare over her shoulder, but he didn't release her foot.

Clara placed the food on the dresser beside two cups of steaming coffee, since Joe and Sarah obviously weren't in any position to take the tray. Sarah was prone on her stomach, one hand over the side of the bed, one foot in Joe's hand.

"You girls be careful," Joe said as they left the room and closed the door behind them. "And be sure to give our regrets to the Reverend and that nice Mayor Drake," he yelled as he held steadfast onto Sarah's foot.

With the girls on the other side of the door, Sarah yanked her foot from Joe's grasp and scooted from the bed. She lost her balance as she escaped and slipped over the edge, ending up on the floor with a thud and an oomph.

By the time she took a deep breath and regained a portion of her dignity, Joe was leaning over the side of the bed, peering over the edge.

"You all right?" he asked, a much too healthy dose of humor in his voice.

She glanced up, out of the corner of her eye. "I'm fine," she said frostily. "Just exactly how long have you been in the bed?" *With me?* she didn't add.

"Not long," he said, making himself comfortable as he peered over the edge of the bed. "Someone was coming, and after all," he grinned. "We *are* supposed to be pretending to be married."

It had seemed like a good idea last night, but that was before she'd spent a sleepless night talking to Joe, before she'd awakened to a large bare foot and a hairy leg inches from her face. Before she'd glanced over her shoulder to find an apparently naked man lounging in her bed, looking big and warm and much too beautiful.

A handsome man who hunted people for a living. A killer. A fast gun, she assumed, like the gunslingers she'd read about in the Eastern newspapers and the dime novels she'd had to hide from her parents. What had Joe said late into last night when she'd broken down and asked if he was fast? A cryptic and very softly whispered, "Not at everything, darlin'."

She should be frightened, she supposed, but she didn't see death in Joe's blue eyes, nor did she see anger and hate and murder. Instead she saw a reluctant softness, a diffident harmony. A hint of the restlessness she felt herself.

It occurred to her, in a foggy, half-asleep moment, that Joe White was everything she'd come West looking for. He was excitement and beauty; he was everything the life her father had planned for her *didn't* have. This bedroom was smaller than any room in her father's house, and yet she didn't feel trapped here. Not at all. In fact, she felt wonderfully, dizzyingly, frighteningly free.

Sarah gathered what dignity she could muster and rose to her feet. She was being as foolish as the girls! Joe wasn't going to stay. He was temporary here, a diversion to deceive the people of Jacob's Crossing, a false father and husband, the convenient solution to a very serious problem. To look at him and see more than was there, well, that was more than foolish, it was downright stupid. Sarah Prince was many things, but stupid was not one of them.

"I'm going to get dressed," she said calmly as she made her way to the wardrobe and the nearby privacy screen.

"Need any help?" Joe offered casually.

She looked over her shoulder to scold him with a glance, only to find him comfortably ensconced in the bed with his hands behind his head, a smile on his face, his eyes pinned boldly on her, and most of his body thankfully covered. "No, thank you."

"Anytime," he said softly, then he closed his eyes.

After church, everyone wanted to know about Joe and Sarah Shorter and the unexpected marriage that was the talk of the town. Alice curbed her impatience to politely answer all questions with as much truthfulness as possible.

She was so tired. Bone tired, and not from the extra physical work that had been required of her since her mother's death and the desertion of their one hired man. It was worrying that wore her out more than anything. Worrying over big things, like whether some judge was going to split up her family, and small fears like what Clara was going to fix for dinner and if Faith was going to wear out her Sunday dress before Evie had outgrown hers and passed it down.

Having Joe at the house offered a respite from all the worries, but Alice knew his presence and the comfort it offered was temporary. Once he was healed and had fulfilled his promise to her, he'd leave. Sarah said she'd stay, but Alice had her doubts. Why should Sarah take on seven girls that were no relation to her? One day she'd likely take a look around and realize that the Shorter sisters were not her children, not her responsibility, and she'd leave, too.

And then where would they be?

She and her sisters shouldn't be separated, not ever. It wasn't right. Somehow, Alice knew Joe White had been sent to them so that would never happen. Why else had he wandered right to their door? He'd been sent by an angel, maybe. A guardian angel. Her mother.

Mayor Drake approached, arrogant in his bearing as always. Red-faced and pucker-lipped, he always looked like he'd been sucking on a lemon and had gotten too much sun.

"Well," he harrumphed as Alice helped Faith into the wagon.

Two minutes later and they would've made a clean getaway! "Good afternoon, Mayor," Alice said politely.

"I'm surprised your father and his new wife would allow you to come to town alone." He pursed his lips into a tight little bow.

"It's not far," Alice said as she climbed into the driver's seat to sit beside Becky. "We've made the trip many times, by wagon and on foot."

"Yes," he said absently. "But you'd think they'd want to make a good impression, given the unusual circumstances of their marriage."

Alice was ready to bid the mayor goodbye and head for home. It was Evie who spoke up in defense of the newlyweds.

"I don't think Poppy and Sarah got much sleep last night. They both looked *very* tired this morning when we took them breakfast in bed."

"Really," Mayor Drake said, and impossibly, his face flushed redder than usual. His mouth shrunk to something resembling a raisin.

Faith leaned over the side of the wagon. "Yeah. I know Sarah didn't sleep well. She was upside down!"

"Upside down?" Mayor Drake asked softly.

Faith nodded vigorously. "Yep. Her head was down by Poppy's feet."

The mayor turned redder still, until Alice thought he might explode on the spot. Why, she didn't know, but it seemed best to make a quick getaway.

"We must be heading back," Alice said, nodding to the mayor while Becky slipped on her driving gloves. "It was nice to see you, Mayor Drake."

He seemed unable to answer as they drove away, headed back to the farm.

Becky drove, and the girls in the bed of the wagon chattered happily, so Alice had a chance to stare at the countryside and let her thoughts run free. A few precious moments with no worry; was that too much to ask for?

Yet one worry she was not able to dismiss, no matter how she tried. Faith and Glory had been so young when their father died they had no memory of him. None at all. It had seemed like such a small lie at the time, to tell them that Joe really was their father. She'd been so sure that one of the littlest girls would slip up and say something to give away the game long before the judge came to Jacob's Crossing, if they knew the truth.

But how would she break the news to them when Joe left? They were already becoming much too attached to him, much too comfortable with this man who was *not* their father. She remembered Albert Shorter as a loving but stern man who worked a lot and didn't want to be bothered at the end of the day. He hadn't smiled and laughed and teased the way Joe did. They hadn't called him Poppy, like they did Joe, they'd called him Father. If Joe was stern and distant and aloof, maybe it would be easy to be rid of him when the time came, but the truth of the matter was that even Alice was becoming fond of him.

If only he would stay. It was a foolish hope, she knew, but if a guardian angel had sent Joe to them, then it wasn't an impossible hope. He could stay, truly become their Poppy, and the Shorters could be a whole family again.

What would make a man like Joe White stay on a farm with seven little girls who were not his own? Not obligation, she knew, or charity, or loyalty. Not even the machinations of a guardian angel. What would make him stay forever?

Love, she thought as the house came into view in the distance. If Joe fell in love with his wife, then he'd stay. And so would Sarah. They would be a real family and no one would ever again threaten to split them up.

She should squelch this spark of hope now, before she began to believe it was possible. The marriage was a sham, a hoax, a contrived plan to fool the town and the judge. Sometimes Joe and Sarah seemed not even to like one another very much, and they were so different. Opposites, in many ways.

But if that guardian angel who'd guided Joe to them was still hanging around, then maybe . . . just maybe . . . with a little help. . . .

Chapter Eight

Sarah yawned as she opened the schoolroom door, lifting a gloved hand to cover her mouth. Goodness, she probably hadn't gotten six hours of sleep in the last two nights combined! One way or another, she was going to have to get accustomed to sleeping in the same room with Joe. At least this morning when she'd awakened she'd been alone in the bed. Joe had been sound asleep on the floor at the foot of the bed, sleeping like a man who had no worries, no troubles. No conscience.

As the door swung in and morning light spilled into the one-room schoolhouse, she was surprised to see Lawrence Drake sitting at her desk and the widow Lottie Handy, dressed in black as always, standing directly behind him.

"Tired, Mrs. Shorter?" he asked, his voice dripping with sarcasm.

The hairs on the back of Sarah's neck stood up, and an unpleasant chill worked its way down her spine. "A little," she confessed.

The mayor rose to his feet, lifting his chin in a challenging way.

"You girls play in the schoolyard until it's time for class to begin," Sarah said without turning to see that Dory, Evie, Faith and Glory obeyed. They would, she knew.

She closed the door behind her and walked to the desk, knowing that whatever was coming wasn't good. Mayor Drake looked too smug, and Lottie Handy looked even more sour than usual. That, in itself, was quite a feat.

"Your services as schoolteacher are no longer required here," Drake said quietly. "Mrs. Handy will fill in until a suitable permanent replacement can be found."

"I'm prepared to stay on as long as necessary," Sarah said. "There's no reason for an immediate change."

"Your unseemly conduct is reason enough," Drake said, a hint of anger and superiority in his voice.

Sarah made no move at all, as she searched her mind for an explanation for the mayor's animosity. Was he speaking of the unconventional wedding? Goodness, she'd never done anything in her life that could be called *unseemly*. Never. That was, after all, part of the problem that had spurred her westward. She could probably use a little unseemly behavior in her life.

Of course, she knew the answer, she knew why Mayor Drake stared at her with superior, beady eyes. He now knew that she'd been staying at the farm with the girls for several days after Joe's arrival. Perhaps, in his small mind, those brief living arrangements were sufficiently immoral to make her unsuitable as schoolteacher.

"Well, whatever you think best," she said calmly. She'd known that eventually someone would come in and take over her job here. Still, Lottie Handy would not have been her first choice. A woman so hopelessly bitter couldn't possibly be good with children. "Mrs. Handy, if you need any help getting started I'd be happy to stay on a day or two and assist you."

"Thank you," Lottie answered without so much as a speck of warmth in her voice. Her spine seemed to straighten, as if she were preparing to do battle. "But no."

Even though Sarah had wanted someone to come in and take over her job as schoolteacher, having it happen so suddenly made her feel disoriented, out of place and rather awkward. She'd hoped for a chance to tell the children goodbye, to ease the transition to a new schoolmarm. This was so unexpected, so . . . abrupt.

Still, there was nothing she could do but gather her few personal belongings and wish

Mrs. Handy well. In the schoolyard she told the girls what had happened, smiling as if all was well, ignoring the sinking feeling in the pit of her stomach and promising to be there to pick them up when school was dismissed.

As she headed, alone, back toward the farm, she realized that this sudden end to her contract with the town meant she'd be spending more time in Joe's company. A good deal more time, to be honest. She didn't know whether to be pleased with the prospect, or terrified.

The children could've walked home from school. Sarah knew that. But it was a long walk, and she really didn't mind getting away from the house for a while. Joe could be rather . . . disturbing, with very little obvious effort. A smile, a softly voiced wisecrack, he seemed to know just how to get under her skin.

"I wish you'd been there today," Dory, seated beside Sarah, said forlornly. "I don't like Mrs. Handy much." All the Shorter girls were pretty, but Dory had the look of one who would be uncommonly striking when she grew to womanhood.

"I'm sure you'll get used to her," Sarah said with a small smile. "She has a rather daunting personality, but I'm sure beneath that austere exterior there's a warm, caring woman." She didn't see any evidence of that warmer person, but she could hope . . . for the sake of the children. "Besides, Mrs. Handy is temporary. As soon as the town council finds a permanent replacement, she'll step aside."

Dory glanced into the back of the wagon. Evie was asleep, and Faith and Glory were talking softly, conspiring and giggling in one corner of the wagon bed. "Perhaps it will be all right. Since you're not teaching, you'll be spending more time with Poppy."

Sarah cut a suspicious glance toward Dory. "I suppose I will."

Dory lifted her chin and stared straight ahead. "He's very handsome, don't you think?"

"Well," Sarah hedged. "I suppose. . . ."

"Have you ever known a man who's *more* handsome than Poppy?" Dory pressed.

"Beauty is in the eye of the beholder," Sarah said primly. "It isn't something so superficial as an attractive face that makes a good man." But oh, the thought of that face did give her chills, on occasion.

"But Poppy *is* a good man," Dory insisted. "He's handsome and he's good. Doesn't that make him the perfect husband? Aren't you just *so* lucky to be married to him? He's lucky to be married to you, too." Dory leaned slightly closer. "Maybe you should tell Poppy he's the perfect husband. Tell him how glad you are that you're married. And then," Dory said dramatically, lowering her voice to not much more than a whisper. "Maybe you can *kiss* him. I hear men are real suckers for that sort of thing."

"Dory Shorter!" Sarah admonished. "Where did you hear such a thing?"

Dory straightened her spine. "At recess," she said, trying so hard to sound grown up. "Frances Dorset turned sixteen last week, you know, and she likes boys a lot." Dory lowered her voice. "She knows everything."

"I don't think you should be spending time with Frances. She's much too old to be your friend." *And much too world-wise, apparently.* "You should play with children your own age." "Children my own age are so tiresome," Dory said with a sigh. Without missing a beat she continued, "Are you going to tell Poppy he's perfect and kiss him? Today?"

Sarah sighed deeply, thanking heaven that the house had come into view.

Joe wasn't surprised to open his eyes and find Sarah peering over the end of the bed, her chin in her hands and her long braid falling past one cheek and down to tempt him. In the three days since they'd become man and wife—of a sort—this had become a nightly ritual. A bit of conversation in the dark, a way to pass the hours when they couldn't sleep.

He wondered if a part of Sarah's sleeplessness stemmed from the distress that was currently driving him slightly crazy; an uneasy attraction he couldn't quite shake, a teasing arousal he knew he could never satisfy. Miss Priss? Not likely.

"I can't believe that Mayor Drake was so offended by our briefly inappropriate living arrangements that he'd dismiss me without so much as a grace period." She frowned as she looked toward the window and the moonlit night beyond.

"Inappropriate living arrangements my ass. Old Larry wanted you for himself, honey," Joe said casually. "That's why he fired you."

Her frown deepened. "He did ask me to marry him a few times, but I didn't take him seriously."

Joe squelched a flash of anger. "He pitched a fit because you violated your contract with the town by marrying me, and all this time—" he began.

"Well," Sarah interrupted, "he did suggest a long engagement." She laid a cheek on her folded hands, and in the soft light of the moon that illuminated the room she looked a little lost, afraid. "I never took him seriously. After all, he barely knew me. I think I'd been in Jacob's Crossing two weeks before he asked me the first time."

Joe felt an unpleasant sensation in the pit of his stomach at the very thought of Sarah and that pompous ass Lawrence Drake together. It was more than anger, more than revulsion. It was as if a sense of wrongness settled in his gut—like he'd swallowed a boulder. Would the mayor pursue Sarah again, after her *husband* deserted her? Most likely.

He thought it best to change the subject. "Alice said that since you and I will both be here during the day, that she and the others will go back to school. Starting tomorrow."

"That's good," Sarah said, relief in her voice. "I don't want their education to suffer, and they're all so smart. Alice, especially." She cast her eyes down at him, and the way they widened he knew she'd just realized that with the girls at school they'd be alone at the farm all day. All day every day until the judge came through town. Two more weeks or so.

"Yep," he agreed, his eyes pinned to hers. "Maybe while they're at school I'll teach you a thing or two."

She swallowed, and licked her lips, and blinked quickly. Three times. God, he wanted to teach her a thing or two. He wanted to peel that prim nightgown off her body, unbraid her hair, and keep her up all night doing something besides talking.

What a stupid idea! He didn't need to be any more involved here than he had to be.

"I thought I might teach you how to shoot."

Even in the near-dark, he could see her face light up. "That would be wonderful."

"After all, eventually you're going to be out here away from town with seven little girls and no man around to protect you. You'll need to know how to defend yourself." And besides, learning to shoot was one of the things on her silly list. It seemed like the least he could do.

"No one's ever bothered us before, and Elizabeth never mentioned having any problems." Sarah's smile faded. "Do you really think I'll need to defend myself and the children from . . . from what? Goodness, I don't think I could actually shoot anyone."

She was so naïve, so incredibly trusting. She didn't see danger in the world around her. Before he left this place, he'd have to make sure that she knew what she was up against, that she understood how danger lurked around every corner, that she couldn't trust anyone.

Moving slowly and cautiously, he sat up. In this position he was face to face with Sarah. She scooted back, just slightly, so her face wasn't *too* close to his. He kept moving, rising to his knees and reaching out to grasp her arm. Luckily for both of them they'd reached an agreement as far as sleeping attire was concerned. He wore a pair of red flannel drawers in compromise.

"Let go of me," Sarah whispered, and Joe heard a hint of fear in her voice. Good. She should be scared. She should be terrified.

"Not yet," he said, holding her arm tight. He crawled onto the bed with her. The mattress dipped beneath his weight and Sarah rolled toward him, landing solidly against the length of his body; her breath on his chest, her legs tangled in white muslin and pushing ineffectively against his.

"Release me, Stumpy," she said coldly, the slightest of tremors in her voice.

"That threat might work on me, Miss Priss," he said, his breath in her hair. "But trust me, if you ever try it on a bad man it'll be a waste of breath."

"A . . . a bad man?"

He rolled Sarah onto her back and pinned her down, his hands on her thin wrists, his full weight pressing her into the soft mattress. Her legs were trapped between his, her breasts, soft and yielding, pressed against his bare chest. "What do you do now, Miss Priss?" he whispered. "Scold? Threaten? Cry?" He placed his face close to hers. "No. You shoot. You get your hands on the gun, point it at me, and pull the trigger."

"All right," she said, her voice relatively calm. Beneath him, her breasts rose and fell, her legs wriggled to no avail. His arousal pressed into her soft flesh. "You've made your point."

"Have I?" he whispered.

Heaven help him, he didn't want to move from this spot. He wanted to lie here a while longer, feel her beneath him, kiss her, touch her, slip inside her . . .

"I'm a helpless female," she said. "Helpless against the assault of the superior strength of a man." Incredibly, there was a touch of something like humor in her voice. A lightness, a serenity. She was definitely no longer afraid.

"Teach me how to shoot, and if the time comes, when it's absolutely necessary, I'll pull the trigger."

"Good," he whispered.

Beneath him her entire body relaxed. He felt it, as if inch by inch she softened beneath him. Her hands no longer pushed against his, her legs no longer wriggled in an effort to be free. The entire night was still and soft and dark. And waiting. Waiting.

Sarah's chin lifted almost defiantly, as if she offered her mouth to him for a kiss. Her lips were soft, and so close to his . . . so damn close.

As much as he wanted to, he knew he couldn't kiss her. Not ever. She'd likely read more into a simple kiss than was there. She'd sense love, not lust. Caring, not passion. Promise, not pure, carnal pleasure.

And pure carnal pleasure was all he wanted from a woman. He definitely did not want some prissy woman looking at him all moony-eyed and wanting, like she expected him to move into her life and fix all her problems, like she wanted more of him; all of him.

"Lesson over, Miss Priss," he said as he rolled off of her and from the bed in a move that was quick and smooth and necessary. Very, very necessary.

A moment later Sarah whispered. "Good night, Stumpy."

* * *

With the morning sun in his eyes, Deacon stood on the spot where Leonard and Isaac had claimed Joe White died. For days he'd been obsessed with the certainty that Rosie had run off with the bastard, that they were out there somewhere, together, laughing at him.

Leonard and Isaac, those incompetents, were gone. Deacon had sent them north to Kansas City with the promise that he'd meet them there in a month or two. In truth, Deacon hated Kansas City. He had no intention of ever going back.

From the spot where Joe White had been shot, Deacon pondered the possibilities. Maybe White had made his way back to Silver Creek and had stolen away with Rosie after he'd had a few days to heal. Then again, maybe he'd taken off from here and sent word to the saloon, asking her to join him. There were three small towns, other than Silver Creek, all within a day's ride of this spot. One to the east, one north-northwest, and one west-southwest. None of them was much more than a wide place in the road. The railroad ran through Silver Creek, but bypassed the other three towns. Each town's population was sparse, and strangers would be remembered.

Especially wounded strangers, or beautiful, blonde, female strangers.

Something unexpected welled up inside him

when he thought of Rosie, something he didn't understand. Why couldn't he just let her go? There were lots of other women in the world, beautiful, sweet, willing women.

Why did Deacon want to kill Joe White simply because Rosie said the bastard was better than him? That he had a quicker shot, a prettier face, was a better lover. A man shouldn't set much stock in a whore's opinion. That's all she was, after all. A whore.

But she was also the only woman who had ever made him laugh. The only woman he'd ever felt anxious about seeing, days before he knew he'd arrive in Silver Creek. The only woman he couldn't get enough of, the only woman who'd ever made him feel jealousy.

She was the only woman he wanted.

Deacon stepped into the stirrup and settled himself in the saddle, taking the reins and choosing a direction. West. Away from the morning sun.

Chapter Nine

Joe had spent part of the morning cleaning the single revolver in the house. He grumbled as he held the handful of bullets, all they had, in his hand. He couldn't believe that Sheridan hadn't been more well-armed than this, as far from town as his place was. Still, the six-shooter was the only weapon Joe had found. Before he left he'd buy a new six-shooter, plenty of ammo, and maybe a rifle. Even a woman as small as Sarah would look intimidating with a good Winchester rifle in her hands.

The girls had gone to school. All of them. Joe had assured Alice that he could handle the chores they hadn't gotten to before school, and Sarah had been quite confident as she'd informed Clara that she could handle all the housework. Only Joe had heard Sarah mutter, as she'd turned away, "How hard can it be?"

Since he'd heard her utter more than one dignified "Blast!" from the kitchen this morning, things were turning out to be more difficult than she'd imagined. He smiled as something heavy clattered against the kitchen floor, and Sarah said "blast" again, with a smidgen less dignity this time.

When she stepped into the dining room, drying her hands on a towel, she wrinkled her nose in his direction. "Teach me to shoot now, and those pots and pans will be my first targets."

He grinned at her. Alice was right. What had she said this morning before leaving for school with her sisters? *My, Sarah certainly is looking pretty today, don't you think?* The dress she wore was plainer than her usual attire; a calico, soft with wear, in shades of green and blue. Doing battle with the dirty dishes had put a bloom in her cheeks, a flush of frustration, perhaps. Her hair was pulled back into a long wavy ponytail. He'd watched her this morning, while she thought he was still sleeping, as she unplaited her hair and brushed it out and then secured it with a blue satin ribbon.

"No kitchen duty in New York?" he asked, trying to ignore his futile train of thought. So what if she did look uncommonly pretty today? She was still off limits.

"Never," she said, perching on the edge of a nearby dining room chair identical to his own.

"And I must say it's rather tedious. Somehow, Clara gathers a sense of accomplishment from setting everything in order, and she does a marvelous job. I don't seem to have her gift."

Joe pushed the gun away and stared hard at Sarah. "If you have second thoughts about this arrangement, now's the time to say so. A lifetime of caring for seven children isn't a chore to take on lightly."

She gave him a small smile. "I didn't mean to complain. I know what I'm giving up to take on this family. To become a part of it."

He wondered if she really had any idea. If she knew how hard it could be just to survive. "I thought you came out here to find life. Adventure."

The serenity on her face never wavered. "I think raising seven little girls will be quite an adventure." Her smile widened. "Why, just this morning, Alice pulled me aside to have a little woman-to-woman chat."

A tickle of warning crawled up Joe's spine. "Is that a fact?"

"There's going to be a town social this weekend, and she wanted to know if I'd teach her to dance. She assumes we'll go as a family, and I just didn't have the heart to refuse her. She's had so little joy in her life, especially lately."

"A social," Joe repeated.

Sarah leaned forward slightly. "She even offered to help me choose a pretty dress and fix my hair more becomingly for the occasion. Isn't that sweet?"

Joe didn't think Alice's offer was *sweet* at all. He thought it was cunning, subtle, maybe even brilliant. He couldn't possibly dance with Sarah. Sarah, in a pretty dress with her hair down. Sarah in his arms, moving with the music, with him.

Alice was trying to fix them up. Pointing out to him how pretty Sarah was, offering to help her "stepmother" prepare herself for a night of dancing with her new husband.

"Yeah, sweet," he repeated softly as he reached for the gun. He liked the familiar feel of the grip in his hand, the click of the bullets in the palm of his hand, the hum of the chamber as he spun it around. This was his world, the only world he wanted or needed.

He thought of Charlie Lockhart, the men he'd killed and would kill, the lawmen who had disappeared in their search for the elusive outlaw. Finding Lockhart and bringing him in, dead or alive, was Joe's mission; not taking care of a house full of women.

"You're giving up everything for these little girls," he said harshly. "A chance for a real marriage, a real husband. Children of your own. Aren't you afraid that one day you'll wake up filled with regret for what you don't have? For what you gave up?"

"No," she said, with such gentle assurance that he had no choice but to believe her. "What about you? Surely you'd like to one day settle down. Raise a family, perhaps." She smiled. "Haven't you ever thought of getting married and having your own little Stumpys?"

She was teasing him, but he didn't feel like laughing, or teasing, or even smiling back. It was best to make sure she knew where he stood on the subject, just in case Alice's meddling put any ideas in her head. "I don't want family," he said softly. "Hell, a wife and kids'll suck the life right out of a man."

Sarah's smile faded. "So you have no intention of settling down."

"Nope."

"You're going to hunt outlaws and wander from one town to the next until you're old and gray," she said, forcing a lightness into her voice.

"That's the plan."

She stood quickly. "Well, I must get back to the kitchen, I suppose." As she turned around she muttered, "Blast," very softly, once again.

Sarah sat back in the parlor rocking chair and enjoyed the silence. She closed her eyes against the lamplight. Goodness. Her feet hurt, her legs ached, the burn on her thumb stung, and she was bone weary. It was a good thing the girls had all decided to retire early tonight.

Which was strange, when she thought on it a bit. Becky and Faith always stayed up as late as possible, and then grumbled when they were ushered to bed. Tonight all seven of the girls had climbed the stairs to their bedrooms shortly after supper, one after another, claiming to be exhausted.

The front door opened and closed, and Sarah allowed her eyelids to drift up. It was Joe, returning from the barn, no doubt. The man did love his horse.

She allowed herself to look at him for a moment, to admire his handsome features and the way his black hair lay so softly against his neck and face. To appreciate, just for the span of a heartbeat or two, his wide shoulders and long legs and strong forearms. Too bad he was so set against marriage. He'd surely make some lucky woman a marvelous husband, one day, if he found a woman who could change his mind about the institution.

"Where are the girls?" he asked as he stepped into the parlor.

"Asleep," she answered tiredly. "Strangely enough, they all decided they were uncommonly sleepy this evening, and scurried off to bed."

For some reason, he scowled and grumbled.

She didn't really care what had struck him the wrong way. She was too tired to care. Her eyes closed again and she rocked once.

"What's wrong with you?" he asked testily.

Without opening her eyes, Sarah lifted her hand. "I burned my thumb on a pot fixing supper. It hurts."

She did open her eyes as Joe took her hand and examined the wound. "Where?"

"Right there." She pointed to the spot on her thumb, a blemish that was barely red. There was no blister, no severe damage to the skin. "I know it doesn't look like much, but it stings."

He dropped her hand with a scoffing glance at the injury.

"I've never burned myself before," she said. "I'll probably get used to it." In fact, the sting was much less now than it had been. Barely a tingle. "And besides, my feet hurt," she added.

"Your feet," Joe said softly.

"Yes. At least in the schoolroom I got a chance to sit on occasion." It had been such a long day. Cleaning, cooking, cleaning again. Nothing was ever quite finished.

"Poor Miss Priss," Joe said, and to her surprise he sat on the floor in front of her and took her right foot in his hand. "Having second thoughts about taking on the house and the sisters?"

"No," she said quickly. "What are you doing?" she asked sharply as he began to unlace one of her short boots.

"You said your feet hurt," he said, slipping the unlaced boot from her foot.

Before she had a chance to protest again he dropped the boot to the floor and began to rub her foot, grasping her entire foot in both hands, pressing his thumbs into the ball of her stocking-covered foot. The sensation was heavenly, and as the pain fled from her foot her entire body was filled with warmth until she felt as if she were floating. Her eyes drifted closed again.

Surely she should protest. This was certainly not proper between two people who were in a relationship of convenience—especially when he kept questioning her decisions. And yet, it felt so good, so wonderful. She was still tired, but she had regained some strength with his touch. Even the burn on her thumb no longer pained her.

When Joe began to unlace the boot on her left foot she didn't say a word. She didn't open her eyes or shy away or draw her foot back in modesty. As Joe began his ministrations once again a faint, pleasant tingle spread slowly and surely through her entire body. She was filled with warmth, and comfort, and . . . and life. All at the same time.

Joe placed Sarah's foot very gently on the floor. Well, the foot rub must've worked, since she now wore the most sinful smile he'd ever seen. Dammit, she didn't look prissy at all, at the moment; her eyes were closed, and a soft smile was on her relaxed lips.

So the girls were all *tired* tonight, huh? Joe White was no fool. He could tell what was going on here. The Shorter sisters seemed to think that if he and Sarah spent enough time

alone together that something would happen.
He knew a trap when he saw one. He'd just
never had the urge to willingly fall headfirst
into one.

"Better?" he asked as he stood.

"Oh, yes," Sarah said softly. "You're an angel.
A paragon of manhood." Her smile widened as
she teased. "A saint."

He placed his hands on the arms of her chair
and rocked her forward, toward him until her
face was close to his. Her eyes flew open.

"No," he said softly. "I'm not."

By the light of the morning sun, Rosie surveyed
the small building that would, in a few days'
time, become her café. For years she'd saved
and planned, knowing that one day the time
would come when she'd start a new life.

Once or twice, she'd wondered if Jacob's
Crossing was far enough away from Silver
Creek to start that new life. If she'd had more
money saved she would have moved farther
west, maybe even all the way to San Francisco,
but Deacon had forced her to make her exodus
sooner than she'd planned.

Deacon Moss, that bastard. He'd ruined
everything! For the past year she'd done her
job, kept her distance, and remained, through
it all, her own woman. She'd been lied to so
many times in her twenty years of life she'd
finally sworn that no lie would ever cross her
lips, no matter what the cost. It was a promise

she'd kept. But it was a promise that had cost that lawman his life.

That wasn't why she'd decided to leave Silver Creek, though. Falling in love was out of the question for her, absolutely out of the question, but every now and then she'd look at Deacon Moss and she'd feel . . . something. For years she'd known without a doubt that love was a false dream, anyway. What had love done for her mother? Broken her heart and killed her. What had love done for Rosie? Nothing, and she didn't believe in it.

She'd always liked Deacon, that was true. And that was fine. There wasn't any danger in liking a man. But lately that liking had grown stronger, until she'd begun to believe that maybe, just maybe it was turning into more. And that was more than she wanted.

She couldn't possibly fall in love! And if she did, well, it wouldn't be with a man who'd have another man killed just because . . . just because she'd opened her big mouth and told the truth.

Deacon had seemed to be most concerned about the fact that she'd not charged poor Joe White on his one visit to her room above the saloon, but he'd never asked why. She would've told him the truth if he had—that Fast Eddie had been coming around in Deacon's absence, that he'd gotten territorial once or twice and scared off paying customers. She might even have told him that Eddie had hurt her once, and that she'd been so relieved that Eddie was dead she'd gotten . . . carried away. As a woman who'd slept with many men, she did appreciate what a fine specimen of manhood Joe White was, but that had nothing to do with her generosity. Eddie being out of the picture was simply good for business.

If only Deacon had asked one more question, after his stream of silly *who's the best*? queries. If only he'd asked, "But who do you want to be with now, Rosie?" She could've truthfully answered, "You, Deacon Moss."

"Good morning, Miss Sheppard." The greeting, coming from behind her, startled Rosie. She turned, her raised hand shading her eyes from the bright sunlight. She recognized the mayor right away. Fortunately he didn't recognize her, but then, on his visits to Silver Creek he had never once looked at her above the neck. His was the only familiar face she'd seen in Jacob's Crossing thus far, and he had no idea who she was. Who she'd *been*.

"Good morning, Mayor Drake," she said sweetly. "How nice to see you again."

"Going ahead with your plans for the café?"

"Indeed," she answered.

He smiled at her, a tight, stingy grin. "Seems to me a pretty lady like you would be looking for a husband instead of planning to start your own business."

"Maybe I'll marry one day," she said demurely. *But not to you, you ass, and not for a very, very long time.*

His tight smile widened, a little. "There's going to be a town soiree this weekend. I do hope you'll save me a dance."

"That's very sweet of you, Mayor Drake, but—"

"Call me Lawrence," he interrupted. "And I'd love to be allowed the privilege of calling you by your given name."

"Mary Rose, Lawrence." It couldn't hurt to have the mayor on her side, but she was *not* going to dance with him. No way would he ever put his hands on her again, not even for a dance. Even if she weren't afraid of him somehow connecting her with her past. "I must be going," she said. Spinning away quickly, she walked back toward the boarding house.

Chapter Ten

Joe stifled a curse beneath his breath. He'd had every intention of refusing to attend this damn shindig, but here he was, stepping into the town square with eight lovely ladies surrounding him. The Shorter sisters, all seven of them, had dressed in their brightest, finest gowns. Petite blondes in red, blue, green, pink and lavender all but danced around him, they were so excited.

There was still enough light in the sky that the lanterns strung around the square were not yet called for. A small band played lively music, and a few couples caroused on the wooden platform that served as the makeshift dance floor.

The girls caught sight of friends and scattered like bird shot. All but Alice, who stayed close. Joe was bracketed by Alice, who twiddled her thumbs and squirmed in her pretty blue dress, and Sarah, who looked lovelier than ever in a fancy copper-colored gown. It wasn't exactly a revealing outfit, but the neck was much less severe than what she usually wore. The indentation at the base of her throat was revealed, and a very small amount of skin beneath caught the light of the sun. As his gaze lingered there, a light, delicate sprinkling of freckles caught his eye. He wondered if it were possible to lick them off, one at a time. He sure as hell wanted to try.

Instructions of one sort or another had filled the past week. During the day, he gave Sarah a brief education on handling, cleaning, and firing the revolver. At night, Sarah gave Alice dancing lessons.

Also, on more than one occasion, he'd caught Clara teaching Sarah how to mend or cook or clean. And each time, the expression on the woman's face had made Joe want to laugh. Sarah was learning, but she didn't seem to like her new domestic chores much. Hell, for all he knew she'd be on her way back to New York in a day or two.

He hadn't rubbed Sarah's feet any more, not since that one time. She'd liked it too much, and dammit—so had he . . .

"Isn't it lovely?" Sarah asked softly, interrupting his thoughts. Joe looked down at her, at her softly styled hair and the tempting sprinkling of freckles.

"Surely you've been to fancier dances than this one, Miss Priss," he answered in a voice as low as her own. "Lavish balls and soirées and cotillions that would put this town social to shame."

She glanced up at him and smiled. "Of course I have, Stumpy. But the people there never had this much fun."

Joe noted that she was, perhaps, right. Children ran and laughed and played on the perimeter of the stage, and those who danced had huge smiles on their faces; these people partook of an almost mindless joy as they moved with the music. He'd sworn he wouldn't dance with Sarah, but then he'd also sworn not to change his sleeping habits for her, not to attend the town shindig—not to want the woman everyone thought was his wife.

"Oh, there he is," Alice hissed, drawing Joe's attention reluctantly away from Sarah.

"Where?" Sarah asked, her voice conspiratorially low.

"Over there." Alice barely motioned with a raised finger and, lifting his eyes, Joe caught sight of a dark-haired young man rounding the stage.

"He's very handsome," Sarah whispered. "Why have I not seen him at school?"

"He used to go to school, but after his older brother left home he had to start helping his father full time with their ranch."

By this point the young man in question was upon them, and the conversation ceased. Alice forced a wavering smile, and the young man answered with a grin that was just as uncertain.

"Oh," Alice said, as if she hadn't been aware until that very moment that the boy was in the state of Texas. "Quincy, how nice to see you."

Quincy? Joe glared at the boy, as any self-respecting father would.

"Poppy, Sarah, this is Quincy Thomas. Quincy, this is my father and his wife, Joe and Sarah Shorter." She handled the introductions formally and quickly.

Sarah, proper as always, greeted the young man with a smile and a prim, "How do you do?" Joe, on the other hand, glared unrelentingly, until the young man was red in the face and had broken out in a sweat.

He remembered too well what it was like to be that age, sixteen, seventeen at the most. Not a boy anymore, almost a man, this Quincy's thoughts would be turning in new and interesting directions. Like what was hidden beneath a girl's skirts.

Suddenly, he wanted to scare the kid. He wanted to threaten to rename him Stumpy if he got any indecent ideas. And unlike Sarah, he wouldn't be threatening Quincy's *hands*.

When Quincy asked Alice if she wanted to

dance, Joe gave her a soft, very serious, instruction. "Stay where I can see you."

As he watched the two young people make their way to the dance floor, Sarah slipped her arm through his. He flinched as she leaned into him. "That was quite good," she whispered.

"What are you talking about?"

"Anyone who saw that scene will never doubt that you are an overprotective father. Why, you had that young man shaking in his boots, and all with that threatening expression you mustered for the occasion."

He didn't know how to tell her that he hadn't manufactured anything. "Wanna dance?" he asked. Hell, if he were going to break all his promises to himself, he might as well have some fun.

Sarah couldn't wipe the smile from her face. *This* was what she'd come West looking for, *this* was why she'd left New York and her family and her father's plans behind.

The town square bustled, its occupants laughing and dancing, talking loudly to be heard above the music and the roar of the crowd. The girls all smiled and laughed, playing with their friends and eating more sweets than they should.

And Joe danced with her. Goodness, Sarah thought as he spun her gently around and she looked up at him, there were times when she looked at him and he took her breath away. It was quite amazing, really. No one else had ever affected her this way, and she suspected no one else ever would.

She chided herself for being silly, for allowing herself to be swayed by the girls' obvious efforts to push her to the man they had taken in and made their Poppy. A perfect husband, indeed. A man who believed a wife and children would suck the life out of him was certainly *not* the ideal mate.

He held her close as they danced, perhaps a little bit too close. He was only keeping up appearances, she imagined, putting on a show for the townspeople.

She decided to enjoy this while it lasted, to smell and touch and move with abandon, to enjoy this almost perfect moment in time. She decided not to care why Joe held her so close, not to think about what would happen tomorrow or the next day or the next.

Because tonight . . . tonight was truly perfect.

Eventually everyone from Jacob's Crossing and well beyond had crowded into the town square. Food, music, and conversation kept the crowd alive through the hours, past sunset and well into the night.

Whenever someone tried to claim Sarah for a dance, Joe found a reason to whisk her away. One of the kids needed her, or he was suddenly hungry, or he wanted to dance with her himself. Joe knew it shouldn't matter to him that the mayor and the shopkeeper and the saloon owner all wanted to claim a dance. But it did.

Hellfire, she looked too good tonight. In that dress, with tendrils of waving hair falling from a loose knot, and the soft smile she wore throughout the evening, she was more alluring than ever. How had he ever thought her prissy and plain? When the light hit her just right she looked like a sunset, all golden and copper radiance.

He spun her around, leading her to the edge of the dance floor, determined not to let her or anyone else know that his thoughts had begun to take a dangerous turn. "Quincy seems to be behaving himself," he said, just to have something to say. Something safe.

Sarah's smile widened. "Aren't they adorable? It's so sweet the way they dance and talk and never actually look at one another. I think they're both terrified."

He growled down at her. "You won't think Quincy's so *adorable* when he decides to sneak Alice behind the barn one afternoon and toss up her skirts."

"He wouldn't dare," she said, her smile dimming. "They're just children."

"They won't be children for much longer," he said in a serious tone. He cast a sideways glance to Quincy and Alice, who stood a few feet away sipping punch. "Maybe you should talk to her, woman to woman. Warn her to be on the lookout for boys with less-than-honorable intentions."

"Maybe I should," Sarah said softly.

Dammit, someone should have the talk with Sarah, because his own intentions were far from honorable at the moment.

Anxious to change the subject, he glanced about the crowded dance floor. "At least Mayor Larry's found some other poor woman to harass." Drake was asking a blonde to dance, and his unfortunate prey was shaking her head vigorously. All he could see was the back of her head, but the woman seemed to be quite adamant.

"I do believe that's Miss Sheppard," Sarah said. "She's renting the room I vacated at the boarding house. She said she's planning to open a café in town. Wouldn't that be lovely?"

Joe spared only a glance for Miss Sheppard, who made a hasty retreat from the mayor. About that time Faith ran into his line of vision, her bright pink checkered dress whipping around her legs.

"Poppy," she cried as she wormed her way past dancers to stand at his side. His dance with Sarah came to a too-soon end. "What side of a chicken has the most feathers?"

Joe considered the riddle for a moment, stroking his chin and shutting one eye briefly before turning his gaze down to Faith. "I have no idea. What side of a chicken has the most feathers?"

"The *out*side," Faith said, delighted to have stumped her Poppy.

Sarah laughed brightly as Evie arrived on the tail-end of the punch line. "That's a dopey riddle," the other little girl said, "and you are a dope." She turned her eyes up to Joe. "I'm tired, Poppy. When are we going home?"

"Soon," he said. He caught Alice's eyes, and when she came to the edge of the raised dance floor he told her to round up the others and get to the wagon. It was time to go home. When Evie asked if he and Sarah were going to help, Joe turned his eyes to Sarah again.

"One last dance," he said, not yet ready to let her go.

Sarah knew she'd remember this night always. Years from now, when she was an old woman, she would close her eyes and remember in great detail watching the full moon rise above Jacob's Crossing, laughing at Faith's silly riddle, smiling at Alice's awkward first romance. Dancing with Joe all night.

He was a good dancer, better than she'd expected. In deference to his healing wound, he'd sat out the more vigorous dances, the jigs that required more effort than was wise at this point, but there were lots of more sedate, slower dances in which he participated.

She'd never enjoyed a ball this much, had never enjoyed a dance partner more. Goodness, she still had on her face the silly smile she'd worn all evening.

They walked now toward the wagon, away from the stage and the noise of the town social. Sarah was tired, warmly and pleasantly sleepy, and ready to go home and collapse into her comfortable, warm bed. Alice had rounded up her sisters, and the girls waited for Joe and Sarah so they could begin the journey home. They had parked the wagon at the end of the street, a fair distance away but not terribly far.

The farther away from the town square they walked, the darker it became. The light from the lanterns strung about the square didn't reach this far into the night. Of course, since there was a full moon they were never in danger of walking into complete darkness, as long as they avoided the shadows beneath the boardwalk awning. Sarah kept her eyes on the end of the street, waiting for the wagon and the girls to come into view.

All of a sudden, Joe came to a halt. In the middle of the street he just stopped. He crooked his head and set his eyes on her. "Hear that?"

"What?" she asked, wondering if he heard something threatening, or one of the girls crying or calling.

"A waltz."

It *was* a waltz she heard when she strained her ears to listen. Though the band that had played all evening was less than magnificent, somehow there was a magic in the air. "So it is."

Joe reached out and grabbed her, and spun her into the middle of the deserted street. The move surprised Sarah, took her breath away, made her heart stop beating for a long moment. But she recovered quickly, falling into step as he twirled her around to the faint strains of the waltz.

This she would remember, too. The rush of her blood, the way Joe's hand felt in hers, the way he led her so gracefully across the dusty street and back again. She looked into his face, a visage more beautiful than ever in the moonlight.

She glanced up and her smile widened. Goodness, here she was, dancing by the light of the moon just as she'd dreamed. She was free, and happier than she'd ever been.

Joe had made two of her whispered wishes come true in the span of a week. He was teaching her to shoot the revolver, and now he danced her about by the light of the moon. A cool breeze washed over her face and her heart beat furiously. She savored everything, every breath, every heartbeat. The way Joe cradled her in his arms. Dust rose about their feet, and in another unexpected move Joe pulled her closer than was proper. As a matter of fact, the way he held her as he whirled her toward the boardwalk, his body pressed against hers from chest to knee, was quite unseemly.

She liked it. She liked it very, very much.

The music ended, and they came to a halt near the shadows. Joe didn't release her, but held on as if he weren't ready to let go, as if he enjoyed embracing her this way.

She wondered what he'd say if she told him about her other wish. The one she'd kept to herself. The kiss she still dreamed of. A real, true, heart-stopping kiss.

Perhaps she didn't need to tell him. His mouth moved toward hers slowly; dipping, slanting, softening. He hesitated when his mouth was almost touching hers, but his moment of reluctance didn't last any longer than the span of a heartbeat. He touched his lips to hers.

A rush of something wonderful and exciting raced through her blood at the touch of his mouth. It was as if the whole world changed in an instant. She tasted Joe with all her senses, felt his spirit to the center of her soul, and became a part of him in one instant.

His mouth lingered on hers for a moment longer, moving gently in a way that affected her heart and her knees and finally the pit of her stomach. She found herself reaching for Joe's arm, holding on for support, answering the kiss with a gentle brush of her own lips.

He pulled her close, so that the length of her

body pressed tightly, intimately, against his. How shockingly wonderful it was. She leaned into him, falling bonelessly against his solid warmth, resting in the shelter of his arms while she tasted him more deeply as his mouth moved over hers.

Joe broke the kiss, moving away slowly, as reluctantly as he'd approached. "I shouldn't have done that," he whispered huskily.

"Probably not," she answered, her voice surprisingly feeble. And then she reached up to boldly place her lips to his again. Just once.

Chapter Eleven

Joe lay in his place on the floor at the foot of the bed, aching, aroused, and miserable.

What had he been thinking? To be with Sarah was impossible, he knew that. Taking her to the town social had *not* been a good idea, and dancing with her had been foolish. And to kiss her—that had been downright stupid.

If only she hadn't kissed him back. Where was her prudish, "Oh, Joe, stop that!" when he needed it? Where was the nonchalance that he had expected?

He closed his eyes when he heard her moving about on the bed. Surely she wasn't going to torture him with their nightly ritual, soft conversation in the dark.

Sure enough, her head appeared just over

the foot of the bed. "You're not asleep, are you?" she whispered.

"No," he said, soft and low and almost menacing. Didn't she know what she was doing to him? Probably not. She was so naïve, his Miss Priss.

She didn't immediately launch into conversation, as she usually did, but rested her head in her hands and looked down at him for a moment. She seemed to be studying him. Uncertain. Maybe even curious.

"Can I ask you a personal question?"

"Sure."

"Who's Tess?"

It wasn't exactly the question he'd been expecting. "Tess is my sister."

She sighed, a long, seemingly relieved sigh. "Your *sister*. That's wonderful. I mean, I was just curious and . . ." She leaned a bit further over the end of the bed. "I just wanted to be sure that she wasn't a sweetheart or a . . . maybe even a wife."

"Nope."

"When I asked you about her before, you said she was a *friend*." There was accusation in that soft voice.

"I was pretending to be Albert Shorter at the time, remember? And Albert didn't have a sister, according to Alice."

"I see," Sarah said thoughtfully. For a moment she was silent, her head in her hands, her eyes cast downward. "Well, do you have a sweetheart or a wife out there somewhere? I know you have some very strong opinions about the institution of marriage, but that doesn't mean you've never been tempted."

Tempted? Who was she kidding?

"I hate to think that maybe there's someone out there who's worried about you right this very minute and wondering where you are," she finished softly.

"Nope," he said with certainty.

He hoped his short answer would put an end to this conversation. Heaven help him, he couldn't handle it. Not tonight.

"You know," Sarah continued. "They say the moon calls out the madness within us."

"Do they," Joe muttered.

"Yes. I never believed it until now, but as I am about to do something completely mad . . ."

He pinned his eyes on her. All he had to do was reach up and grab her, pull her to the floor to lie beside him, kiss her again and then there would be nothing left between them. No walls, no promises, nothing. "Completely mad," he repeated.

For a few seconds he thought the conversation was over. Sarah said not a word, but stared out the window. "Do you remember what you said to me a few days ago, about giving up so much for these girls, about how I'd never have a real marriage and a real husband?"

"Yep." Was she having doubts now about

staying here with the girls? Ah, he couldn't blame her. It was a lot to ask of anyone.

"You're right about that, of course. No man will want to take on a woman with seven children. And of course, I'll have to pretend to wait for you for a while, after you desert us. Years, I imagine."

He said nothing. There was no argument, no persuasive logic he could use. Even though he had grown fond of the girls, he certainly could not fault this beautiful young woman for wanting a life of her own.

"So I imagine I'll live the rest of my life right here. Alone, but for the girls and perhaps one day their families. I don't mind, really, but . . . but . . ." She continued to stare out the window.

"But what?" he prompted, a little surprised that she hadn't backed out.

She cocked her head slightly to the side and took a deep breath he both heard and felt. "But I should like to know what it's like to . . . to lie with a man the way a wife lies with a husband."

Joe was stunned speechless. Surely he'd misunderstood.

"Sorry," Sarah said as she backed away where she had leaned off the bed. "I shouldn't have said a word," she muttered, her voice no longer clear. "It's the moon, I tell you. The moon."

Joe came slowly and quietly to his feet. The moonlight streaming through the window illuminated the bed and the squirming lump beneath the quilt. Sarah had pulled the covers all the way over her head again. She was hiding. Possibly from him and maybe even from herself.

If he was smart he'd lie down and suffer in silence all night. He was already too close to this woman, he liked her too much. He wanted her too much. Leaving this place was already going to be harder than it should be.

He moved to the side of the bed and reached down to pull the quilt away from her head. She immediately turned her eyes up to him.

"I'm sorry," she said again. "I shouldn't have asked. It's too much to ask."

He smiled down at her. "Too much to ask? If you think that's true the moon really has made you mad."

"You wouldn't mind?" she asked.

"Mind?" He sat on the bed and peeled the quilt away from her body. Even in her prim nightgown she looked tempting and delicious and seductive. He reached out, and with one hand unfastened the top buttons of the unnecessary garment she wore. He felt himself giving in, letting go, releasing every doubt that had filled him just a few minutes ago. "I've wanted to do this for a long time."

"You have?" She trembled beneath his hand, but not with fear. He knew she wasn't afraid of him. She never had been.

He peeled muslin away and kissed the skin

just beneath her throat, flicked his tongue slowly across the sweet flesh there, sucked lightly as he settled one hand at her waist.

"Wh . . . what are you doing?" she whispered.

He lifted his head and smiled at her. "Licking away your freckles."

She knew with all her heart that this was right. Joe was her husband. Though the name he'd signed on the marriage certificate was not his own, and he didn't intend to stay with her, the words they'd said in a church had to mean something. They had to.

She didn't know exactly what to expect. Basically, yes, but exactly . . . no. She only knew she didn't want to spend the rest of her life an oblivious virgin, wondering what she'd missed and berating herself for passing up the chance to lie with the only husband she'd ever have.

Joe unbuttoned her nightdress as far as possible, nearly to her waist. He didn't seem to be in a hurry at all, but lingered over each button, touching, kissing her. She wondered, as he kissed her chest once again, if she had any freckles left.

He peeled back the fabric of her nightgown, exposing her flesh to the night air and then covering her breasts with his roughened yet tender hands. Her nipples pebbled against his palms, and when he shifted his hands and flicked his thumbs over those hardened peaks she sucked in her breath and held it. Sparks shot through her body, faint, deep, surprising shocks of sensation.

"Sit up," he whispered, slipping one hand behind her head and lifting her into a sitting position. Here she could look him in the eye, see his face as he began to unbraid her hair in smooth, unhurried motions. She reached out to caress his cheek with nervous fingers, to feel the rough warmth beneath her fingertips. When that simple touch was no longer enough to satisfy her, she moved her hand to his neck, settling it comfortably there. Her fingers rocked against his skin, and she leaned her head back slightly so that she felt his hands in her hair and at her back. She was overcome by the need to touch him, to have him touch her, to absorb his warmth and energy.

When her hair was free Joe speared his fingers through it, finally cupping the back of her head and pulling her mouth to his for a long, slow kiss.

His mouth was more demanding than it had been on a Jacob's Crossing street. Harder. Hotter. Finally forcing her lips apart to allow his tongue access to her mouth. As his tongue danced with hers, the throb low in her belly that had been tormenting her all night increased, grew more insistent and distinct. She wanted this. Wanted him. A cry from deep in her throat broke free.

Joe grabbed the hem of her nightgown and

worked it upward. His fingers brushed her legs as he slowly lifted the nightgown away, his hands slipping beneath her hips to lift her away from the mattress until the muslin was bunched at her waist. Cool night air brushed her bare legs.

An unexpected trembling wracked her body, but not because she was afraid. She was anxious, and curious, and a flickering of uncertainty shot through her, but she was not afraid. She knew full well why she wasn't afraid of what was to come, how she had found the courage to ask Joe to lie with her.

She loved him. In the days since she'd first seen Joe lying in this bed, she'd fallen in love. Slowly, certainly, and deeply. It was impossible, but oh, so true. She wanted him, not just with her body but with her heart.

Taking the muslin in his hands, Joe made quick work of ridding her of the nightgown completely, lifting it over her head and dropping it to the floor. She sat before him completely naked, vulnerable and achy and uncertain about what she should do next.

She didn't know what came next, but she did know that Joe was going to have to divest himself of his sleepwear, as well. She reached out and untied the tapes at his waist, and slipped her hands beneath the waistband. Even his hips were hard, his thighs, the way he looked at her . . . when the red flannel was on the floor

171

next to her white muslin, she glanced at his manhood. A glance, only, since she was not so bold as she sometimes tried to be.

He pressed her back, pushing her into the mattress and hovering above her. Sarah held her breath, trying to ready herself for what was to come. Pain, perhaps. An end to this ache within her, surely.

But Joe didn't delve between her legs and push to enter her. He hovered above her, kissing her deeply, then flicked his thumbs over her nipples once again. A deep tremor snaked through Sarah's body, hot and tingly and insistent.

Joe moved his warm kisses to her throat, to her freckled chest, and then to a nipple he sucked deep into his mouth. Sarah came off the bed, arching instinctively into the man above her. Her entire body was one exposed nerve, and she felt everything; the cool of the night air, the breath in her mouth, the brush of Joe's body against hers, his tongue, his lips, the throbbing between her legs—and then his gentle hand forcing her thighs apart.

She waited, again, for an insistent thrust that would put an end to her virginity. But again, Joe surprised her. He touched her, brushed his fingers against her throbbing flesh. She felt herself melting at his touch, her entrance growing wet for him. Her thighs fell further apart in invitation. He stroked harder, and then slipped a finger inside her.

Her entire body was unsettled, shaking, pulsating. When she felt the tip of him pressing against her she rocked down and up, searching for the touch that would bring her ease. Wanting, at last, the fulfillment of having Joe inside her.

He moved slowly, stretching her impossibly with his invasion, inching inside her until he met the barrier of her maidenhead. He hesitated, and then he plunged forward, bursting inside her, filling her at last.

There *was* pain, and a moment of panic. What had she done? Joe became very still, and then he kissed her, gently, as he had on the street. With sweetness and promise. With trepidation and affection. The sharpness of the pain faded, her body adjusted to him, and her panic fled.

He rocked within her, stroking her aching body, reviving the rhythm of her desire. Her own hips rocked with his, into and away from his thrust. A tension built within her, a pounding, pulsating pressure that drove away everything else.

"Relax," Joe whispered.

Relax? Was he mad, too?

"Don't fight it," he whispered.

Don't fight what?

He locked his lips to hers and slipped his tongue into her mouth, pushing, demanding. Her mouth answered, her hips twisted and reached. She lifted her legs and wrapped them around his. She couldn't get close enough, couldn't ever, ever get close enough.

A shock wave burst through her body, ripping her apart, splintering her body into a million tiny pieces. She cried out against a pleasure so intense it blinded her. Stole her senses. Washed away the rest of the world.

As the pleasure faded, Joe plunged deep inside her once again. She felt his long, hard body shudder above and inside her, and she held on to him as if for dear life as the shaking lessened and died. He drifted down to cover her. Goodness, they were both sweating and shaking and weak.

She laid her hand against Joe's head, flicked the ends of her fingers through his hair. They were still connected, still together, and she felt no rush to remedy that state. There was something very right about it, very comforting.

"Did I hurt you?" he asked, rising slowly above her.

"A little," she confessed.

"I didn't want to hurt you." He lowered his head to kiss her, another sweet, gentle kiss.

She found herself believing, as surely as the Shorter sisters no doubt believed, that Joe would never leave. That he would stay here forever, and spend night after night just like this. Surely this was something special, something not to be tossed aside.

Those were irrational thoughts, and she was not a woman given to such foolishness. Still, she wondered if Joe would stay if she told him she loved him.

* * *

They bathed at the basin near the dresser, and Joe stared down at the spot of blood on the washcloth he held. In the moonlight it looked black, dark, ominous. Something in his gut tightened and twisted. He'd never slept with a virgin before. Never. And for good reason. It was a hell of a lot of responsibility, making love to a woman for the first time. One uneasy side effect he hadn't expected; right now he was feeling much too proprietary about Sarah, much too protective.

There weren't many virgin prostitutes, he thought wryly, and most of the women he found himself with were employed in that profession. After all, prostitutes weren't looking for more than a way to make a living. They didn't liken passionate sex with nonsense like love and marriage. They usually knew what they were doing in bed, and how to prevent unwanted babies.

Babies. Joe looked over his shoulder to catch a glimpse of Sarah reaching for her nightgown, her movements fluid and graceful. Those movements seemed almost lazy, and she appeared content as she tried to straighten the tangled garment. It hadn't occurred to him, not once, that Sarah's whispered request might result in a baby. She didn't need another mouth to feed, and he didn't need or want the obligation and worry a child entailed.

Of course, he'd be gone before she knew if

there was a child or not. He could lie with her again and again and leave before they knew. Though, he felt like a selfish coward for even thinking that way.

He didn't want to ruin this night thinking about leaving or responsibility or babies. Tossing the washcloth aside, he returned to the bed and grabbed the nightgown from Sarah before she could slip it over her head.

"Nope," he said, grabbing her around the waist and pulling her into the bed with him. "You don't need that, honey."

"Joe," she said, indignation and laughter in her voice. "I can't sleep without my nightgown."

"Yes, you can," he said, drawing the quilt over them both and lying down with Sarah in his arms, her back against his chest, her backside nestled against his lower belly. "I'm living proof of that fact."

"But I feel . . . I feel . . ."

"Naked?" he finished for her.

"Naked," she whispered.

He brushed her hair aside and kissed her on the back of the neck. "Go to sleep, Sarah," he said softly.

"Oh, goodness," she breathed, relaxing in his arms already. "I don't think I can. My brain is spinning, my heart is pounding, and I can't quite catch my breath."

Joe didn't say so, but his own heart was pounding pretty damned furiously, and he was having trouble catching his own breath.

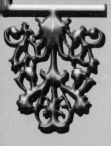

Thrill to the most sensual, adventure-filled Romances on the market today...

FROM ◆ LOVE SPELL BOOKS

As a home subscriber to the Love Spell Romance Book Club, you'll enjoy the best in today's BRAND-NEW Time Travel, Futuristic, Legendary Lovers, Perfect Heroes and other genre romance fiction. For five years, Love Spell has brought you the award-winning, high-quality authors you know and love to read. Each Love Spell romance will sweep you away to a world of high adventure...and intimate romance. Discover for yourself all the passion and excitement millions of readers thrill to each and every month.

Save $5.00 Each Time You Buy!

Every other month, the Love Spell Romance Book Club brings you four brand-new titles from Love Spell Books. EACH PACKAGE WILL SAVE YOU AT LEAST $5.00 FROM THE BOOK-STORE PRICE! And you'll never miss a new title with our convenient home delivery service.

Here's how we do it: Each package will carry a FREE 10-DAY EXAMINATION privilege. At the end of that time, if you decide to keep your books, simply pay the low invoice price of $17.96, no shipping or handling charges added. HOME DELIVERY IS ALWAYS FREE. With today's top romance novels selling for $5.99 and higher, our price SAVES YOU AT LEAST $5.00 with each shipment.

AND YOUR FIRST TWO-BOOK SHIP-MENT IS TOTALLY FREE!

IT'S A BARGAIN YOU CAN'T BEAT! A SUPER $11.48 Value!

Love Spell ◆ A Division of Dorchester Publishing Co., Inc.

Get Two Books Totally
FREE —
An $11.48 Value!

▼ Tear Here and Mail Your FREE Book Card Today! ▼

PLEASE RUSH
MY TWO FREE
BOOKS TO ME
RIGHT AWAY!

Love Spell Romance Book Club
P.O. Box 6613
Edison, NJ 08818-6613

AFFIX
STAMP
HERE

He heard Sarah's breathing slow and become more even, felt her body relax against his. "That was quite marvelous," she whispered.

Quite marvelous, indeed.

"I'm glad I found the strength to ask, now that it's said and done," she said sleepily.

"Me, too," he said reluctantly.

"But I think I know what you mean about having a wife suck the life out of you. I swear,"—she sighed—"I feel completely . . . drained."

A minute later she was asleep.

The woman in his arms was the worst kind of trouble. Sweet. Loving. Giving. A *good* woman. Hell, a good woman was the last thing he wanted or needed. But right now . . . in his muddled state of mind . . . he could almost believe differently.

Joe whispered into her hair. "What have you done to me, Miss Priss?"

Chapter Twelve

There were a hundred reasons why she should regret last night, but as Sarah wakened to the sight of Joe's sleeping face she felt not an ounce of remorse.

The sun barely peeked above the horizon, and softly filtered light filled the large bedroom and fell across the bed. She'd fallen asleep with her back against Joe's chest, but in the night she'd squirmed and twisted so that they'd slept face-to-face.

A prudent woman would slip quietly from the bed, dress quickly, and leave the sleeping man to his dreams. She would berate herself for being so bold as to actually *ask* a man to lie with her. She would blush at the remembrance of what she'd done under the cover of darkness.

Sarah had been raised to be a prudent woman. It no longer appealed to her.

Burrowing into the soft mattress, she hugged the quilt to her chest. Yes, she was tired of being prudent. She wasn't going anywhere, not right this minute. Why run, when she could lie here and study the man she loved?

Joe's mouth looked soft in sleep. It was full, wide, and tempting. Last night he'd kissed her with that mouth; he kissed her over and over again. He'd tasted her lips and her freckles and her breasts.

He'd been inside her, a part of her. The memory made her tingle, deep and certain.

There had been a time when she'd been tempted to kiss those sleeping lips of his, when just the sight of them had tantalized her. She'd chickened out, then, afraid to be caught, afraid to take even the smallest chance. She didn't feel at all like a coward, now.

Scooting slightly forward, she brought her face close to Joe's. His dark, stubbly beard looked strangely adorable by morning's light, the way his hair lay slightly mussed was endearing. And his mouth . . . relaxed and soft, it waited. She lifted her chin and placed her lips softly over Joe's.

He responded almost immediately, coming awake slowly, gradually, with a sigh and a leisurely dance of his mouth over hers. Her heart pounded, her blood rushed, and something that could only be called love settled firmly in her heart.

As he came more awake, his body shifting against hers, his kiss becoming more demanding, Joe snaked his arm around Sarah and pulled her close. There was no longer anything sleepy about this embrace, no longer anything innocent. He devoured her with those soft lips, forced her lips apart and tasted deeply with his tongue.

And when the kiss finally ended, slowly, reluctantly, Joe drew back slightly to settle his most unsettling eyes on her face.

In the morning light, she could see him much more clearly than she had in the shadows of the night. His eyes were blue and clear, the stubble on his face rough and dark, the lines and ridges of his neck and shoulders rugged and masculinely beautiful.

She laid her fingertips tentatively on the ridge of his collarbone, needing to touch, hungry to feel. All along he'd said his stay here was temporary. The marriage was a sham, a hoax. He had *important* business to tend to. But right now she felt so much more between them than a ruse to help seven little girls. She sensed love on her part. Need on his. They shared a bond she didn't understand and refused to deny.

She'd come West to make every moment count, to open her heart and experience everything life had to offer. This time with Joe was a gift she would not deny herself.

With a finger crooked over the edge of the quilt, Joe slowly slipped the covering down so that the globes of her breasts were exposed. She didn't try to stop him, even when the sunlight fell on her exposed nipples. She did, however, hold her breath, a little shy, a little afraid. She was well aware of all her faults, imperfections that could be hidden under the cover of darkness but were more than clear by the light of day.

But the way Joe looked at her, she didn't feel plain at all. He looked at her as if he liked what he saw. As if she were truly beautiful. He touched her as if she were the most fragile, delicate creature on earth, as if he cherished her.

"You still have a few freckles left," he said sleepily, rocking his thumb softly over one nipple and then the other.

"I see that," she whispered.

He scooted the quilt down a few inches more, as if he were intent on studying her entire body. Something in her wanted to yank the quilt from his hands and pull it over her head, but another instinct, a stronger force, compelled her to study him as he did her.

Wide and strong in the chest, he could easily overpower her. But he didn't. His touch remained gentle, his hands offering the most tender touch she'd ever known. Dark hair was sprinkled across that wide chest, and as he raked his hands down to her hips to caress her there, she reached out and touched his own tiny, flat nipples.

He continued to wear a small bandage over the wound in his side, and her searching eyes found other evidence of his dangerous profession; a long, thin scar high on his chest, another on his upper arm. She ran her fingers over both scars, wondering how he'd gotten them, trying to offer silent comfort for every pain he'd ever suffered.

She still ached from last night, and yet she wanted him again. She felt her body responding to his touch, felt a deep quiver and a strange, hot tingle that warmed her from head to toe. The throb between her legs became more insistent as he caressed her backside and thighs, a heavy heat settling there.

With a quick move, Joe tossed the quilt to the end of the bed, revealing their bodies so close, her pale legs entwined with his longer, darker ones. His manhood, hard and long, nudged against her insistently, pressing into her belly.

"You're so beautiful," he whispered.

It was a lie born of passion, so she didn't argue with him. Perhaps, behind a cloud of desire, he did see beauty in her at this moment.

He was the beautiful one, so powerful and handsome, with a body marred only by his healing wound and those other, much smaller scars. She reached down to touch his bandage with fingers as tender as Joe's own.

"Does it still hurt?"

"A little."

She moved her hand from his wound to rake over his lean hip, savoring the warmth beneath her hand. The softness of his skin, the passion in his eyes.

He kissed her deeply again, demanding and hungry. She opened herself to him, completely and without reserve. For the moment, she was his in every way. His wife. His lover. And he was everything to her. Most of all, he was her heart.

He rolled her onto her back, and she went willingly, languidly, her thighs spreading instinctively. He didn't immediately place himself above her, but remained on his side beside her, slipping his hand between her legs to caress her inner thigh.

She looked down the length of their bodies, her eyes falling on the fascinating sight of his dark hand on her pale thigh and then on the shaft of his manhood, so long and hard it was amazing to her that she'd taken it inside her; and would again.

"Well," she muttered softly, her eyes on the evidence of his desire. "I don't think I will ever be able to call you Stumpy again, not with a straight face."

She raised her gaze to watch him grin; he

had such a lovely, enticing smile. His fingers slipped higher to touch her intimately, to caress and stroke her. Her body responded immediately, with tremors and a rush of moisture.

"That's all right," he whispered. "I feel sure I won't be able to call you Miss Priss again."

She laughed lightly as he rolled atop her, but her laughter died as he forced her legs further apart, pushing himself against her, into her, stretching and stroking her until there was nothing in the world but the joining of their bodies and the love in her heart. And the world was complete.

Sarah went back to sleep within minutes, but Joe couldn't. What had he been thinking to take her again? Ah, he hadn't been thinking at all. He'd come awake with her mouth on his, and her body so close he could feel it with every fiber of his being.

He'd never lost control before, never ceased to think rationally because a woman kissed him, because she looked at him with impossibly hungry eyes. Damnation.

When he heard small feet and voices above stairs, he left the warm bed and dressed silently. This would not be a good morning for the girls to decide to deliver breakfast in bed. Sarah, beneath the quilt once again, looked too well loved; her hair was loose and tangled, her face flushed and smiling, her nightgown on the floor.

He met Clara, the first to rise, in the kitchen.

She looked surprised to find him up, and then smiled widely. "Are you going to church with us today?" she asked.

Joe shook his head. "No. You girls go ahead. Sarah needs her sleep, and I have things to do."

"What kind of things?"

What did he have to do?

He had to tell Sarah that there wasn't anything lasting between them. He hadn't been blind to the look in her eyes this morning, as he'd pushed inside her. He'd seen tenderness as well as passion. Hope. A need that went far beyond anything the joining of their bodies could satisfy. He had to tell her that last night . . . and this morning . . . had been mistakes, that it couldn't happen again, that no matter how real it had felt last night, they were not married. He was going to leave as soon as the judge came through town and settled the matter of custody of the Shorter sisters.

But damn, he wanted her again. Tonight and tomorrow night and every night until he pulled up stakes and left town. He wanted to spend all night and every day learning every sensitive inch of her skin, tasting her, touching her, stroking her until she cried out the way she'd done last night. He wanted to feel her crumble in his arms again and again. Last night he'd taken her virginity, and that somehow made her *his*. The possessiveness that rushed through him at the thought scared the hell out of him.

185

"What kind of things around the house, Poppy?" Clara asked again.

"I'm going to put a lock on my bedroom door," he answered.

"Why?" she asked.

Because I'm a weak, cowardly bastard, that's why. "For privacy, why else?" he said gruffly.

"Oh." Clara set about preparing breakfast without another word.

Alice actually groaned aloud when she saw Mayor Drake coming her way. She'd shortened her step to match Faith's, and they hadn't even reached the wagon yet. Becky probably had the wagon ready to go, but Dory and Glory were behind her, so there was no hope of a quick escape. She wondered if lagging behind to speak to Quincy for a few moments had been wise, after all.

"Alice Shorter," the mayor called, huffing as he hurried to catch up with her. "Once again I was surprised to see that your father and stepmother decided not to grace us with their presence in church today."

"Sarah overslept," she said. "Surely you understand. It was quite late before she got to bed, after getting all the little ones settled down and to bed last night. The town social kept them up far past their usual bedtime."

As always, Mayor Drake looked red and angry, like he was about to burst. "There is no acceptable excuse for missing services. I thought better of Miss Prince . . . Mrs. *Shorter*," he snorted, "but obviously I was mistaken about her character. I will pray for her soul," he added darkly.

"You don't need to pray for Sarah," little Faith piped up, her voice bright and innocent. "She prays all the time, even when she's not in church."

The mayor looked pleased to hear this, and nodded approvingly as some of the unnatural redness left his face. "I'm glad to hear it. Still—"

"I got up last night to get a drink of water," Faith continued. "I think I swallowed some dust on the ride home last night, 'cause I woke up in the middle of the night with a terrible dry throat. When I came downstairs, I heard Sarah in her room praying."

"You did?" A strange look of puzzlement settled over the mayor's florid face.

"Yes," Faith said. "I heard her, clear as a bell. *Oh my God!* She sounded like she was praying *real* hard."

Mayor Drake's lips tightened and his eyes bulged. "I see. What else did you hear?" he asked quietly.

"Nothing," Faith said with a shrug of her shoulders. "Just that one *Oh, my God!*" She gave the second rendition even more exuberance than she had the first.

Alice bit her lip, a little shocked but also a little pleased. Faith had no idea what she'd heard, but Mayor Drake obviously did. And Alice suspected she did, too.

She'd suspected, last night on the ride home, that something had changed. Sarah and Joe had remained silent, but she'd sensed something different about them.

And now she knew what that something different was. Her plan had worked. Joe and Sarah were falling in love, and that could only mean one thing. They were going to stay. Forever.

Chapter Thirteen

Joe found himself oddly grateful for the opportunity to saddle up Snowdrop and ride to town. Grateful for the opportunity to get away from Sarah for a while. Dammit, it had gotten to the point where he could hardly think when she was around. He sure as hell wasn't thinking clearly. He looked at her and his mind and his body headed unerringly in one direction.

He forced his mind in another direction; business. He had to have a weapon of his own before he left. It wouldn't be wise to ride back into Silver Creek unarmed, not knowing what awaited him there. Too, Sarah needed ammunition for the six-shooter and a decent rifle. For protection. After he left she'd be out there all alone, with seven little girls. She wouldn't be safe unless she was well armed and knew how to handle the weapons.

He smiled, not knowing exactly why. She was a quick learner, and was already a pretty decent shot with the six-shooter. She wasn't afraid of the gun, didn't take the power in her hands lightly, and listened intently to every word of instruction he spoke.

Yep, Sarah continued to surprise him. Every day, every night . . .

So much for training his thoughts away from Sarah.

The general store wasn't crowded on a midweek morning. The shopkeeper who'd been so shocked on Joe and Sarah's wedding day, Garland Dutton, was friendly and helpful when he saw that Joe was a serious customer. The selection of weapons and ammo was small, but what was available suited Joe just fine. He quickly selected a Colt Peacemaker for himself, a lever-action Winchester rifle and a box of shells for Sarah, and bullets for both six-shooters. He charged the purchases to the Shorter account. Once he was out of here he'd send money to Sarah to cover these and other expenses. She'd need a little cash now and then. Unfortunately his traveling cash was stored in his room in a Silver Creek hotel, and the rest was in a Dallas bank account. He couldn't very well have money wired from Joe White's account without raising a few questions he couldn't answer, and he wasn't ready to return to Silver Creek. Not yet. Once the judge came through town next week, then he could return to Silver Creek and resume his pursuit of Charlie Lockhart and his gang.

A small, irritating knot formed in his stomach. Leaving Sarah would be hard, harder than he'd ever expected. Hell, he'd even miss the seven runts.

"Joe?" An unfamiliar, soft, shaking voice called his name, and he turned from the counter. The woman in the doorway looked familiar. Attractive, well-dressed, and pale with what appeared to be shock, she stared at him with wide blue eyes and an open mouth. "I . . . I thought you were dead."

"A common assumption, darlin'," he said lightly, wracking his brain to remember her. Hell, he didn't know anybody from Jacob's Crossing, hadn't even been in Silver Creek for more than a few days before. . . .

Silver Creek. "Rosie?"

The shock on her face faded, and she ran forward with open arms and threw herself at him. Having no other choice, he caught her. She buried her face against his neck and started to cry. Dammit, he barely knew the woman. What was she blubbering about?

Dutton cleared his throat with evident disapproval, and Joe realized that with a word or two Rosie could ruin everything.

He looked over her pale head to the frowning

shopkeeper. "My cousin. I guess she hadn't heard the news about me not really being dead and all."

Rosie sniffled once and lifted her head. A savvy woman, she only stared at him accusingly. She didn't give him away.

He put her on her feet and took her arm. "We need to have a nice, long talk, me and Cousin Rosie. I'll be back shortly to pick up my purchases."

Dutton snorted in disapproval or disbelief, but moved the weapons and ammo to a shelf behind him for safekeeping.

She'd made progress with the café, but it would still be another week or two before she was ready to open. The place was a mess, and the supplies Garland Dutton had ordered for her were not all in yet. She'd spent most of the week getting her room above stairs in order. Living there would save her the cost of her room at the boarding house.

She made Joe White a cup of coffee and cut a slice of the caramel cake she'd made yesterday, trying out a new recipe. He sat at a small round table and cradled the coffee cup like it kept him earthbound. He ignored the cake.

"Deacon said you were dead," she said, sitting down across from him.

His eyes lifted to meet hers. "Deacon," he repeated softly.

She nodded, slow and easy. "Deacon Moss.

He sent his boys after you, and they came back and said you were dead." Tears stung her eyes and she fought them back. Relief rushed through her. Deacon wasn't a murderer, and Joe White wasn't dead just because of her unwavering honesty.

"Did you tell him I'd been asking about Charlie Lockhart?"

She nodded, ever so slightly.

He put his coffee cup on the table and leaned back, silent but wound so tightly she could see the tension in his neck and jaw.

He didn't ask, but she felt like she had to add an explanation. "That's not why he sent Leonard and Isaac after you, though."

"It's not?" Joe raised his eyebrows in evident skepticism.

She shook her head. "Deacon's no angel, but he would never work with someone as mean as Charlie Lockhart. He was just jealous, the dolt." The anger that had been building for weeks overcame her.

"Jealous?"

She leaned slightly forward. "Deacon is kinda insecure, and he's always asking me, *Who's the best, Rosie?* He has to be the best at everything, or else it just makes him crazy. So that night, when he got back to town and came to see me like always, he asked me, *Who's the best, Rosie?* and I told him the truth." He waited for her to continue. "You, Joe. I mean, you beat Fast Eddie."

"He wanted me dead because I beat Fast Eddie to the draw? Were they good friends?"

Rosie bit her bottom lip. "I don't think that's why he sent those boys after you."

He waited, silent and patient and angry.

"See, I told him you were better-looking and a better lover, and that after you killed Eddie I let you come upstairs with me for free. I think that's what made him the maddest, that I didn't charge you."

"I paid you," Joe said, his face expressionless.

"I slipped the money back in your pants pocket while you slept. Damn, I was so glad to see that bastard Eddie dead, and giving you a free visit was the only way I could think of to repay you."

Joe shook his head in disbelief. "Great. I hunt these outlaws for months, and because some—" he caught himself just in time. "Because a lady makes her sweetheart jealous, I get ambushed."

"Deacon Moss isn't my *sweetheart*," she said fiercely. "I don't have a sweetheart and I never will. He was just a . . . a regular customer. I've retired from my previous profession, and I'm opening myself a café, and if I never see Deacon Moss again as long as I live I'll die a happy woman."

Joe looked around the café, taking in the half-finished eating area and the counter where she'd eventually sell sweets and breads. "You're retired, huh?"

She nodded. "I've worked for this place all my life."

He raised his eyebrows at her again, skeptical, almost amused. "All your life. What's that, twenty-five years or so?"

"Twenty," she said, raising her chin defiantly. It had been a damn long twenty years, not that she'd tell him or anyone else that.

He should be angry with her, furious that because of her, Deacon had tried to have him killed. But he didn't look angry at the moment. "Well, you just about blew my cover back there at the general store," he said calmly. "You're going to have to help me put things back in order."

"I'll do whatever I can," she swore.

He sipped at his coffee and broke off a piece of caramel cake, popping the morsel into his mouth. She could tell by the expression on his face that he liked it, so she smiled. She did two things well, and cooking was one of them.

When Joe finished his bite of cake he fixed cold blue eyes on her. Her smile died. "You're going to have to lie," he said softly.

She'd sworn she'd never lie. It was a promise she'd made to herself, and she always, always kept her promises. Nothing good had ever come to her because of a falsehood. Her mother had lied to her for years, the man she'd fallen in love with at the age of sixteen had lied with a charming smile on his face. The man who'd given a distraught Mary Rose her first job, swearing that all she'd have to do was sing and serve a few drinks . . . liars all.

"I don't know if I can."

Joe sat in the parlor after supper, looking over the new rifle in his lap. His eyes were on the weapon, but his mind was elsewhere.

If Rosie would play the long-lost distant cousin of Joe Shorter, that wouldn't hurt. He prayed that she wouldn't decide she had to be true to her long-standing rule of honesty above all else. She had, at least, promised to think about the idea.

He was going to have to tell Sarah about the additional player in their ruse, and he had to tell her tonight. Damn, he dreaded telling her. She'd ask her usual questions, and the first would no doubt be, *How do you know Mary Rose Sheppard?*

What was he supposed to say? *Gee, honey, she's just a calico gal I used to know. Only bedded her the one time.*

Prim and proper Sarah would certainly not approve. She'd probably become indignant and cold and turn her back on him. Or else shove him onto the floor and make him take up his old place at the foot of the bed. He didn't want to sleep on the floor anymore. He'd gotten much too accustomed to sleeping with Sarah.

The girls, all eight of them, were getting ready for bed, so he had the dimly lit parlor to himself. The house was quiet, and soon Sarah would be ready and waiting, as she had been every night this week. Every day he said he was going to put an end to that part of their relationship. But every night she changed his mind with a look or a kiss or a softly spoken word.

He heard little feet on the stairs, stealthy and almost silent. A moment later a pale head peeked around the corner. When he smiled, Glory burst into the room, her white nightgown floating around her legs, and threw herself at him. He set the rifle down just in time, and caught her as she jumped into his lap.

"I wanted to tell you goodnight, Poppy," she said, settling warmly against his chest.

"Goodnight, sweetheart," he said softly. "Have only good dreams."

"I will," she said. She didn't leave her place in his lap, but settled herself more comfortably, snuggling against him, squirming her little legs and arms until she finally drooped snugly against him. "But before I go to sleep I just wanted to tell you that I love you, Poppy."

His heart sank. Sarah was right. Somehow the girls *had* begun to think that this was real, that he was going to stay. What did one say to a five-year-old who opened her heart so easily? "You're a pretty remarkable girl yourself, Glory," he said softly. "I like you a lot. Now, get to bed. Tomorrow will be another busy school day."

She didn't make a move to get down from his

lap, but lifted her head to assault him with wide green, innocent eyes. Ah yes, she was a beautiful child, rosy cheeked and innocent.

"I hope you won't go away again," she said softly.

Again?

"Alice says we shouldn't bother you, but I just wanted to speak my mind. Sarah always says it's okay to speak your mind as long as you're mindful of other people's feelings. I like having you back, and I don't want to do anything bad to make you leave us again, so I'm going to be especially good." Her eyes seemed to get impossibly wider. "I don't remember what it's like to have a father, so I really, really, want you to stay this time."

Joe's heart sank, and he felt suddenly, impossibly ill. He should've known. The little ones, especially Faith and Glory, had taken to this game too quickly, too easily, without a single slip-up. Of course they thought he was going to stay; of course they thought his marriage to Sarah was real.

They thought he was really their father.

Chapter Fourteen

Joe walked into the bedroom, closed the door and put the latch he'd installed in place, and began to undress. All without looking at her or saying a single word.

From her place on the bed, Sarah watched him intently. Something was wrong. She knew it, as surely as she knew that no matter what disturbed him he'd soon put it aside to come to bed and love her.

In the past few days she'd put aside every reservation, every doubt, to be Joe's wife. To love him. He was everything she'd come to Texas looking for. Excitement, beauty, love. And he needed her. She knew it was true every time he came to her, every time he smiled at her or touched her or kissed her.

Well, she hadn't been able to dismiss one small, nagging doubt. Next week the judge would come to town. They'd make an appearance as a family, and if all went well the Shorter sisters would no longer be in danger of being split up. Joe would have no more reason to stay.

And yet she kept expecting him to tell her differently. To whisper in her ear, as they lay together in the dark, that he wasn't going to leave her, ever.

She was as foolish as the girls.

"What's wrong?" she asked as he sat on the side of the bed and removed his boots.

There was a short pause before he answered, "Nothing."

She reached out to caress Joe's back, trailing her fingertips along his spine. In all her life, she'd never felt close enough to another person to touch him so easily, to reach out at will and lay her hands on someone else's body. She kept her hands, and her deepest thoughts and desires, to herself.

"Everything," he said softly.

Sarah sat up and placed her hands on his shoulders, running her palms over the warm, hard flesh, reveling in the feel of his skin under her hands. Even if Joe wasn't going to stay, she didn't regret what had happened between them in the past few days. This time with Joe might be her only chance for love, these nights the only nights of passion she'd ever know.

"Tell me," she whispered, and then she kissed his shoulder lightly. She closed her eyes and savored the taste of his skin, salty and male beneath her lips. Heavens, she had begun to crave him, thinking about him in the middle of the day and looking forward to this time together. She slipped her arms around his waist and pressed her chest to his back, needing to be close to him.

He didn't say anything right away, but she was patient. It was Joe's way, she'd discovered, to think for a while before he spoke, to consider his words.

She didn't want to be careful with her words. She wanted to tell Joe, right now, that she loved him. She wanted to whisper the words in his ear, and then, more than anything, she wanted him to turn around, take her in his arms, and say the words back to her. *I love you, Sarah.* She wanted that more than anything.

"We have a problem," he said softly.

"Another one?" she asked lightly as she kissed his shoulder again and held on tight.

"A big one."

Suddenly she was truly worried. It wasn't like Joe to be this pensive. "Tell me," she said again.

Sarah took the news better than he'd expected, and apparently much better than he had. She chided herself for not seeing the truth herself, for not understanding why the littlest ones called him Poppy with such affection and took to him so naturally.

They'd have to be told the truth, she agreed. That was the first, and the simplest, step. Neither of them could come up with a tolerable way to handle that dreadful chore.

What a day. There was still the matter of Rosie to address. Ah, he was a coward. He wanted to make love to Sarah first, and *then* tell her.

He stripped off his denims and crawled beneath the quilt. A single lamp burned low, lighting the room softly, dulling the colors and the edges around them. Beneath the quilt Sarah wore no more than he did; nothing at all. After the first two nights she'd quit coming to bed with her nightgown on. It was just a waste of time. Precious time.

"I saw someone in town today. Someone I know."

She sat up, bringing the quilt with her so that her breasts were covered. "Someone you *know*?" A touch of panic made her voice smaller, thinner. "Who?"

He reached out and twirled a long strand of red hair around his finger. "A woman. It's just . . . bad luck that she ended up in Jacob's Crossing. She hasn't been in town long. Came here to open a café."

Sarah's eyes got wide, and even in the dim light he could see her normally pale face go white. "Miss Mary Rose Sheppard," she said softly. "I've met her. She's a very attractive woman. How do you know her?"

Joe shrugged. "I met her in Silver Creek, a while back. I don't really know her all that well." He couldn't look her in the eye, dammit. Still, he felt like he owed her the truth. "I don't . . ." he stumbled over his explanation. "She worked at the saloon there, and I . . . I was a, uh, a one-time client."

Sarah's face went a bloodless, ghostly white.

"But she knows my real name, so I had to take her aside and explain what was going on," he continued quickly. "In the general store I had to come up with a quick account, so I said that Rosie's a cousin. She's going to consider playing along with the story."

"She's going to *consider* it. How very kind of her," Sarah said, her voice small. As he watched in horror, unshed tears came to her eyes, sparkling, threatening to spill down her cheeks.

"Don't," he whispered.

She tried to smile, but the effort was weak and ultimately sadder than her threatening tears. "You must think I'm so silly."

"Never."

"I know, logically, that there have been other women in your life," she said softly. "I suppose I secretly hoped they were all ugly and . . . and forgettable." She pinned her eyes accusingly on him. "But Miss Sheppard is a stunning beauty, and a sweet woman with a bright smile. I'm sure your time together was *not* forgettable."

"Actually, it was," he admitted. "I'd had too much to drink, and it had been a very, very long day." He didn't want to tell her that he'd gone to the saloon to drown his sorrows after killing a man. A lawman shouldn't be so achingly sentimental. "Besides," he reached up to touch her face, to stroke her soft cheek. "She's not as beautiful as you."

Most women would have smiled at such a compliment. Not Sarah. In fact, his well-meant words seemed to anger her. "Don't lie to me," she said hoarsely. "I know you're just trying to make me feel better and your heart is most likely in the right place, but *do not* lie to placate me."

"I'm not lying."

She shook her head, forcing his hand away from her face. "All my life, I've been surrounded by women who look like your Miss Sheppard. They have perfectly shaped faces, and golden or sable-dark hair, and pert noses, and lovely smiles."

"She's not *my* Miss Sheppard—" Joe began. He got no further before Sarah interrupted.

"All my life, I heard the whispers. *What a shame that Sarah doesn't look more like her mother. Oh well, at least she seems to be intelligent, and she is a pleasant enough girl.* I was taught early on that I didn't have to worry about my less-than-perfect physical attributes. Father's money and Mother's social standing assured me a good marriage."

"They're crazy," Joe whispered.

"When I was fifteen years old," Sarah said angrily, "I endured a shopping expedition with my mother and her good friend, Barbara, and Barbara's two spoiled, beautiful daughters. They were already filling out, and there I was, flat as a pancake. They were graceful and lady-like and composed, and I was nothing but gangly arms and legs. I kept running into things and knocking them over, and after a while they were all looking at me with pity, shaking their heads, bemoaning the fact that I take after Father's side of the family instead of Mother's. One of the little twits actually called me a *giraffe*, when I tried on a dress that made my neck look a mile long. And another thing—"

Joe had heard enough. He reached out, grabbed Sarah, and dragged her from the bed. She squealed once, but didn't fight him as he carried her across the room and set her on her feet before the dresser. He kissed her quickly, and then, with his hands on her shoulders, spun her about so she could see her reflection and his in the mirror above the dresser.

"What do you see?" he whispered in her ear.

She pulled against him in an obvious effort to escape, but he held tight.

"Know what I see?" He held the sides of her head and made her look, forced her to gaze upon their reflection in the mirror. All they could see from this distance was her body before his from the waist up, but it was enough. "I see a beautiful face." He stroked her cheeks with his thumbs. "Smoldering dark eyes, a lush mouth, and a perfect nose."

"It's too long. . . ." she whispered.

"It's perfect," he insisted lowly. "Regal and lightly freckled."

"And look at this hair," he said, spearing his fingers through the red waves. "God, I love your hair. I love the smell, and the silky feel of it in my hands, and the way it flames in the light of the sun. Look, Sarah, and see what I see."

At last, she willingly lifted her eyes to their reflection.

"And this neck," he whispered. "This is the perfect neck." He kissed the side of her neck. "Pale and soft and elegant, with lots of freckles that need to be kissed away. That girl who called you a giraffe probably has a stumpy little neck. Or did her head rest directly on her shoulders?"

Sarah smiled, and in that moment he knew that everything was going to be all right.

"And honey, you might have been flat-chested at fifteen, but as far as I'm concerned these are perfect." He cupped her breasts in his hands, then watched in fascination the reflection of his dark fingers moving against her pale skin, caressing the globes of her breasts and the nipples that became hard at his touch. "As a matter of fact, your entire shape is perfect." He skimmed his hands to her waist, over her hips, and down her thighs.

He wanted her more than he ever had, and that was saying something. The overwhelming need was alarming. It wasn't right, wasn't natural. He'd never stayed with a woman this long before. Had never wanted to. He moved fast and frequently, no ties, no obligations.

What had happened between him and Sarah went much deeper than satisfying her virgin curiosity. What drew him to her now was more than simple physical need, and that knowledge terrified him.

But it didn't terrify him enough to make him walk away.

She turned in his arms and lifted her face to kiss him, deeply, passionately. He could take her this instant, hard and fast, where they stood or on the floor. He didn't care.

She wrapped her arms around him, holding on tight, pressing her breasts against his chest. A deep tremor worked through her body and he felt it as if the tremble of desire were his own.

He carried her to the bed and dropped her onto the mattress. She spread her thighs, and as he fell to the bed to cover her he guided himself inside her, sheathing himself in her wet heat.

He forced himself to love her slowly, to savor every long, slow stroke, to hold back until she began to fall apart in his arms. As her inner muscles squeezed him he allowed completion to overcome him, to rule his body and his mind for a few moments of complete, powerful consummation. Beneath him Sarah lifted her hips, and moaned, and wrapped her arms around his neck.

And then she ruined it all, stealing the moment of perfection from him. She whispered, "I love you," as the last waves of completion wracked her body.

Joe doused the lamp before joining her under the quilt. As he slipped into the bed she sidled against him and took a deep breath. This was her place at night; at his side, in his arms.

How could she ever thank him for making her feel, for the first time in her life, beautiful?

She hadn't meant to whisper *I love you*, but the soft words had come to her lips unbidden. Words so soft, so unintelligible even to her own ears, he surely hadn't heard them. In a way, she wished she'd shouted the words, taken his face in her hands, looked him in the eye, and said *I love you, Joe White. Love me*.

He was tense tonight. Usually she melted into his arms and fell asleep, but tonight he was stiff, unyielding as she tried to cuddle against him.

Of course, he was worried about telling the littlest girls that he was not really their father. She wasn't looking forward to that moment, herself.

"Everything will be all right," she whispered.

"No, it won't."

He sounded so dismal, so lost. She came up

on her elbows to look into his face. With the light doused she could see very little. She saw enough to know that he was truly miserable.

"I want to take care of you," he said.

In the dark, Sarah smiled. "Do you?"

"After the judge comes through, and everything's sorted out with the girls, I'll get back on the trail of those outlaws. There's a hefty reward for Lockhart, and for some of his men, too. Raising seven little girls, you're going to need all the money you can get, I imagine."

Her blood went cold. "You're talking about sending me *money*, after you leave?"

"Sure," he said softly.

"I don't want your money." Did he think he could *buy* what they had? That what she wanted from him was cold, hard cash?

"Sarah, I think maybe . . . maybe . . ." Joe began, faltering. "I think maybe I need to get out the extra bedding and start sleeping on the floor again."

"Why?"

"There are ways to prevent babies, Sarah darlin', but we haven't been using any one of them."

"I've thought of that," she whispered. "It's unlikely that our few nights will result in a child, don't you think?"

Joe took a deep breath and sighed. "Many a baby has been made in the echo of those very words, honey. Besides"—he shifted in the bed as if he couldn't quite get comfortable—"I don't want you to get the wrong idea about us, Sarah. I do like you, more than I've ever liked any other woman, but—"

"You heard me, didn't you?"

He sighed, deep and forlorn. "Like I said, I want to take care of you, check on you now and again, but . . . but . . ."

"You heard me say 'I love you,' but you don't love me . . . so now you're running scared," she said, her voice amazingly calm. It seemed her heart grew smaller, drier, colder. She'd known all along that Joe didn't love her, so why did this hurt so much?

"I do want to take care of you," he added quickly. "Send money when I can, maybe come through and see you and the girls now and again. I can—"

"No," she said, her voice strong and unwavering. "I won't have you riding in and out of my life as it suits you. Welcoming you every time you get lonely and decide to warm my bed for a few days, crying my heart out when you leave again." Her eyes had adjusted to the dark. She saw his forlorn face well. Too well. She reached out and took his face in her hands and looked him in the eye. "I love you, Joe White," she said clearly. "But I deserve better than that."

He rolled from the bed and reached for his trousers. "Yeah," he said as he stepped into them and headed for the door. "You do."

Chapter Fifteen

It was easy to avoid Sarah throughout the day. The barn needed a good cleaning, the animals needed tending to, and the large garden behind the house . . . that needed a lot of work. Weeds were decimated, rocks were dug up and flung aside, clumps of hard dirt were pounded into grains of yielding soil. This was work the girls couldn't possibly do. They'd worked around the unmanageable areas, skirting the rocks and the clumps of hardest dirt.

Joe had almost forgotten what it was like to work the land. Almost. By the time the girls returned from school his shoulders and back were aching. He'd worked Tess's garden, after she'd married Sheriff Harvey Draper. Harvey had been the one to survey and assess Joe's work, always finding fault, always finding something he'd missed. Nothing was ever quite good enough for Draper—nothing he did, and nothing Tess did.

Still Joe couldn't make himself hate Harvey, even though there were times he truly disliked the man. His brother-in-law had taught him to shoot, given him his first job in law enforcement, and introduced him to Marshal Webb. Harvey hadn't purposely set out to make Tess miserable. In fact, there were times when Joe was sure Harvey loved his wife, in his own way. He just had a hell of a time showing it.

He sighed.

The only time he'd seen Sarah today, except for the occasional glimpse through an open window, was when she'd stepped out the back door to call him in to lunch. After he'd washed up and stepped into the kitchen, he'd found his meal waiting on the table. And no Sarah. She didn't even want to sit at the same table with him, and in a way he was glad. He couldn't possibly make idle conversation with her and pretend nothing had happened between them.

But for the evening meal she sat in her usual place. Better not to disturb the girls' routine, he supposed. With seven children seated around them and chattering about their day, it was . . . easier.

"I don't like Mrs. Handy," Glory said, pouting as she poked her fork at a pile of butter beans. "She made me stand in the corner."

"And why was that?" Sarah asked calmly as she passed a bowl of corn to Clara.

Faith piped up. "Mrs. Handy said that Glory is a little chatterbox and she needs to learn to mind her manners."

"I am not a chatterbox!" Glory insisted. "Poppy, you go to town tomorrow and tell Mrs. Handy that I'm not a chatterbox. I *do* mind my manners! Sarah *never* made me stand in the corner when she was my teacher."

Joe started to tell Glory that he didn't have time to go to town and confront her teacher about making her stand in the corner, but he never got the chance.

"Mrs. Handy does have a mean face," Dory said as she cut a bite of ham off the slab on her plate. "She always looks like she's mad at somebody."

"She's an old grouch," Clara added.

All the girls jumped in at once, each of them voicing their unflattering opinion of the new schoolteacher.

Sarah silenced the children with her soft, commanding voice. "We should show compassion for poor Mrs. Handy. She's a widow, and from what I've seen has no friends or family. I'm sure her sour disposition stems from the fact that she's lonely."

"Of course she's lonely," Becky said unkindly. "Who would want to be friends with that sour old battle-ax?"

"Becky," Sarah said. "That's unkind of you."

213

Linda Jones

Becky was unrelenting. "But it's true. Should I not tell the truth because it's unkind?"

"Besides," Alice added. "She has friends *and* family. I see her with the mayor all the time, and she has a son who comes to town now and again to visit her. I think the sheriff checks in on her now and again. Her husband was sheriff, before he was killed."

"How did he die?" Joe asked.

"He was murdered," Becky said brightly. "Shot in the back not long after we moved here. They never did find the man who did it."

"Murdered?" Joe repeated, his interest in the subject of the evil Mrs. Handy rising.

"This is not suitable dinner-table conversation," Sarah said primly. Her statement was followed by a long moment of silence, while the girls dug into their meal. Sarah had done a good job, he had to admit. She was getting the hang of working around the house. He heard fewer and fewer "blasts!" from her during the day.

"You know," she added. "I might just go to town myself tomorrow. We need a few things from the general store, and I've been meaning to see the dressmaker about purchasing a new bolt of fabric. Alice, you need a new dress. You all do, but we'll have to manage one garment at a time, I suppose." She glanced at Joe out of the corner of her eye. "I've been meaning to check out the new café that's being built, and while I'm there I might as well have a word with Mrs. Handy and see how things are going for her. Perhaps she needs my help settling in."

"Hooray!" Glory said brightly.

"Besides," Sarah said softly, ignoring Glory's outburst, "There should be word by now on the judge's exact date of arrival in Jacob's Crossing. We'll want to be prepared." It seemed her spine stiffened, her chin lifted stubbornly, and some of the color drained from her face.

Sarah hid in the kitchen as long as possible. With Clara and Dory's help she made quick work of cleaning up after the evening meal.

With any luck, she'd go to town tomorrow and find that the judge would arrive before the end of the week. The sooner this was over and Joe was gone the better off she'd be. It was going to be impossible to move forward as long as Joe was living in the house and they had to pretend to be married.

It would be easy if she didn't love him. If she just liked him, perhaps cared for him a little, she could look at their pretend marriage and their nights of passion as an experience, a slice of the life she'd always known she was missing, an experiment of sorts.

She'd wondered about love for years, and now she knew the truth. Love hurt. It was uncontrollable, reached deep inside and grabbed her heart, filled every waking hour and her dreams, and *blast* it was painful.

Maybe when Joe was gone the hurt would go away. Maybe she would be able to forget this terrible aching feeling when she didn't have to look at him every single day.

Clara and Dory hurried up the stairs to join their younger sisters in getting ready for bed. Only Alice remained downstairs, washing down the dining room table and straightening the chairs.

As the oldest girl headed for the stairway, Joe stopped her with a softly spoken, "Alice, we need to have a word."

Sarah's heart stopped. Oh, she didn't want to be a part of this, she didn't. It was going to be ugly, and painful, and she just wanted to hide in her room they way she'd hid in the kitchen.

And leave Alice to deal alone with Joe's anger? Not likely.

Joe sat down in the wide rocking chair he seemed to prefer, and Alice stood before him, her hands clasped demurely. Oh, she looked so small and defenseless next to Joe, so fragile. Sarah stood back and to the side, where Joe could see her—in case he even thought of losing his temper with the child.

"Alice," he said, his voice stern but controlled. "We have a problem."

Alice said nothing. Her spine was stiff, her head held high. She waited for Joe to continue. Maybe she knew what was coming.

"Glory thinks I'm her father. Her *real* father," Joe said softly. "Why is that?"

Darn his hide, he could be a little more compassionate, his eyes softer, his posture less . . . less threatening. How could a man seated in a rocking chair look so intimidating?

Alice glanced over her shoulder to Sarah. Tears already filled her eyes. Sarah left her post at a safe distance and came to stand beside Alice. "It's all right. We just need to know."

Alice looked down at a seated Joe. "Only Faith and Glory think you're really our father. They didn't remember him, and I was afraid they'd . . . they'd . . ." Her voice cracked.

"How are we going to tell them the truth?" Joe asked quietly, just a touch of anger in his voice. "Did you ever think of that?"

Alice's lower lip trembled, and her shoulders slumped. "No. I made a mistake." A few silent tears ran down her cheeks. "I'm sorry. I try not to make any mistakes, but sometimes I just don't know what to do. I'm sorry."

Joe's anger softened. Sarah could see the change in his eyes, the pain he took on himself. "Everybody makes mistakes," he said. "There's no reason to . . . to cry." It was obvious the prospect dismayed him, but his words only made matters worse. Alice's few tears turned into a flood.

"I *can't* make mistakes," she blubbered. "I'm in charge of everything now, and if I make a mistake they'll take my sisters away."

Joe reached up, grabbed Alice's wrist, and with a gentle tug he pulled her onto his knee.

217

Alice was startled, but after a moment settled comfortably in his lap.

"You're a kid," he grumbled. "You're supposed to make mistakes."

Alice was trying so hard not to cry, holding back, breathing abnormally. Her entire body was tense.

"Go ahead and cry," Joe said so softly Sarah almost couldn't hear him. "You're entitled."

Alice laid her head on his shoulder and sobbed, just once. "I want my mother," she said softly.

"I know," Joe whispered, cutting his eyes up to Sarah. He looked so lost, so agonized, that she could only love him more. And that wasn't good.

"I can't do this alone," Alice sobbed. "I want my mother!"

"You don't have to do anything alone," Joe said softly. "Sarah's here, and . . . and I'm here."

For now, Sarah thought.

Joe let Alice cry; for her mother, for her unwanted responsibilities, for her mistakes. He laid a hand on her back, patted it a few times, then began to rock.

Sarah had never been one for tears. As a child she hadn't cried much, and when she had given in to tears she'd been alone. Always. No one had ever comforted her. If her lip so much as trembled in front of her father, he'd tell her to *buck up and act like a Prince*. Her mother always did her best to avoid any unpleasantness, disappearing quickly if her only child ever looked as if she might shed a tear.

No one had ever held her, and rocked her, and told her to wipe her tears on his shirt, the way Joe did with Alice. No one had ever told her that she was allowed to make mistakes.

As Alice's sobbing lessened, Joe's eyes found Sarah again. He said he didn't want a family, didn't want kids or a home or roots of any kind. But he was better at this family business than she was. He knew how to comfort a distraught child, when to scold and when to hug.

Since he wasn't going to be here much longer, she would have to learn.

Alice finally regained her composure and headed up the stairs to bed. All was quiet above stairs, so the other girls were already asleep or well on their way.

Joe looked a little bewildered, sitting there in the rocking chair with a teardrop-dampened shoulder. He seemed a little lost. They still had no real answers, no solution to this new problem.

Yes, she wished she only liked him, that she didn't love him at all. If she simply *liked* him, she'd kiss away the bewildered look and take him to bed, and together they would forget this horrible day and the argument they'd had last night. But she loved him more every time he looked at her, every time he touched her, and that meant his leaving would only hurt more.

She loved him, and she couldn't make him love her back.

So when she went to bed she fastened the latch Joe had put on their bedroom door and crawled into bed alone.

Deacon loved the sound and smells of a saloon and the taste of good whiskey. Together, they usually held the power to soothe him after the worst, longest of days. But not tonight.

"Don't you want to buy me a drink, you good-looking thang, you?"

He looked up into the face of the woman who placed herself in his lap. As his eyes met hers she smiled, revealing a gap where one of her front teeth should've been.

"Uh, no," he said, giving her a gentle shove to force her off his lap. She did move, reluctantly, but was back a moment later, snaking her arms around his neck to secure her position. "Maybe you've got other things on your mind," she said suggestively, straddling him lewdly.

It was a fact that he did have other things on his mind, but none of them had anything to do with this saloon gal; who was, with the exception of the missing tooth, a nice-looking woman.

"I'm looking for a lady," he said. Dammit, he'd asked everyone else in this godforsaken place, the second town he'd stopped at in his search. He'd stopped at every ranch and farm in between, too, zig-zagging his way across the land.

She ground against him. "You got one right here, handsome. And you look to me like a man who knows how to handle a lady, if you know what I mean."

He was tempted to toss her onto the floor, but maybe that would have to wait until after he'd gotten an answer to his questions. "Lovely as you are, I'm looking for a specific lady. Her name's Rosie, and she has pale hair and blue eyes, and she wouldn't have been here more than a couple of weeks."

The gal's smile faded. She did look a lot prettier with her lips together. "Haven't seen her."

Deacon reached past the woman to grab his whiskey, downed it in one swallow, then gently disengaged her arms from around his neck and shoved her from his lap. Again. "I gotta get moving."

There was just one town left of the original three he'd decided to search: Jacob's Crossing. And after that . . . after that he wouldn't know where to look. The thought that Rosie might not be there either gave him an unpleasant and unexpected chill. If she wasn't there, where would he look next? How would he *ever* find her?

He shook off the chill. He would find her, dammit. He had to. And when he did . . . when he did . . . Dammit, Rosie had no idea what she'd put him through, how she'd tortured him. One part of him wanted to make her pay dearly for hurting him this way, but another part knew he'd be so glad to see her he'd probably kiss the ground at her feet.

And after that, maybe he'd ask her to marry him. He'd never thought much of the idea of legally tying himself down to one woman, but it was a sacrifice he might be willing to make to keep Rosie in once place.

Deacon shuddered as he came to his senses. Married! Hellfire, he wasn't ever getting *married*. Still, maybe Rosie wouldn't mind being his woman, exclusive-like. Maybe she'd let him put her up in a little house somewhere and when he came off the road she'd always be waiting for him. He kinda liked that idea.

He smiled as he rode toward Jacob's Crossing. *His woman*. Rosie would like that, he was certain of it. And she'd be so happy when he asked her she'd forget all about the Joe White incident.

Chapter Sixteen

Since Joe hadn't been to this part of Texas before, he wasn't worried that he might have even a passing acquaintance with the judge he and Sarah were set to appear before. Still, he was nervous as they approached the saloon, which had been closed and converted to a staid courtroom for the afternoon.

His nervousness had nothing to do with the fact that Sarah had taken to locking him out of their bedroom at night. That she fastened the latch *he'd* installed against him every night. That he'd been sleeping on the floor in the parlor or in the barn for the past three nights. He'd slept in worse places.

This new predicament should make it easier for him to walk away when this chore was done, to load up his saddlebags and head back to Silver Creek with no regrets. No reservations.

"Hold my hand, Poppy," Glory said, skipping forward and taking his hand before he had a chance to respond. She tucked her little fingers in the palm of his hand and hurried to keep up with his pace. He shortened his stride to accommodate her.

"Me, too," Faith said, scurrying forward to take his free hand. "I'm a little nervous," she said. "I've never seen a judge before."

"Judges are just regular people, like you and me," Joe said calmly. Some were good, some bad, some power-hungry. Better not to divulge that bit of information to a child. "We have nothing to worry about."

Evie decided to take Sarah's hand, and as she did Joe glanced in that direction. Sarah was at her Miss Priss best today, in a severe gray gown and a prim hairstyle. Looking at her he could hardly believe this was the same fiery woman who'd shared his bed for days, who'd whispered about learning to shoot and walking in the rain, who'd wrapped her legs around him and cried out in the dark.

Dangerous direction for his thoughts to be taking, he decided, glancing over his shoulder. The four older girls trailed behind, silent and unsmiling and as worried as Faith professed to be.

They pushed through the batwing doors and

filed into the back row. There were just seven seats in the row, so Glory climbed into his lap and Faith sat on Alice's knee. The judge was seated at the front of the room, at a small desk that had been placed there for him to preside over. His was the only chair in the room that was not hard and wobbling. Someone had moved a wide leather chair into the closed saloon for court day.

The justice, Judge Wilkins, according to the placard that had been placed before the large man, dominated the room with his size and his booming voice. Gray-haired, with a well-tended mustache and gold-rimmed spectacles, he was fit for a man of his apparent years.

As Judge Wilkins and the sheriff debated the fate of a petty thief, Sarah leaned close to Joe and whispered, "See the lady two rows up and to your left? The fair-haired woman in the dark plum gown."

Joe easily found the woman, and just as he laid his eyes on her she turned her head. When she saw Joe watching her, she quickly returned her gaze to the judge.

"That's Felicity Halberg, the woman who'd wanted to adopt Glory."

Joe was a little surprised. The woman was younger than he'd expected and looked perfectly normal, if a bit tired. He'd expected a monster, he supposed, an evil witch. But Felicity Halberg, who now kept her spine rigid and

Linda Jones

her eyes straight ahead, appeared to be just an average, nice-looking if not spectacular, woman.

When the Shorter family was called forward, Faith bit her lower lip and moaned low in her throat, and Glory clutched at Joe's shirt. Rather than fighting, Joe lifted Glory as he stood, holding her in his arms as they made their way from the back row, past Mrs. Halberg and all the others, to the front of the saloon. Glory encircled his neck with her thin arms and held on tight.

"It's all right," he whispered.

"I don't want to go away," she whispered back.

Her words crept under his skin, made their way inside him and found a home. Something in his heart clutched and released. These girls had lost enough. They didn't need to lose one another.

Judge Wilkins studied the single sheet of paper before him. "What are these people doing here?" he asked grumpily, casting his eyes to the front row where Sheriff Potter and Mayor Larry sat side by side.

"Your honor," the mayor said dramatically, coming to his feet with an awkward stagger. "The situation is not as wholesome and typical as it seems at first glance. Two months ago the mother of these children passed away. At that time everyone believed the father to be long deceased, and the town banded together and

226

did its best to make proper arrangements for the girls. Before those arrangements could be implemented this . . . this stranger came to town claiming to be Joseph Shorter. He then married this . . . this hussy and—"

Joe set Glory on her feet and turned threateningly toward Mayor Larry.

"Mr. Shorter," Judge Wilkins said calmly and sternly. "While I understand your natural response to the mayor's unfortunate words, I must warn you. I allow no violence in my courtroom. Not even if it's well-deserved," he added in a lower voice.

Joe stopped short. Oh, he'd dearly love to put his fist through Larry's red, puffy face. Glory tugged at his pants leg, and when he looked down she offered her arms up to him. He lifted her up into her place, and together, with Sarah and the other Shorter sisters standing around him, they faced the judge.

"The town's *arrangements*," Joe seethed, "included splitting my girls up, putting the older kids to work in inappropriate situations, and sending two of them to an orphanage hundreds of miles away. They were going to hand Glory over to . . ." He looked into the wide green eyes so near his own. How much did Glory know? Probably more than she should. He glanced briefly to Felicity Halberg, seated in the third row with her eyes wide and desperate, leaning forward expectantly.

Joe returned his attention to the judge. "They were going to hand Glory over to strangers. I arrived just in time—"

"Your honor, I have inquiries as to this man's identity that are pending. If we can just wait until your next visit to—"

"Mr. Shorter," Judge Wilkins interrupted Larry with little patience. "Are you these girls' father?"

He was lying in a courtroom. If Marshal Webb ever found out . . . "Yes, your honor, I am."

"And this lady is your new wife, I take it," the judge added.

"Yes, sir, she is."

"But your honor—" Larry began.

The judge silenced him with a frigid glance. "I really see no reason for the court to get involved. But just to ease the mayor's mind, is there anyone here who can vouch for your identity?"

"I can," Alice said quickly, her voice trembling slightly.

The judge gave in to a small smile. "Anyone besides his children."

Joe held his breath. Dammit, this should be easy. The judge should look at Sarah and know she would provide the best possible home. What else could they do to prove it?

A sweet, soft voice came from the back of the saloon. "I can vouch for Cousin Joe."

Joe, along with Sarah and all the children, turned to watch Rosie walk down the aisle toward the desk. Ah, she might change her dress and her hairstyle and her profession, but the walk with the gentle sway of her hips still said *woman. All woman.* The Shorter family parted to let Rosie come to the front of the crowd. With a smile, she faced the judge fearlessly.

It was clear to Joe, if not to everyone, that Wilkins knew Rosie. The flicker of recognition, the friendly smile, came and went quickly.

"This is my Cousin Joseph Shorter, your honor. I haven't seen him in years, it's true, but I can certainly attest to his identity." For one who never lied, she spoke this one quite easily.

When Rosie smiled the judge actually blushed. His cheeks turned pink and a spot of perspiration broke out on his forehead. Yep. He knew her. And Honest Rosie's word couldn't hurt.

"Mayor Drake," Judge Wilkins said testily. "Don't waste my time again with this case. Leave this family alone."

"But your honor—" Larry began.

"And that's an order!" Wilkins bellowed.

It was all over in a matter of minutes. Long, tense minutes. Joe was glad to usher the girls and Sarah out of the saloon and into the sunlight.

It's over, Joe thought as he placed Glory on her feet so she could jump up and down and squeal with her sisters. *Sarah is here, and the judge is satisfied, and no one will try to split the sisters up again.* His job here was finally over.

He backed away and watched the sisters hug and squeal and twirl. They were so happy. So relieved. Evie and Dory tugged at Sarah's skirts, and she gave them a soft smile as she laid her hands on their shoulders. Yeah, they didn't need him. He'd served his purpose and now it was time to move on.

Sarah lifted her eyes to look at him and her smile faded. Hell, it was past time. He had work to do, people to find, bad men to arrest. He shouldn't even be thinking of staying for a few more days, a few more weeks. Indefinitely. He sure as hell shouldn't be thinking of heading home to rip that damn lock off the bedroom door.

"Mrs. Shorter," a wavering voice called.

Sarah spun around, instinctively reaching for Glory and pulling the youngest girl to her side. "Mrs. Halberg," she said, resting her hand on Glory's shoulder.

There were no greetings, no polite inquiries into each others' health. The women just looked at one another for a moment, and then Mrs. Halberg's gaze drifted down to linger lovingly on Glory.

"I'm happy for you all," Mrs. Halberg said softly. "I just wanted to tell you that. If things had come about differently, we would have been more than happy to—"

"Thank you," Sarah interrupted crisply, confirming Joe's suspicion that Glory had no idea what her fate might have been.

Mrs. Halberg raised her eyes and smiled. It wasn't a strong bright smile like Sarah's could be, but a touch of happiness flickered there. Just a touch. "I'm going to have another baby," she said softly.

"Oh," Sarah said, obviously surprised. "How wonderful for you."

The smile widened almost imperceptibly. Yes, there was the beginning of happiness there. "Jake and I, we didn't think we'd ever have another. We've wanted one for so long. I'd given up hope." Her smile wavered again. "I just wanted to let you know that I am happy for you. And Jake said if you ever want to sell the old Sheridan place, he wants first crack at it."

"He'll have it," Sarah assured her.

As Felicity Halberg stepped away, movement over Sarah's shoulder caught Joe's eye. A woman in black and a younger man approached quickly and then brushed past. Sarah smiled and said, "Good morning, Mrs. Handy," and the man nodded absently to Sarah and then to Joe.

The man passed so close to Joe he could've reached out and snagged him. The familiar image was practically burned into his mind; the hook nose, the long, curling, dark brown hair, the scar above the right eyebrow.

Tristan Butler wasn't working in Silver Creek, he was right here in Jacob's Crossing. And if Butler was here, Lockhart wasn't far behind.

* * *

Sarah was relieved and heartbroken at the same time. The girls were safe and together; the judge had all but ordered Mayor Drake to leave them alone . . . and Joe would soon be leaving. He might even go tonight.

Something was certainly on his mind. While the girls laughed and celebrated and dug hungrily into their supper, Joe remained silent. Perhaps he was still wondering how to tell the younger girls that he wasn't their father and that he wasn't going to stay.

Together they made short work of cleaning up after supper. Alice and Clara and Sarah whirled through the kitchen, while Becky and Dory got the little ones ready for bed. With the chores done, they all went to bed happy and content, together and safe. Watching Alice, the last of them to go, climb the stairs, Sarah was assured that this moment and all the moments to come were worth any sacrifice she had to make.

Joe was waiting in the parlor. She knew he waited, the way he rocked so slowly and stared at her as she came into the room. She reached behind her back to untie the apron and slip it off.

"A job well done, Stumpy," she said coolly. There was certainly no need to get emotional over something she'd known all along was inevitable.

"You did well yourself, Miss Priss," he said softly.

She walked toward him. Brave. Serene. Determined not to let him see how scared she really was of raising seven children all alone. "What on earth are you talking about? I didn't say a word."

"You didn't have to. One look at you and the judge knew these girls were in good hands."

Looks can be deceiving. "We'll be fine, I'm sure," she said, assuring Joe without actually saying so that they did not need him. He was the kind of man who would stay, if he were needed enough. He would remain out of obligation. Duty. A commitment he'd made to a family that was not his own.

She wondered if that was the reason he'd become a lawman; that need to take care of everyone. She wondered if that was part of the reason she loved him.

"When will you be leaving?" she asked. Chin high, eyes wide and dry, she maintained her composure. Best to get this over and done with so she could move on.

Restless, as if he was so tired of sitting he couldn't stand it a moment longer, Joe came to his feet. Again, she could see that something was bothering him. "I don't know. I think I might stick around a while longer. It'll look suspicious if I disappear the minute the judge leaves town."

Sarah's heart leapt into her throat. Oh, she couldn't take much more of this living with Joe. *Not* living with him. Turning around and seeing him there. Rolling over at night and realizing, half-asleep, that he was *not* there.

"We'll manage," she said calmly. "Telling Glory and Faith that you're not their real father will be much harder than telling the people in town that you're gone." She wondered if the reason he was hesitant to leave was his reluctance to confront the little girls who so lovingly called him Poppy. "As a matter of fact, you can leave anytime you like and I'll tell them myself."

He pinned his blue eyes on her. They were hard, deep, startling blue eyes. They made her throat dry and her knees wobbly. "I wouldn't ask you to do that."

"You didn't ask, I offered," she said sensibly. "You've done enough." *More than enough.*

He took a step toward her, and her knees began to wobble again. Her instinct was to turn and run . . . but she was not going to run from Joe. She *would not* let him see how he continued to disturb her. She stood her ground.

"Have I?" he whispered as he reached her. He stood close enough to reach out and touch her, but he didn't. "I feel like I've muddled everything horribly, like I've made a bigger mess of things."

"You saved the girls," she said sensibly, just a slight tremor in her voice. "That's certainly not. . . ."

"What about you, Sarah? Who's going to save you?" he interrupted.

"I don't need saving, Stumpy, thank you very much."

Joe took the last step, the one that placed him so close to her his body was mere inches from hers. She could barely breathe, and the wobble in her knees turned into a definite shaking. He hovered over and above her, around her. She didn't step back, not even when Joe touched her cheek with his hand, not even when he moved his mouth toward hers. She saw his lips part slightly, could taste them seconds before he gently touched his mouth to hers.

Oh, she'd missed this. She hadn't realized how much, not even when she seemed to suddenly and inexplicably crave a simple kiss, the feel of his body close to hers, the way his mouth moved over hers. So soft and sweet, so tempting and sinful.

The kiss ended too soon, as Joe backed slowly away. He looked as dazed as she felt.

"Miss Priss," he said huskily, "Sometimes I think you need saving most of all."

She backed away, heading toward the bedroom door, unable to turn her back on Joe.

"Lock the door," he whispered. "And if I lose what's left of my senses and come knocking, don't let me in."

"I won't," she said, though not as firmly as she'd intended.

"Sarah," he whispered as she backed into the door and reached behind her to grasp the handle. "I'm not leaving yet. It's too soon."

She didn't ask Joe why it was too soon, didn't ask him why he'd kissed her. Her heart wanted to believe that he felt some of what she did, that he was learning to love her. Her more practical mind wondered if his wound still bothered him too much for the long trip ahead, or if he simply wanted more time before telling the girls the truth. She knew how he dreaded that chore, and knew just as well that he would not leave it to her alone.

Without another word she slipped into the room and closed the door behind her, slipping the latch firmly into place. Would she have the strength to leave it in place if Joe knocked on the door in the night?

From the parlor window, Joe looked out into the black night. He was close, too close, to stalking to the bedroom door and knocking soundly, just as he'd promised not to do. And if Sarah obeyed him and didn't answer? Hell, it was a flimsy lock.

He shouldn't stay another day. Tomorrow morning he should tell the girls, quickly and efficiently, how the truth had been bent or discarded here and there for the sake of pulling off the farce in front of the judge, and then he should saddle up Snowdrop and ride away.

But he couldn't.

236

Tristan Butler was right here in Jacob's Crossing, of all places. He was a deadly young man, and his face was recognizable to anyone who made a habit of perusing wanted posters. Joe had recognized him right away.

Sarah and the girls were oblivious to Butler's reputation. How many others in town had no idea what kind of man walked their streets? A small town was a good place to hide. People kept to themselves, for the most part. They were isolated, quiet, almost purposely blind to the world around them. But dammit, the sheriff had to know who Butler was. Possibly the mayor and a few others, too. And the woman with Butler? His mother, the notorious Mrs. Handy?

Too many questions danced uneasily through his mind. Sarah. The kids. Butler and Lockhart. Hell, he couldn't leave now! How many men had Butler and Lockhart killed? How many lawmen had lost their lives looking for those outlaws? Yeah, it would be easier to ride away in the morning.

But he wouldn't. Much as he hated to admit it, he had the best cover he could possibly ask for. A wife. Seven kids. A struggling farm. He could walk right up to Butler and arrest him before the man knew what had happened.

But that wasn't going to be enough. Charlie Lockhart was out there somewhere. Close. Within reach. Feeling safe in his quiet little town. Joe knew that if he played his cards right, if he nosed around and kept his eyes open, he could ride out of here with Butler *and* Lockhart in custody.

Or slung over their own horses, if necessary. After all, the outlaws were both wanted dead or alive. And one way or another, he was going to get them.

Chapter Seventeen

Last stop. Last chance.

Since the other two towns in close proximity to Silver Creek had yielded nothing, here he was. Jacob's Crossing.

Like the other two towns he'd searched, this one was quiet and plain and small. If anything, it was even smaller. In a way it reminded him of the little town in Mississippi where he'd grown up.

There he'd been a bastard. Poor. Always on the outside looking in. Until he'd discovered his talent for handling a firearm. Then he'd settled into a life of petty crime.

This town had one church. One general store. One saloon, for God's sake. A dilapidated

Linda Jones

hotel and a few small establishments completed the dusty main thoroughfare.

Oh, but there was one thing Jacob's Crossing could boast that the other towns didn't have, or so he'd heard; the crookedest sheriff in Texas.

Deacon slid from the saddle and tossed his horse's reins over the post in front of the hotel. It was already well past midday, and if he kept a low profile he'd be here a few days, at least. He needed a clean soft bed, and a bath, and a good hot meal.

The hotel didn't look like anything special. The boardwalk was unswept, the windows in need of cleaning, and as he stepped inside, Deacon's hope for a clean bed and a decent meal evaporated. This place was not much better than a barn. Dirty, dark, and dusty, it was one of the most unappealing hotels he'd ever set foot in. Dammit, he was already depressed enough.

A young clerk dozed behind the front desk, but he awakened quickly enough as Deacon slapped his palm on the bell.

"Yes, sir," the kid said as he snapped up to his feet.

"I need a room," Deacon said, surveying the layer of dust on the desk before him. "Preferably a clean one."

"Yes, sir." The clerk slid a dog-eared registration book across the desk, and Deacon took the proffered pen to sign his name. That done, he flipped through the last several pages, skimming for a Joseph White or a Rosie. Dammit, why had he never asked Rosie her last name? It hadn't seemed important. Until now.

He found no Joe and no Rosie, so he angrily slammed the book shut. The clerk jumped, and then handed Deacon a room key. "This is our very cleanest room, sir. Room 204."

Deacon snatched the key from the kid and turned away. At the foot of the stairway he spun around to face the wide-eyed boy. "Any place around here I can get a decent meal?"

"Miss Sheppard's Café next door," the boy said eagerly. "She just opened it today, and I heard she served a real nice noontime meal."

Deacon climbed the stairs to his room, intent on cleaning himself up before venturing out again. Hell, if Miss Sheppard's Café was no better than this place, he'd be living on jerky until he left Jacob's Crossing.

Something very strange was going on. Sarah had time to ponder as she dried the last of the dishes she'd used for the simple noon meal she and Joe had shared.

For one thing, Joe was still here, and from the look of things, he had no intention of leaving. He'd even insisted that they all go to church on Sunday, and he'd socialized and said hello to just about everyone he saw. He'd even made a point of having a word with Mrs. Handy, asking her how the girls were doing in school and asking after her son, who was in town for an extended visit but not present at church.

This morning he'd gone to town again, for a few supplies, he'd said. And then he'd come home with canned peaches and flour they didn't need—and tobacco. She'd never seen him use tobacco.

Sarah wondered, with a sinking heart, if Joe had gone to town this morning to see Miss Sheppard. To thank her, perhaps, for her help with the judge. Perhaps he had searched the lovely businesswoman out for some other reason. After all, Sarah *did* keep him locked out of her bedroom at night, and he *was* a man. . . .

She was an idiot to even consider that he might still be here because he had developed feelings for her. If he was staying close to Jacob's Crossing for anyone, it was likely the beautiful Miss Sheppard.

With the dishes done, she returned to the parlor and her sewing basket. If there was anything she disliked more than cooking it was mending, but with seven children and a careless man in the house there was always mending to be done. Always.

Sarah looked down at the sewing basket and sighed. She didn't want to ply needle and thread on a worn calico skirt or one of Willem Sheridan's old shirts. She truly, truly didn't want to do this.

She felt only a grain of guilt as she shirked

her duties and stepped onto the front porch. The days were growing hotter, but on this afternoon there was a welcome cooling breeze. She stepped to the edge of the porch and closed her eyes, allowing the wind to rush over her face and her body. She took a deep breath of the fresh air and exhaled slowly.

When she opened her eyes and looked forward, she saw nothing but land and grass and blue sky before her. How could something so beautiful be so harshly unforgiving? Not everyone could make it here.

Could *she* make it here? With seven children to love and care for and protect? She felt only a brief moment of indecision before straightening her spine. She *could*. Heaven help her, she had no choice. Her decision had already been made, and there was no going back.

"It's going to be a hot summer." Out of the corner of her eye, she saw Joe slowly approaching. After his excursion to town and a quick luncheon, he'd immediately gone outside. To the barn, to the garden. Anything to increase the space between them, she supposed.

"I'm sure it will be," she said, watching him come toward the porch with long, slow strides. Her heart skipped a beat and she chided herself. A sweaty working man with rolled up sleeves and dirty denims and mussed hair should be repulsive to her, unattractive and coarse and vulgar. Her mother would certainly think so.

But then, Sarah had discovered early on that she had very little in common with her mother.

Joe climbed halfway up the steps and then took a seat to gaze out over the same landscape that had captured her attention a moment earlier. She wondered if he saw beauty or hardship there. Perhaps he saw both, as she did.

The wind ruffled his black hair, cooled him as it had cooled her.

Sarah bit her lip in indecision before taking a single step toward Joe. She cast off the indecision as she opened her mouth and asked, "Why did you go to town this morning?"

He glanced over his shoulder. "We needed—"

"We didn't need any of the supplies you came home with. They will be used, eventually, all but the tobacco, but there was no urgent demand for more peaches or flour."

"I sent a telegram to Marshal Webb," he said. "I hope to hell he understands what I wrote. I had to be careful not to give myself away. Telegraph operators can be the biggest gossips in town."

So, of course, he couldn't use his real name. He had to continue to pretend to be Joe Shorter. "Oh," she said, feeling a touch of relief. "I thought maybe you'd gone to town to see your friend. Cousin Rosie," she added.

Joe scooted over on the step and patted the space beside him, silently asking her to sit. Sarah's first instinct was to refuse. She even shook her head while she looked at the back of his. But her legs were tired, and her feet would ache by the end of the day if she didn't give them a rest on occasion.

So she sat beside him. Not so close as to be touching, but with her hip mere inches from his. For a few minutes they just sat there, side by side, enjoying the breeze and the quiet. With seven children in the house, quiet was meant to be treasured.

"You're going to burn up in those clothes," Joe said without looking in her direction. "Why don't you live a little and unfasten a few of those tiny pearl buttons at your throat so you can breathe."

"I can breathe just fine, thank you," she said primly.

Beside her, Joe broke into a wide grin. "Don't try to pull the Miss Priss act on me, Sarah honey. I know you better than that."

Fresh heat suffused her face; from an embarrassing blush, she was quite certain. "I am not acting," she said. "I . . . I . . ."

She was burning up. Her high lace collar had grown tighter and hotter as the day went on.

"Fine," she said softly, and just a little grudgingly. "If it will make you happy."

She unfastened the top three buttons and folded back the collar slightly. Oh, the breeze against that previously constrained skin felt heavenly. Absolutely heavenly.

"And if you think that feels good," Joe said, as if he could read her mind and sense her relief, "wait till you feel this."

Without further warning, he reached out and grabbed her skirt, lifting it slightly so that a hint of wind slipped beneath. The breeze against her legs *did* feel good, but she wasn't about to tell him that.

"Behave yourself," she said, slapping lightly at his hand.

"I'm not very good at behaving myself," he admitted.

"So I've noticed."

"And you need to learn how to relax."

"You're quite relaxed enough for both of us," she admonished.

He turned his eyes to her; hard, piercing eyes that touched her as surely as the hand on her knee. The hand she had only tried to slap away once. Only once.

"I don't feel *relaxed*," he admitted, his voice low and tight. "Not since you started locking your door at night. I know it's for the best. I know I should leave you alone, quit looking at you, quit thinking about you all the time."

Her heart skipped a beat.

"But I miss you," he admitted.

He pulled her skirt up slightly once again, and a rush of cool air slipped beneath. This time she didn't slap at his hand, or tell him to stop, or pretend that she didn't like sitting so close to him.

246

"I miss you, too," she said, knowing that if she said *I love you* she'd lose this moment. She didn't want to lose the moment; she wanted to savor it.

Without warning, Joe lifted her legs and draped them over his lap, twisting her around in the process. He pushed the heavy skirt to her knees.

"Joe," she admonished, smiling as she leaned back to regain her balance.

"I've seen your legs before, Miss Priss," he said with a smile of his own. "Not by the full light of day, mind you." He studied her exposed limbs thoughtfully. "I'm not at all surprised to find that they look as fine this afternoon as they did by lamplight. Or moonlight." His smile faded. "Or in the dark."

Neither of them smiled as Joe placed a hand behind Sarah's head and drew her face slowly toward his. By the time her lips were inches from his she was practically sitting in his lap; her body pressed against his, her arms around his neck.

He brushed his mouth against hers, barely touching, barely tasting. "One kiss," he breathed. "No harm can come of that, right?"

She murmured her assent. "One kiss."

His lower lip stroked hers, teasing, scarcely coming into contact. It didn't count as a kiss, she reasoned. It was simply getting ready for the kiss. The *one* kiss. She felt his breath, felt his heartbeat.

With every simple brush of his lips against hers her insides twisted. Butterflies fluttered in her stomach. Her knees, exposed to the cooling air, trembled. Oh, it was a good thing she wasn't standing, because she felt quite sure she couldn't manage the feat.

Soon she was hungry for the one kiss, for the full force of Joe's mouth on hers. She moved forward and he moved back, teasing her. Always, their lips touched lightly, feathery, damp almost-kisses that had her insides churning.

Finally he laid his mouth completely and fully over hers, and she sighed deep and long in relief. Heavens, he tasted and felt so good, so familiar and alluring. This one kiss was full of promise and passion, longing and, whether he knew it or not, love.

As long as their lips didn't part, this was still just *one* kiss. Right? She found she wasn't in any hurry to break contact, and apparently neither was Joe.

In a smooth, fluid motion, he laid her back against the porch steps and slipped his tongue into her mouth. Once. Twice. And again. She held on tight and answered his bold tongue with an exploration of her own. This was no sweet kiss, no gentle tease. Not any longer. It was passion, heat, a joining as surely as any of the nights they'd spent together.

Her back arched, and she pressed her body

against his. She ached all over, and only Joe's touch promised to take the ache away.

Somehow her legs ended up wrapped around Joe in an entangling manner. Her knees bracketed his waist, her calves rested on the backs of his hard thighs. He rocked against her, and she felt the length of his manhood pressing against her. All that lay between them were a few layers of annoying clothing. Denim and linen. Nothing that couldn't be moved out of the way. He rocked against her again, and a long, slow tremor worked its way through her body.

And as long as he didn't move his mouth from hers this was still just one kiss.

But he did lift his head. Slowly, reluctantly. He looked down at her and brushed a strand of hair away from her face. "Someone's coming," he whispered, sliding his body away from hers, moving her skirt into its proper position. "Don't lock the door tonight," he whispered.

"I won't," she promised, and she meant it. She wanted Joe for as long as she could have him.

They sat side by side and silently watched the wagon with the girls approach the house. She hadn't heard a sound, not a single sound! If Joe hadn't heard . . . but he had, of course. Maybe he hadn't been as enthralled by that one kiss as she'd been; so enthralled the rush of blood in her veins drowned out everything else.

Joe had made so many of her dreams come true. Little things like shooting a gun and dancing in the moonlight. Bigger things, like making her behave in an unseemly manner and feel beautiful, and leading her to the edge of forever. Thanks to him she knew what love was. Unfortunately, her wish list wouldn't be complete until he loved her back, and she didn't think that would ever happen.

Rosie was pleased. Business on her first day had been brisk, the customers obviously satisfied. Yes, she could settle in Jacob's Crossing nicely, build a business, and make a home.

The last of her customers had left, and she wiped down the tables with a damp towel before tackling the kitchen. She'd been at it since sunup, and was exhausted. But it was a good exhaustion, she decided with a tired smile on her face.

She heard the door behind her open. Inwardly she groaned, but there was no way she'd turn away a paying customer. Business was business.

"I'll be right with you," she said as she gave the table one last swipe.

The customer voiced no response, and she didn't hear so much as a chair leg scraping against the floor. There was just silence. A deep, almost ominous silence. She turned around to face her newest customer, surely the last for her first day.

Her heart leapt into her throat. "Deacon?" she squeaked.

"Rosie," he whispered. "Hot damn, I've been looking all over for you."

"You shouldn't have," she said, her voice a little stronger than his. Not much, though. "What do you want?"

Slowly, a smile grew on his face. "I want you."

Her heart began beating so rapidly and hard she was certain he and everyone else in Jacob's Crossing could hear it. "I'm not in that trade anymore, Deacon Moss. I'm no longer for sale. Now if you're hungry . . ."

His smile faded. "It's that Joe White fella, isn't it. He ain't dead at all."

"Joe has nothing to do with this," she insisted softly. "I've been planning to start my own café for a long time. Since I started working in Silver Creek, as a matter of fact." She lifted her chin bravely.

"But he's here," Deacon said with menacing softness.

"I don't see what that has to do with—"

"He stole you away from me."

Rosie tossed the damp towel onto the nearest table. "You are such a idiot, Deacon Moss," she said angrily. "I swear, I don't think you have any more smarts than Isaac and Leonard. The three of you make a great team. If you pooled your resources you *might* be able to come up with one brain!"

Deacon narrowed his eyes and took a step forward. "Tell me you love him and I'll leave you alone," he whispered. "Dammit, I want to

251

kill him, I want to shoot him deader than hell, but if you love him—"

"Joe?" she asked.

Deacon stopped dead in his tracks. "Of course, Joe. Who else?"

You, you moron. "Well, for one thing, Joe's got a wife and seven kids."

Deacon stopped in the middle of the room. "Is that a fact?"

"It's a long story," she sighed. "I'll tell you all about it over supper, if you're hungry."

His smile crept back. "So you don't love him?"

"Good heavens, no," she snapped.

He quickly closed the distance between them and swept her into his arms. She could almost swear he was laughing as he spun her around and buried his face in her hair.

"Put me down," she insisted breathlessly.

He did put her down, but he didn't let her go. Instead he kissed her, fast and hard, stealing the last of her breath.

"I want you, Rosie. I swear to God, I need you. Tell me there's a bed upstairs. I don't want to take you back to that nasty hotel."

Gathering her strength, she gave a shove against his chest. "Deacon Moss, I'm not that kind of woman."

He lifted his eyebrows as he took a single step back. "Excuse me?"

"Not anymore," she added. "I'm trying to be respectable. You can't just ride in here and . . . and . . . try to make me fall back on all my promises to myself." *No matter how much she wanted to do just that*.

"Respectable, huh?" he said softly.

"Yes," she tried to make her voice prim and distant, but a soft tremor likely gave her away. "Did you think I would be content to work above a saloon forever? Did you think I never dreamed of anything else?"

Home. Family. Love. She didn't dare voice those unrealistic dreams aloud.

Deacon looked around the small café, at the plain wooden tables and the counter she'd polished until it shone. "This is what you want?"

"Yes," she whispered.

He took the nearest seat and sat down, stretching his long legs under a small round table. "Fine. I'm starving. What you got to eat, Miss Sheppard?"

Chapter Eighteen

How could something that felt so right be wrong? He wanted Sarah, she wanted him . . . so why shouldn't they enjoy what time they had left together?

In the back of his mind Joe knew this was a bad idea. Sarah's involvement went much deeper than wanting. She thought she loved him. She'd convinced herself that there was more to this relationship than lust. He knew better.

The girls had gone to bed hours ago. Sarah had made busy work for herself for a while after that, and then she'd retired, herself. Without a word. If the door was locked he'd turn away, he swore it. If she'd changed her mind . . .

The door swung open easily with a gentle push. A single lamp on the bedside table burned low and steady, illuminating the woman who sat on the bed. Waiting for him. Her hair was down, and she wore one of those prim nightgowns of hers, buttoned to the neck. And her eyes . . . wide, deep, beautiful eyes were pinned on him with such expectation. Well, maybe there was more than lust going on here. He liked Sarah. He liked her a lot. If he ever decided to allow himself to fall in love and settle down, he couldn't pick a better woman.

He stood in the doorway, wanting Sarah more than he'd ever wanted anything, knowing the longer he stayed here, the more he *liked* her, the more dangerous this part of the game became. He could love her, too damn easily.

"Poppy?" Little hands tugged at his denims, and he looked down. He hadn't even heard Glory approaching, he'd been so lost in the vision on the bed.

"What's the matter, sweetheart?" he asked, resting his hand on the top of her head.

She stuck her lower lip out, pouting, and her eyes went wide. "I had a bad dream," she said.

He gave her a smile. "It was just a dream. They're not real."

Her lower lip trembled. Ah, it wasn't going to be that easy.

"What did you dream about?" he asked, ready to dispel her unnatural nighttime fears.

255

Monsters? Storms? What made Glory's eyes water and her lower lip tremble.

"I dreamed I woke up and you and Sarah were gone," she said softly. "Everybody was gone but me. I was here all by myself, and I didn't like it." She looked threateningly close to tears.

He could assure Glory that she'd never wake to an empty house, but he couldn't promise that he would always be here.

Maybe Sarah knew how awkward the moment was for him. She left the bed and came to the doorway, and then she did something he'd never seen her do before. She swept Glory from her feet and gave her a big hug.

"That sounds like a very scary dream," she said. "You know I'm not going anywhere, don't you?"

"Not ever?" Glory asked tearily.

"Not ever," Sarah said with assurance.

Glory laid her head on Sarah's shoulder and took a deep breath. "You're my new mother, aren't you?"

Past the tangle of pale curls on the child's head, Sarah's eyes met his in the dim light. "Yes, I am."

Glory snaked her arms around Sarah's neck and held on tight. "Sometimes my Mama used to let me sleep with her when I had a bad dream, so I wouldn't be scared."

The look Sarah gave him was apologetic and

even a little sad. "Would you like to sleep with me tonight?" she asked.

Glory answered with a soft nod of her head. As Sarah carried her to the bed, she lifted that head of blonde curls and tossed a glance to Joe.

"And you too, Poppy," she said. Her lips no longer trembled; her eyes were dry. "I'm little. I don't take up much room."

"I'll just . . ." he began, already stepping back into the hallway. Shoot, he was getting accustomed to the floor, anyway.

"You too, Poppy," Glory ordered, her soft voice insistent. She pinned those large green eyes on him. "You, too."

He closed the door behind him.

"Your nightshirt's in the bottom dresser drawer," Sarah said, a hint of humor in her voice as she placed Glory on the bed, covered her with the quilt, and crawled in to lie beside her.

Grumbling, Joe found the detestable article of clothing, neatly folded, right where Sarah had said it would be, and stepped behind the privacy screen. Still grumbling, he undressed and yanked the nightshirt over his head. He prayed he didn't die in his sleep, because he did not want anyone to see him in this monstrosity.

When he stepped from behind the screen he found Sarah watching from her place on the bed. Glory was snuggled up to her new mother, comfortable and secure, nightmares vanquished.

Sarah smiled widely as Joe stepped toward the bed. "I must tell you, Stumpy, it takes a real man to pull that particular outfit off with such grace and elegance."

If Glory wasn't here he'd rip the damn thing off. Again. But then, if Glory wasn't here he never would've donned the nightshirt in the first place.

"The blue in the embroidered flowers on the collar matches your eyes," Sarah said as he crawled into bed on the other side of Glory.

"Don't push it, Miss Priss," he mumbled.

"You can call her Sarah, remember?" Glory said sleepily. "You don't have to call her Miss Prince anymore."

"I forgot," he said, settling himself as comfortably as possible on his side of the bed. Comfortable, hell. There was no way he would ever be comfortable tonight. As soon as Glory was good and asleep, he'd slip from the bed, put his clothes back on, and retire to the parlor. Or maybe the barn. Anywhere but here.

He reached out to the bedside table and doused the light, throwing the room into a long moment of complete darkness. His eyes adjusted quickly, until he could make out the little girl curled so comfortably in the center of the bed, the enticing form of Sarah beside her.

It wouldn't take more than a few days, a week at the most, for Webb to arrive with his contingent of deputies. Hopefully, by then he'd know where Charlie Lockhart was, but if not . . . getting Tristan Butler behind bars was a step in the right direction. Maybe the man would talk. Joe had discovered early on in his peacekeeping career that there was no honor among thieves. They ratted on one another without a second thought, if they thought it might buy a judge's good favor.

And then . . . he'd be gone. He didn't want to get married and settle down, didn't want to be trapped the way Tess had been. Tied down. Imprisoned. Spending long days caring for someone else's children.

"I'm sorry," Sarah whispered softly, her voice no more than a breath in the night.

"Don't be," he said, his voice not much louder than hers. "It's probably for the best, anyway." Glory rolled over and burrowed her face against his arm, squirming to make herself cozy.

"Probably," she said so softly he almost didn't hear her.

"Another week or so and I'll be gone," he said sensibly. "No reason to complicate matters."

She didn't answer, not right away. She scooted further beneath the quilt, it seemed, and burrowed into her pillow. "Good night, Stumpy," she said as she rolled over and turned her back on him.

Glory, already sleeping but not soundly enough to suit him, wrapped her arms around his and sighed, long and deep. He wasn't going anywhere until she was deeply enough asleep that he could disengage himself without disturbing her.

"Good night, Miss Priss."

An outing to Jacob's Crossing on Saturday had all the girls in an uproar. Alice was nervous because Quincy would be in town today, too. She didn't know what to wear, how to fix her hair, or what to say when she saw him. Becky had spent the entire morning teasing her sister unmercifully.

Clara's breakfast biscuits had not been up to her usual standards, and she was not happy about that. Not happy at all. She couldn't imagine what she'd done wrong. Dory and Evie argued loudly over to whom the red ribbon they both wanted to wear belonged. Faith snatched the scarlet ribbon and hid it, and refused to tell her livid sisters where it was. Glory, who had awakened with her arms still securely around her Poppy's, was apparently still disturbed by her dream. She was not her usual happy self.

Joe had been quiet all morning, saying very little, but as he loaded the bickering girls into the wagon he bellowed an insistent, "Quiet!" They all obeyed.

Sarah climbed into the seat beside him, wishing she'd pled a headache and stayed home by herself. Still, Joe had insisted. This family outing would support their story, he said. When he left, there would be no question that the marriage had been real. He could be a persuasive man.

Everyone was silent on the ride to town. Joe's bad mood had rubbed off on the entire clan, it seemed. By the time they arrived in Jacob's Crossing, the girls were anxious to escape the family wagon and go their separate ways. Alice was alone, and Becky and Clara were each taking charge of two of the younger children.

Sarah had enough shopping to do to keep her busy for several hours. She had assumed Joe would be with her, but after he assisted her from the wagon he took a step back and told her he was headed for the saloon.

"The saloon?" she asked, taking that one step to keep him close. She didn't, after all, want to raise her voice. "It's not even ten in the morning!"

"It's good cover," he said softly, and then he turned his back on her and walked away.

For a few minutes, Sarah stood by the wagon and watched him go. The saloon! She'd never been in one, even made a point to avert her eyes when she passed Jacob's Crossing's single saloon. But she knew what went on in those places. Wildness. An abandonment of good taste and restraint.

Drinking. Gambling. Women. Hadn't Joe met Mary Rose Sheppard in just such an establishment?

She entered the general store telling herself

she didn't care, silently agreeing with him that it was a good cover. When he deserted her, people would remember how he'd frequented the saloon and left his bride to do the chores herself. Why, if he got intoxicated and kissed a saloon girl or two, all the better.

And to think, for a brief moment she'd foolishly thought he'd stayed for her!

She shopped efficiently, choosing only what they needed but buying enough so they would not have to make another trip this week. Perhaps not next week, either, if they were frugal. Garland promised to wrap her purchases up, charge them to her account, and have his son load them onto the wagon for her.

There was a little cash in the house, still, some of Willem Sheridan's stash, but it might be wise to see about selling another piece or two of grandmother's jewelry. Sarah didn't want Joe to send her money. She wanted to prove to him that she didn't need or want his assistance, to be absolutely certain he knew she was not for sale.

Her next stop was the dressmaker's. She didn't sew very well herself, but perhaps it was time she learned. Good heavens, seven little girls! Just thinking about the clothes they'd need in the years to come made her light-headed. School clothes, Sunday dresses, party gowns. Wedding gowns.

The dressmaker was busy in the back room with a customer, but she stuck her head out and told Sarah to feel free to look around. She'd just begun to browse through the bolts of fabric when the door opened and another customer entered the shop.

Sarah's heart dropped to the floor. She wanted to run, to escape the confines of the shop, but Miss Sheppard, wearing a wide, sincere smile, blocked the doorway.

"Cousin Sarah," she said, a touch of humor in her voice.

"Miss Sheppard," Sarah said stiffly.

Mary Rose Sheppard's smile faded slightly. "I just have a minute before things get busy, and I wanted to see if Iris still has a bolt of fabric I was interested in." She walked past Sarah to a bolt of blue silk. "I really shouldn't, but it's such a pretty shade of blue."

"Yes, it is," Sarah said, trying to be polite. Miss Sheppard had been quite helpful. "By the way, I never did get a chance to thank you for helping us with the judge. I really do appreciate your assistance."

The pretty girl just shrugged. "No problem. I owed Joe a favor. We're even, now."

Oh, she didn't want to know why this woman owed Joe a favor, she really, really didn't want to know. "That's a lovely shade of blue," she said, making mindless conversation. "I'm sure it will look lovely on you."

"Blue's my favorite color," Miss Sheppard said with a sigh. "I do have a weakness for it." She ran her fingers along the edges of several bolts. "Oh, I bet this would look good on you," she said, pulling out a bolt of silk fabric that was neither true blue nor green. When the light through the window hit the fabric it looked like sunlight on a calm sea. "You should definitely have a dress made of this."

"I don't need a new dress," Sarah said primly. She had protested firmly, but her eyes strayed to a bolt of shockingly red silk.

Miss Sheppard returned the fabric to its place. "Well, I'll just come back later when Iris isn't occupied. The café will start getting busy soon." Her hand was on the doorknob when Sarah stopped her with a quick question.

"Miss Sheppard," she said softly. "Are you in love with Joe?"

The beautiful woman turned slowly, and Sarah held her breath. She didn't want to know. She *had* to know.

"No," Miss Sheppard whispered. "There is someone else, though. I'm trying so hard not to love him, but it isn't working. Not at all." She cocked her head slightly. "I wish I was more like you."

Sarah was stunned. "You're beautiful. Men adore you. Why on earth would you want to be like me?"

Miss Sheppard gave in to another small smile. "Men respect you. You're dignified and ladylike and regal, and even when they *look*, they know better than to *touch*."

"But sometimes . . ." Sarah began. Oh, she

did not want to open her heart and soul to this woman she barely knew!

"Sometimes you want them to touch?" Miss Sheppard asked teasingly.

There had been a time when Sarah would've lifted her chin and walked away with her dignity intact. "Perhaps," she said softly.

"Having trouble with Joe?"

It was another question she'd rather not answer. "Perhaps a little."

Miss Sheppard smiled widely. "Cousin Sarah, when you're finished shopping, come over to the café for lunch. I'll feed you, and then I'll run off the late crowd and we'll have ourselves a nice long talk."

"Thank you, Miss Sheppard. I think I'd like that very much."

Perfect. Just perfect. Joe sipped at his whiskey and watched Tristan Butler out of the corner of his eye.

"Do you know," he said loudly to the bartender, "how expensive it is to have a wife and seven daughters? Seven! Hell, feeding them takes a small fortune, and that little farm doesn't exactly bring in a fortune. I may have to go out and find real work. A job." He made sure his words were slightly slurred. No one seemed to notice that in the hours he'd been sitting at the bar he'd spilled as much whiskey as he'd swallowed.

"Nothing wrong with that," the bartender

said, only half-paying attention. "I'm sure you can find something here in town."

Joe snorted, showing his disgust for the possibility, and with his whiskey glass in hand turned to face the room. Butler was playing cards with a couple of local boys, cheating and winning. The boys either didn't know they were being cheated or were afraid to speak up. Smart boys. Tristan Butler had killed more than one man over a betting dispute.

His instinct was to yank the unsuspecting outlaw out of his chair and haul him to the Jacob's Crossing jail. The world would be a better place when Butler was behind bars. But if he could get Charlie Lockhart, too . . . hell, he had to take the chance.

The boys, broke at last, backed away from the table and left the saloon. It was too early in the day for the place to be crowded. Even the saloon girls were still upstairs, resting for a busy night ahead. For the first time, the only patrons in the saloon were Joe and Butler.

Butler lifted his eyes and pinned them on Joe. "Seven daughters," he said, flashing a smile that revealed his mean streak. "Hellfire."

Joe shrugged and downed what was left in his glass. The other man looked him over.

"You look like the kinda man I could use. You really looking for a job?" Butler tossed his dark curls over his shoulder.

"Maybe," Joe said uncertainly, slapping his empty glass onto the bar.

"The money's good and the work is easy," Butler said. Damn, but the man had cold eyes. Sarah's eyes were dark, but they were warm, and alive, and honest. Butler's eyes were dark but dead.

"What kind of work?"

Butler spent the next minute or two looking Joe up and down, trying to decide if he could trust him, perhaps. "You any good with a gun?"

"Pretty darn good, if I do say so myself."

Butler almost smiled. Almost. "Ever killed anybody?"

This was where it got tricky. He had to play his cards just right. Butler might've bought the story about the wife and seven kids, but if he was too anxious, too open, this would be over before it had even begun. "Why should I tell you if I did?"

They stared one another down, sizing each other up in a way that was primal and ageless. Now was the time. Butler would either trust him and ask him in, or dismiss him. Joe tried not to hold his breath.

The batwing door swung slightly open. "Joe," a reserved voice hissed. "Goodness, the girls and I have been waiting for over an hour."

Slowly, Joe turned his head to Sarah. She stood the boardwalk, the batwing door open just enough for her to peek in, the expression on her face so disapproving it was almost laughable. "I'll be there in a minute."

"Well, hurry," she added before letting the door swing shut.

Butler had a wide, amused smile on his face. Damnation, he'd been so close.

"That's the little woman?" Butler asked, still amused.

"Yep." Joe pushed away from the bar. So damn close!

"Shorter," Butler called as Joe reached the exit.

Joe turned around. He hadn't introduced himself to Butler, or anyone else in the bar, as anything other than Joe.

"I keep pretty close tabs on everyone in this town," Butler added. "I've had my eye on you since I got back."

"Is that a fact?"

"When you can drag yourself away from the little lady and the kiddies, come see me. I'm here every night of the week."

"About that job?" Joe asked.

Butler smiled, a crooked, evil grin. "About that job."

By the time Deacon arrived, Rosie was ready for him. Her hair was tightly constrained, and not a single strand escaped. Her blouse was buttoned to the chin, and the conservative gray skirt did not swish when she walked.

The walk was the hardest part. No wiggle at all, Sarah had said. Spine straight, chin high, shoulders back, hips as motionless as possible.

Rosie had practiced all afternoon, gliding across the café floor and back again.

"Hello, sweetpea," Deacon said with a wicked smile. "Miss me?"

He was so sure he could charm his way into her bed! Well, he had another think coming. "Good afternoon, Deacon," she said primly. "Are you hungry?"

His smile faded. "Uh, yep."

"Have a seat." She swept her hand to indicate the nearest table and smiled; the reserved, proper smile Sarah had insisted upon.

She went to the kitchen, walking slowly and carefully, and returned with a plate piled high with food.

"Are you hurt?" Deacon asked as she set the plate before him.

"Of course not," she said in a low voice. "But how kind of you to ask."

Deacon kept one eye on her while he ate. She saw suspicion there, and confusion. When his meal was finished, she cleared away his plate. But Deacon was in no hurry to leave.

"Rosie, sweetheart," he said in his best, most cajoling voice. "I came all this way looking for you. I fretted over you more than I've ever fretted over another woman in my whole life. Doesn't that mean anything to you?"

She maintained her posture and looked down her nose at the seated man. "It was very sweet of you to worry about my welfare—"

Deacon shot to his feet. "I was not worried

about your welfare!" he shouted. "Well, I was, but that's not why I came looking for you. I want you and I need you," he said tightly, grabbing her shoulders to make his point. "Now, you forget this foolishness and let's head upstairs and get reacquainted."

It would be so easy to say yes. Darn her hide, she wanted him, still. She wanted to fall into his arms and say *Yes, Deacon. You're the best*.

But then where would she be? Right back where she had started.

She placed a firm hand on his chest. "I think you should leave now," she said, almost prudishly.

"Leave?"

"I'm not the same girl you knew in Silver Creek, Deacon. I'm a lady now. A proper lady."

He snorted. "You're no lady, Rosie, and I'm no gentleman."

She wanted to shout at him that she *was* a lady, dammit. But Sarah had said absolutely no yelling and no cursing. None! One's voice must be controlled at all times, one's words carefully chosen. "I've changed," she said quietly. "I decided I want more from life than living above a saloon and making myself available to any man willing to pay for my services. I can't go back, Deacon. I can't undo any part of my life, no matter how I'd like to do just that. But I can start again. I'm a lady. There won't be any more men in my bed until, and *if*, I decide to marry one day."

He took a horrified step back. "Married?"

"Perhaps one day."

Deacon shook his head as he backed out of the café. Rosie held her breath. He might never come back. He might leave town tonight and she'd never see him again. She hadn't wanted him to find her at all, but now that he was here she realized that she needed him, too.

She wanted him to stay, but he had to be willing to accept the new Rosie. He'd even have to make a few changes, himself.

What was she thinking? Deacon Moss was never going to change. He didn't want to be a gentleman, to live a normal life, to court a lady.

But in her heart she harbored a grain of hope that he'd be back tomorrow. And the next day. And the next.

All she could do was wait.

As Rosie put up the CLOSED sign and bolted the door, she wondered how Sarah had taken to *her* lessons.

Chapter Nineteen

The whiskey he'd consumed at the saloon was affecting his brain, Joe decided as he watched Sarah walk from the dining room to the kitchen bearing a few empty plates. She looked too good tonight, too tempting. Her hips seemed to sway ever so slightly as she walked away, her hair was loose and falling around her shoulders instead of tightly restrained. It certainly wasn't his imagination that she'd unfastened the top buttons of her blouse after they got home! When she'd leaned across the table to grab a bowl of snap peas, the lace had fallen back, giving him a tantalizing view of a freckled patch of skin.

He'd kissed those freckles, he now remembered too well as he sat in the dining room all alone. The little ones were getting ready for bed, the older girls helping Sarah in the kitchen.

Maybe he only imagined a change in Sarah, since last night's disappointment stayed with him. Logically he knew he had to keep his distance. Sarah wasn't the kind of woman to give her body without her heart. He should've known that all along, should've rejected her when she'd whispered in the dark, asking him into her bed. He wanted her body, but he did *not* want her heart. A woman's heart came with too many liabilities, too many problems.

Sarah came back into the room for the last of the dirty dishes, casting a long, slow smile his way, leaning over the table so that her blouse fell slightly open again. Yep, his mind knew he needed to sleep in the barn for the duration.

But his body had other ideas.

He retired to the parlor, his mind spinning. Butler. The elusive Charlie Lockhart. Sarah. He shook off those thoughts. Time was running out. If he wanted to catch Lockhart himself before Webb arrived in town, he'd have to take Butler up on his offer, meet with him in the saloon one evening and see what kind of "work" the outlaw offered. If he could weave his way into the gang before Webb's arrival and present both outlaws, shackled and cowed, it would be a real feather in his cap.

Alice and Becky and Clara said goodnight as they climbed the stairs. Their mood was much improved from this morning, when they'd been at each other's throats over one trivial matter or another. If he ever wondered why he did what he did, he had only to think of the Shorter sisters. The world would be a safer place for them when Butler and Lockhart were behind bars or hanging from the end of a rope.

Sarah entered the parlor, and for a moment Joe forgot all about outlaws. She gave him another of those slow smiles as she sat on the settee, her wide, lush mouth almost creeping into a grin.

"I don't know how I'll survive a Texas summer," she said softly, leaning back slowly and lifting her hair off her neck, tilting her head back and closing her eyes. Every move seemed deliberate, calculated to tease and arouse, to show off her body to its best advantage.

It had to be the whiskey.

She reclined on the settee, and as she did her skirt shifted to reveal a very small portion of her very fine legs. She seemed not to notice the infraction.

"I swear," she said softly. "It's so blasted hot." With her eyes closed, she flicked open yet another button of her blouse and peeled the fabric away from her skin to allow a little fresh air to creep in.

The certainty that he had to stay away from her bed faded a little, became foggy, unimportant. "The hottest part of the year won't come for another couple of months," he said, trying to make conversation. *Safe* conversation. Surely the weather was safe enough.

"I never learned to swim," she said. "Evie said there's a lake not too far from the house where they swim in the summertime. Maybe I should learn. The very prospect is lovely," she sighed. "Goodness, if I set my mind to it I can almost feel cool water on a hot day. I can just imagine stepping into the lake, and splashing in the water." She finished her musings with a low, "Hmmm."

In his mind he could see her too clearly; stripping off her prim clothes, stepping into the water in nothing but her chemise and petticoat . . . or maybe nothing at all. His mouth went dry. His hands balled into tight fists. His insides grew heavy and tight as he did war with himself.

His body was winning.

Moving slowly, Sarah sat up. She straightened her skirt, but the blouse still hung slightly open. Dammit, there was just a tiny bit of skin exposed! Not enough to have this effect on him, surely. She lifted her hair off her neck again, closing her eyes, tilting her head back and all but thrusting her breasts in his direction.

"Well," she said as she came to her feet. "I must get to bed. We really should go to church in the morning." She flashed another of those annoyingly seductive smiles in his direction. "Good night, Stumpy," she whispered.

Dammit, she even turned differently than

usual. Her movements were leisurely, slow, with a hint of an undulation in each simple motion. She didn't swing her hips, exactly, but there was a gentle, beguiling sway as she turned and walked away.

"Goodnight, Sarah," he muttered. Dammit, he couldn't call her Miss Priss, not right now.

She stepped into the hallway, opened the bedroom door, and flashed him one last smile. And then she closed the door firmly behind her and set the bolt in place. He could hear it, firm but slow. Reluctant but certain.

He closed his eyes and leaned back, aroused, baffled, and uncertain. If he knocked on that door would Sarah let him in? If he knocked on that door and she let him in, would he ever be able to walk away?

He remained on the couch and cursed beneath his breath. *That's it*, he thought bitterly. *No more whiskey for the remainder of my stay here. It's made me a little crazy.*

That craziness kept him awake long into the night.

There were times in the next several days she was sure this wasn't working; other times when Joe looked at her a certain way, she was just as certain it was working too well.

Since Rosie's brief but enlightening lessons on Saturday afternoon, two very long days ago, Sarah had been easing into this new way of moving and dressing. It seemed simple enough, but there were times she had to think about the way she moved, the way she spoke. Mainly, she had to relax. How many times had Rosie drummed that into her? "Relax, Cousin Sarah," she'd said with a smile. "You move more like a soldier than a woman."

But now, as she looked at the outfit on the bed, she wondered if this wasn't going too far. The blouse was more revealing than her chemise, sleeveless and low cut. The skirt was bright yellow and short enough to show off her ankles, if she wore a pair of slippers instead of her usual boots.

Maybe she didn't need to go this far. The way Joe had been looking at her lately, it probably wasn't necessary. He was coming around. If she went to him . . . but, no. Rosie had forbidden her to blatantly make the first overture, and had insisted that Sarah not tell Joe she loved him. "Once a man knows you love him, you lose," she'd said. "He'll think he owns you. He'll think he can get away with anything and then come running to you and you'll have him back without a word of protest."

Sarah unbuttoned the blouse she'd worn all day, those three very important buttons at the neck unfastened, of course. Maybe it was time to take the next step. In another two weeks school would be over, and the girls would be home all day every day. Goodness, Joe might not even be here in two weeks if she didn't do something immediately.

She shucked off her skirt and blouse quickly, before she could change her mind, and donned the outfit Rosie had given her. Her hair was already down—Rosie had insisted it was a feature she could use to her advantage—but she took a moment to brush it out and toss the waving strands over her shoulder.

Joe was in the barn this afternoon, as he was on most afternoons. There were animals to be cared for, the milk cows and his horse, but she suspected he spent much of that time talking to Snowdrop. She'd caught him, on more than one occasion, talking to the mare as if he expected her to talk back.

She fixed two tall glasses of lemonade, a good enough excuse to seek him out, she supposed, and left by way of the kitchen door. Her heart thudded in her chest as she approached the wide open barn doors. She'd never been brazen in her life! With every step she felt more naked, with the sun on her arms and her chest and her bare head, with the yellow skirt swishing just above her ankles.

She caught a glimpse of Joe before she reached the entrance. Sure enough, he stood at a stall talking to Snowdrop, his voice so low she couldn't make out the words.

Stepping into the shade of the barn, she stopped just short of entering. "I thought you might be thirsty," she said softly.

Joe turned slowly, squinting his eyes, shading them with one hand. Of course, she was backlit by the sun, so he couldn't see her clearly. It was just as well.

Taking a deep breath, she stepped into the barn. There had been a time when she'd found the musty smells distasteful, but she'd come to find a strange kind of comfort in the smell and feel of the rustic building. Animals, hay, leather, they combined to form a very homey, comforting scent.

As she stepped closer to Joe, his eyes widened.

"Jesus Christ!" he muttered as he looked her up and down. "What the hell are you wearing?"

She smiled, remembering the word Rosie had drummed into her. *Relax*. "I don't see how I can get through the summer in my old clothes. They were made for New York, not Texas."

He reached out and absently took the offered glass from her. "You mean to tell me you're going to run around here dressed like that all summer long?" He sounded almost angry at the prospect.

She took a long sip of her own lemonade, making him wait for him answer. "Maybe." As she lowered the hand that held her glass of lemonade, the puffy short sleeve of her blouse fell, exposing her shoulder. She lifted it back into place, moving slowly.

A wicked smile crept across Joe's face. "You're teasing me," he hissed.

"I am not," she said, too quickly and too

indignantly. To make up for the lapse, she gave him a small smile. "Don't be silly."

Joe drained his lemonade in one long gulp and set the glass on the ground at his feet. "Two can play that game, honey," he said, reaching out to flick his fingers absently at her sleeve. It fell again. This time she didn't try to right it. He trailed one slow hand over her shoulder, up her neck, and then speared his fingers through her hair. With the other hand he took her lemonade and dropped the half full glass into the hay.

"Looks to me like you've decided not to be Miss Priss anymore," he said huskily.

"I don't know what you mean," she said, only slightly indignant. This was what she'd wanted; for Joe to touch her again, for him to look at her as if he couldn't live without her.

"The hair," he whispered, raking his fingers through the loose strands. "The clothes." To make a point he pulled the low-cut front of her rounded neckline low enough so that her nipples peeked out. "The sway in your walk," he whispered. "You're trying to seduce me."

"I am not," she protested weakly.

He ignored her. "Do you think I don't want you, all the damn time? Do you think I don't look at you and wish everything was different?"

Her heart skipped a beat. No matter how much Rosie insisted, she couldn't be casual about this, she couldn't pretend she didn't care. "Why can't it be?" she whispered. "Different, I mean."

With a low groan he pulled her against him. She felt the beat of his heart, the heat pouring off his body, and the hard ridge of his arousal pressing against her insistently.

"I can't think straight when I hold you," he whispered.

She closed her eyes and melted against him. "I know what you mean. I never felt this way, before I met you. I never felt so . . . so flustered and hot."

"Do I ruffle your feathers, Sarah?"

"Yes, you do," she admitted softly.

"Good."

He slipped the loose blouse lower and brushed his fingers over her nipples. They hardened at his touch, and she felt the sensation to her toes. A heavy heat settled low in her belly, and the long, deep breath she took did nothing to still the uneasiness within her.

Joe dipped his head to lick one hard nipple, to take it in his mouth and suck gently. She watched his lips close over the nipple, watched his eyes drift shut. Her knees went weak and she grasped at his head for support, to hold on, to bring him closer.

He brought his mouth to hers and kissed her deep, spearing his tongue into her mouth while he pulled her close. She held on tight, kissing him back, clutching at his shirt and pressing her breasts against his chest.

Her insides were spiraling quickly out of control, and so were his. She felt it, as if his sensations were her own, as if his desire and hers mingled and grew with every breath they took. Too many days spent apart fed the fire. All those lonely nights of missing and wanting him culminated in a deep, aching need.

Joe lifted her skirt as he kissed her, bunched it in his hands and raised the bright yellow fabric to her thighs. He settled his hand there, caressed her trembling flesh, and then those fingers crept slowly higher to touch her intimately, to stroke and caress. She felt herself grow wet against his hand, throbbing with readiness.

She lifted one leg and hooked it around his hip, bringing them closer together, anxious to have him inside her. She moaned when he slipped a finger inside her, rocked against him when he ground his hips against hers.

There was nothing but this moment in time, nothing in the world but the sensations that grew to an impossible level with each passing second. Tremors danced through her body, tickling, buzzing, filling her ears and her eyes and her blood. She wanted Joe now. Not tonight, after the girls were asleep. Not even in a few minutes in their soft bed. She wanted him *now*.

Through the haze she heard and felt him unbutton his denims while he kissed and fondled her. *Good*. He danced her to the wall by the open door, lifted her gently, and lowered her onto him. The feel of him entering her, stretching and filling her, made her catch her breath in wonder and relief.

She wrapped her legs around him. With the wall at her back and Joe holding her, she swayed against him, into him, unable to stop or even to slow down, searching and climbing toward the ultimate pleasure. Not wanting this joining to end; driving toward the end just the same.

He pounded against and into her, faster, harder, deeper, until she shattered in his arms. She cried out, holding on with what little strength she had left, savoring the last waves of completion, savoring Joe's own fierce release as he gave over to release and pumped his seed into her with a low cry of his own.

Suddenly they were still, and Sarah realized they were both covered with a sheen of sweat. She still had trouble breathing, and apparently so did Joe. His breath came labored and deep as he buried his face against her shoulder and lowered her to her feet.

Satisfied and unbelievably exhausted, what she wanted most of all was to capture Joe's face in her hands, look him in the eye, and tell him she loved him with all her heart. But Rosie's warning came back to her, along with the remembrance of the disastrous night she'd confessed her love for the first time and Joe had suggested that he'd come through and *visit* now and again.

Just as well. She was winded, breathless,

incapable of speech at the moment. She held onto Joe with everything she had, and he leaned into her as if he didn't want to be anywhere else in the world. Ever.

She heard her own pounding heart, Joe's labored breath in her ear, the muted sounds of Snowdrop moving in her stall . . . and approaching horses and creaking wheels.

"Someone's coming," she said, slowly and reluctantly disentangling herself from Joe's embrace.

Joe lifted his head and looked her in the eye. Ah, she could get lost there, staring into his heart and soul, caught as easily by a glance as by his arms. "I really do wish things were different," he said softly.

She smiled at him. Not Rosie's long, slow, practiced seductive grin, but a true heartfelt smile. "Sometimes things only change if you make them. You might be born into one life, but you can make another. I'm living proof of that." She kissed him quickly. "Good heavens, I must look a mess. I wonder if I can sneak through the back door without running into our visitors." She wondered who had come to visit. It was too early for the girls to be returning from school.

Joe cupped her cheek in his hand. "You're beautiful," he whispered. "Shining from the inside out. Glowing and happy and radiant as any sunset." He grinned wickedly. "You look like you've just been well—"

"Joe!" she admonished with a smile, interrupting him before he could finish his sentence.

When she tried to slip past him he caught her arm and pulled her back. "You are beautiful," he said again. "But I don't think I want anyone else getting this particular view."

He straightened her blouse, covering her breasts and righting the misbehaving sleeve. And then kissing her one more time before letting her go.

It was much too late to avoid the guests who'd arrived at the front door by slipping to the back. Sarah pushed her hair over her shoulders and headed for the coach that had stopped in the front drive. She recognized the driver, the man who owned the livery in town and rented this less-than-magnificent carriage on occasion.

Well, perhaps she wasn't dressed to receive company, but then this company had arrived uninvited. A trickle of sweat snaked down her chest to disappear beneath the muslin and between her breasts.

"Hello, Mr. Watts," she said brightly as she came to the carriage. He stared at her wide-eyed in answer.

The carriage door opened, and a finely dressed man stepped out. She was so shocked to see him here, in this place, at this time, that it took her brain a moment to accept what she was seeing. His eyes, when he saw her, went as wide as the carriage driver's.

"Hello, Father," Sarah said softly.

Her father reached up a steady hand, and a feminine gloved hand took it and alit to the hard ground.

"Mother," Sarah said, her voice even softer than before.

One more occupant left the confines of the coach, his mood evidently as morose as her parents'. "Hugh," she said, quite certain no one could understand the croak that escaped her lips.

The eyes of all three were pinned in wide wonder on her, and then, almost as one, those eyes shifted to a view over her shoulder. She turned to see what they saw, just as Joe finished tucking in his shirt.

Chapter Twenty

"James, she's lost her mind," Sarah's mother said dramatically from her perch on the setee. "Look at her. Just *look* at her! Oh, my poor baby," she moaned. "We should have brought Dr. Bennett with us. He'd know what to do."

Joe lounged casually against the wide entry way that separated the parlor from the hallway, observing the scene before him with more than a trace of amusement. Sarah was as flustered as he'd ever seen her, so surprised by this unannounced visit that she didn't seem capable of standing in one place for more than three seconds or forming a complete sentence.

Her mother was indeed an attractive woman. As far as Joe was concerned she didn't hold a candle to Sarah, but with her dark hair and violet eyes and striking figure she was still quite a looker.

The older man, Sarah's father Joe assumed, and a much younger fella were so citified that the sight of them conferring in low, excited voices was almost comical. With their fancy suits and shiny shoes and bowler hats, these men were true city slickers. The older man's suit was dark and plain; the younger man had chosen to dress in a brown check with a little yellow stripe running through it. To Joe's thinking, it was a worse clothing choice than the detested nightshirt.

He dismissed the city folks and set his eyes on Sarah. In spite of the current crisis, a smile crept across his face. He'd been floored when she'd walked into the barn wearing that revealing outfit with her hair down and innocent come-hither look in her eyes; like she wanted to eat him up but didn't know exactly where to start.

He'd never lost control with a woman before. Never. He'd never taken a woman against a wall because the bed was just too damn far away. He'd never wanted anything in his life the way he wanted Sarah. Damn, he could still smell her on his skin, could still feel her soft hands at his back and her legs around his hips.

His smile faded. He could so easily fall in love with her. And right now the fall wouldn't be far—he was already halfway there.

He caught himself. What kind of a fool

would even consider taking on a prissy woman and seven kids in the name of a nonexistent emotion that wouldn't last, in the waning heat of an erotic encounter? Not him, by God.

And then Sarah turned pleading eyes on him. She was lost. Confused. Outnumbered. She needed him.

He walked into the parlor, taking long, slow strides toward her. Ignoring the melee around him, the hissing citified voices and a mother's wailing protests. He concentrated on Sarah, and just Sarah, and when he reached her, he slipped an arm around her shoulder and faced a suddenly quiet room.

"Sarah, honey," he said sweetly. "Aren't you going to introduce me to these folks?"

He grinned at the three unsmiling faces and tightened his hold on Sarah. She seemed to need the support.

"Of course," she said in a slightly trembling yet proper voice. "This is my mother, Katherine Prince." She gestured to the lovely, distraught woman on the setee. "My father, James Prince," she said, nodding to the scowling older man, "and a family friend, Hugh Towerson."

Towerson raised his pert nose in the air. "Sarah is being modest. I am much more than a family friend. I'm her fiancé."

Joe continued to smile at the greenhorn. "Not anymore, partner," he said softly.

Hugh opened his mouth to reply, but Sarah spoke up before he could make a sound. "This is Joe Shorter," she said, her voice a little stronger than before as she glanced almost pleadingly up at him. "My husband."

All hell broke loose.

Sarah felt like she hadn't had the opportunity to so much as take a deep breath since she'd walked into the barn bearing two glasses of lemonade. Her parents were livid. Hugh was self-righteously incensed, and Joe had become perversely silent.

Joe apparently wasn't at all bothered by the fact that the three visitors from New York looked him up and down as if he were an oddity in a traveling circus. He'd smiled absently when her mother had asked, horrified, if Sarah had truly married *that . . . that man.*

At least he hadn't given away their deception. As long as her parents and Hugh believed she was truly married, they'd have no choice but to return to New York and leave her here. Here was where she wanted to be.

Of course, her father had never been one to give up easily. "We can arrange for a quiet divorce," he whispered softly, as if even saying the words aloud would cause a scandal. "Once we return home and you and Hugh are married, no one will ever have to know about this incident."

Sarah set her eyes on Hugh. Surely he wouldn't abide such a disgrace! If nothing else, Hugh Towerson had his pride. Sarah tried not to blush as she remembered the picture she and Joe must've made, coming from the barn. Surely Hugh would not consent to such a ridiculous suggestion.

Hugh surprised her with his soft answer. "I believe that is the only acceptable course of action."

Sarah wished with all her heart that Joe would speak up and tell them all that he didn't want a divorce, that he would not allow it. A show of indignity was surely called for in this situation.

But he didn't say a word. He stood beside her, his arm across her shoulders, but he remained silent. Well, what did she expect? This was her problem, not his.

"There will be no divorce," she said firmly. "I'm very happy here."

Katherine Prince set teary eyes on her husband. "I told you, James, she's lost her mind. My baby's not well."

"I am *very* well," Sarah insisted. "And I have most certainly not lost my mind." She stood firm as her mother turned pleading eyes her way. "I was going to write to you soon, to let you know about my circumstances, but I've been delaying writing that particular letter for this very reason. I am twenty-four years old, Mother. I will decide the path of my own life." She took a deep, stilling breath. Having said that, she felt better. "How did you find me?"

Her father answered. "I hired Pinkerton's the

day after you left. They've been searching for you for months, but they had very little to go on. As soon as they located you we made arrangements to travel to this . . . this . . ." He glanced around the parlor with disdain. "This place."

Sarah watched her mother regain her composure. Goodness knew nothing disturbed Katherine Prince's stoicism for long. Unnecessary displays of emotion were unladylike, beneath her, common.

"I have some bad news, Sarah," she said calmly. "Your Aunt Mabel passed on two months ago."

Her Grandmother Prince's sister had been ill off and on for the past two years, yet still Sarah felt a wave of sorrow that resembled a sudden illness of her own. Grief washed through her. She had loved Aunt Mabel, who had told her stories about the grandmother who had died when Sarah was little. Most of those stories ended with a comparison of Sarah and her grandmother. Apparently she even looked like the unrepentantly audacious, adventuresome redhead who had given birth to Sarah's father.

"I'm so sorry to hear that," she said sincerely. Joe's arm tightened around her, a brief and welcome comforting gesture.

"I would have liked to have you beside me at the funeral," her father snapped. "At such times a man needs his family."

"I'm sorry I wasn't there," Sarah said softly,

and it seemed Joe leaned even closer, comforting her still.

James Prince set angry eyes on Joe. "Would you kindly get your hands off my daughter!" he shouted.

Joe didn't move, but he did, finally, speak up. "Would you kindly quit doing your damnedest to upset my *wife*?"

Sarah watched her father's left eye twitch. Oh, that was not a good sign. Usually when she saw that telling twitch she made her excuses and left the room before things got any worse. Unfortunately, she didn't have anywhere to disappear to at the moment.

"The girls will be home soon, and I don't want them to walk in on an unpleasant scene," Sarah said calmly. "You must be tired after your trip—"

"Girls?" her father asked softly.

Sarah met his penetrating gaze. "Yes. Joe has seven daughters."

Her mother came up off the setee, moving gracefully and slowly. "You married a man who has seven children?" she whispered. "*Seven?*"

Sarah did her best to maintain her composure. "Yes. They're lovely girls, very sweet and bright. You'll like them all, I'm sure."

Katherine Prince looked as if she were about to faint.

Joe leaned slightly forward. "I'm sure they'll love meeting their new Granny."

Sarah watched her mother's face go ghostly

white. The stunned woman even wobbled uncertainly before retaking her seat. "I am most certainly *not* their grandmother," she said softly. "Seven girls," she whispered. "This is proof that you have indeed lost your mind, Sarah Louise Prince."

"Sarah Louise Shorter," Joe corrected in a low voice.

If looks could kill, poor Joe would be dead on his feet. Her mother, her father, even Hugh glared at Stumpy with pure hatred. Sarah leaned closer to Joe, as if she could protect him the way he'd so valiantly protected her. For a moment she felt sure that together they could face anything. Everything.

And then she remembered that it was all a lie.

Deacon straightened his too-tight collar, and then one at a time he rubbed the tops of his boots against the back of his calves to wipe off the dust and bring out the shine. Taking a deep breath, he opened the door to Rosie's café.

He'd almost left last night. He'd even begun to pack his saddlebags with every intention of leaving town for good. She'd miss him then, when he was gone. She'd be sorry for pretending to be a lady when she obviously still wanted him.

But it had then occurred to him that maybe Rosie just wanted to be courted a little, to know that he didn't take her for granted. Women could be funny that way.

The supper crowd had left, and Rosie was wiping off the last of the little round tables that dotted the floor of her café. She looked up in mild surprise when he opened the door.

Deacon took off his hat. "Howdy," he said, his voice a little too soft and a touch nervous. "I though maybe you'd like to take a walk around town with me. We can watch the sunset, maybe talk a while."

The smile she cast his way was worth everything; the bath, the haircut, the tight collar.

"I'd love to take a walk with you," she said. "Just give me a minute to change out of these clothes."

As far as he was concerned, the skirt and blouse she wore were fine for a quick walk around town. If he played his cards right, she wouldn't be wearing them for long, anyway. But he'd fixed himself up for her. Maybe she wanted to do the same for him.

So he waited, glancing only half a dozen times or so to the stairway that led to the upstairs room where Rosie made her home these days. If he climbed those stairs and caught her half undressed . . .

No. She wanted to be proper, and he could handle that. For a while.

He was watching the stairs when she appeared there, and he decided right then, without question, that she was worth any wait. Even with her hair in a neat bun, and her blouse buttoned to her chin, and her skirt brushing the floor so that all he could see was the tips of her boots, she was beautiful. Different from the woman he'd known in Silver Creek, perhaps, but still his Rosie.

Rosie took his extended arm as they stepped onto the boardwalk, and they began to walk. He hoped he was doing this right. Hellfire, he'd never courted a woman before!

It turned out to be not so hard. Mostly he just had to listen. Rosie spoke about her day at the café, her customers and the minor problems she'd had in the kitchen. Her voice was soft, gentle, and she didn't swear one time, not even when she told him about one particularly irascible patron. She even walked differently, though not as stiffly as she had on Saturday evening when she'd moved like she had a stick up her behind. She moved gracefully, sweetly. Like a real lady.

Men still watched Rosie, but the looks cast her way were different this evening. The men didn't leer or holler, didn't ogle her and make lewd suggestions. They looked at her with admiration and respect, and an occasional touch of longing.

Deacon and Rosie walked to the edge of town for an unobstructed view of the sunset, then stood in silence as the sky turned every shade of orange and yellow and pink. Something in Deacon wanted to grab Rosie there and then, kiss her deep and long, and *tell* her that tonight he'd be sleeping in her bed.

But he didn't. He wasn't a complete fool. Rosie had started herself a new life; she wanted to be a lady. It was going to take time to convince her that she was *his* lady and always would be.

"Sounds like you were right busy today," he said as they headed back into town.

"I was," Rosie said, her voice sweet and soft.

"How about if I come help you tomorrow?"

She cast him a suspicious glance. "You? Help in the café?"

"You don't have to pay me," he insisted. "I need something to keep me busy while I'm stuck in this town." She wisely didn't ask why he was still here.

"I can feed you, no charge," she said. "An extra pair of hands would be nice."

Deacon wore a small, satisfied smile as they approached her establishment. So far so good. All in all, he considered this courting thing to be going well. But dammit, he wanted more time. He wanted to talk a while longer, he wanted to convince her that she could be a lady and be his woman at the same time. But too soon they reached the building, and Rosie turned to him to say goodnight.

She smiled. "Thank you, Deacon. This was lovely."

Lovely. "Yeah."

"I'll see you in the morning."

"Bright and early," he added.

Suddenly her smile died and he saw her gaze

shift from his face to the saloon across the street. He looked over his shoulder just in time to see a dark-haired man enter the establishment that was already loud and lively.

"Who's that?" he asked as he turned his eyes back to Rosie.

She sighed. "Joe White."

His teeth clamped together, his hands fisted. A fire of anger welled up inside him. "So that's pretty boy Joe White. Maybe I'll just—"

"No," she said, laying her hand on his arm. It was that soft hand that stopped him. "Please, leave Joe alone. He has enough problems of his own, right now."

"So he comes to you with his problems," Deacon seethed. "That's just great." He kept remembering her words as she sat on the bed in Silver Creek. *Who's the best? Joe White.*

"No, Joe doesn't come to me with his problems. His wife and I are becoming friends, and we . . . we had a nice long talk Saturday afternoon." Her eyes were moony and wide and sparkling, and they touched his heart. Dammit. "I haven't had many real women friends in my life. If you make trouble with Joe, I might never get to be real friends with Sarah."

"All right," he agreed like a chastened boy. "I won't cause any problems."

"Promise?" she whispered.

Deacon wrinkled his nose and shifted on his feet. He didn't like being held back, he didn't like knowing that bastard was across the street and he couldn't do a damn thing about it. But if it was important to Rosie . . . "Hell, I promise," he finally said.

Rosie smiled at him, a wide sweet smile. "Thank you," she whispered, and then she came up on her toes to kiss his cheek. "You're the best, Deacon."

With that she spun away from him, opened the café door, then closed it before he could get out another word. She bolted it behind her.

Chapter Twenty-one

Joe usually liked the sounds and smells of a good saloon: laughter and fighting, cigar smoke and cheap perfume, the shuffle of playing cards and the clink of glasses. Unfortunately, Jacob's Crossing's only saloon wasn't anywhere near the finest he'd ever seen, and in order to be here he'd had to leave a disappointed, disillusioned "wife" behind with her parents and that pompous ass who had been her fiancé.

He couldn't tell Sarah what he was doing, how he was trying to get close to Butler to find Lockhart. Knowing too much might put her in danger, and he wouldn't do that. Not ever.

In the hours he'd been here, he'd managed to slosh and spill more whiskey than he swallowed, so he smelled like a drunk but still had his wits about him. Butler had been playing, and winning, at cards again. Every now and then Joe caught the outlaw's eyes, but he hadn't spoken to him about that *job*. Not yet.

Butler had apparently finally tired of his card game; he was raking in his winnings and dismissing the other players. When the table cleared, he nodded to Joe in silent invitation.

Joe kept his half full glass of whiskey in his hand as he made his way to Butler's table. He'd never been this close before, had never sidled up to an outlaw he was chasing and shared a drink with him. As he plopped into a recently vacated chair, Butler waved off the saloon gal who weaved her way toward the table.

"Still interested in that job?" Butler asked in a low voice.

Joe nodded. "Hell, I'll do anything for money." He set his eyes meaningfully on Butler. "Anything."

The admission brought a smile to Tristan Butler's face. "I'm glad to hear that. I found the perfect assignment for you, just today."

Joe took a sip of the whiskey, then placed the glass on the table. "Let's hear it."

Butler looked amused, but there was something deadly lurking in his eyes. "Three very well-dressed strangers arrived in town this afternoon on the stage from Silver Creek."

"Do tell," Joe said softly.

"By golly, they actually *smelled* like money." Butler's grin widened. "And I want it."

Joe shoved his glass aside and leaned over the table. "You do know you're talking about my wife's family, don't you?"

"I suspected as much when I heard they'd hired a ride out to your place," Butler said, his grin replaced by a wary look. "Does that make a difference?"

Well hell. "I haven't been married all that long. It might put a damper on things if I rob my wife's parents."

Butler found that amusing. He even laughed out loud and slapped his knee. "You've got a point there. But you see, I have another plan."

Joe didn't like the sound of this, not at all. "What kind of plan?"

Butler's smile faded, his eyes went almost black. "I kidnap that wife of yours and hold her for a tidy ransom, and you—"

"No," Joe interrupted. Hell, he wasn't going to get Lockhart after all. He was going to have to arrest Butler and have the sheriff hold him in the Jacob's Crossing jail until Webb arrived.

Butler raised one expressive eyebrow. "No? Shorter, nobody tells me *no*."

"You don't bring a man's family into business," Joe argued. "Not ever. It's messy and unprofessional, and no good will come of it."

"Unprofessional?" Butler repeated.

"I won't have my wife hurt," Joe said in a low growl.

"I'm not gonna hurt her," Butler hissed. "I'm just going to . . . detain her for a spell. The plan is foolproof."

Joe searched for an argument that would sway Butler. He was afraid he wouldn't find one. So, should he try to take Butler here? Or should he wait until morning? "My in-laws are difficult people. They won't just sit back and give you what you want. They'll go to the sheriff."

Butler smiled again. "I certainly hope so."

Out of the corner of his eye, Joe saw Sheriff Potter approaching. Potter seemed to be like a good number of small-town sheriffs Joe had met; self-important and petty, the man walked through the town like he was king and the people of Jacob's Crossing were peasants. Past his prime, he was also just too damn lazy to do his job.

"Evening, Morris," Butler said as Potter took a seat.

Joe felt a brief warning, as dread settled uneasily in his gut. These two looked entirely too chummy.

"Tristan," Potter said with a nod of his head. "How is that lovely mother of yours?"

"Just fine, Morris. She was asking after you just this afternoon. Wants you to come to supper Friday."

"I'd be delighted."

Joe watched the exchange with growing dread. Something wasn't right here. The sheriff turned toward Joe and looked him over with a touch of contempt. "So, has Mr. Shorter here agreed to help us out?"

Butler shook his head. "He's being difficult. Doesn't think it's *professional* to involve a man's family in business."

Dammit, he was going to have to string these two along until Webb arrived. "I don't want my wife hurt, that's all. She's . . . delicate. I need the money, but for God's sake come up with another plan."

Butler looked at Joe as if he were deciding whether to agree or shoot him here and now. "I tell you what," he finally said. "The woman that got off the stage this afternoon was wearing a real nice brooch. Looked to me to be real diamonds, not that mail-order trash. I think my mother would love to have a brooch like that to wear to church on Sunday."

"I'll get you the brooch," Joe agreed. "Just give me a few days."

"Two days," Butler said. "After that . . ." he shrugged as if he didn't care one way or another. "Well, we'll see. We don't need you for this plan. Your participation would make things easier all the way around, but I can and will proceed without you, if I have to."

With that, the subject was closed. Butler smiled as he leaned forward and clapped the sheriff on the back. "We got us a sweet setup here, Shorter. Blow this and I *will* kill you." He set dead, dark eyes on Joe's face. "But not before I take care of the missus and those brats of yours."

Sarah tossed in the big bed, but did so gently since Faith slept on her right and Glory slept on her left.

She could not believe that Joe had deserted her this evening to go to the saloon! He had to see a man about a job, he'd said. It apparently didn't matter that her parents and Hugh were intent on doing battle over their marriage. Oh, no. It didn't matter that he had to throw her to the wolves in order to escape for the evening.

And that's exactly what he'd done. There was no man to be seen about a job! He just wanted out of the house. Could she blame him? Her parents were troublesome, and Hugh was not an easy man to talk to. They were, all three of them, *her* problem. So she really shouldn't blame Joe for taking his chance to steal away.

But she did.

Especially after this afternoon in the barn. There was more to their coming together than simple physical need, she was certain of it. There was heart in their passion, she knew it; she felt it still.

She didn't move when she heard the horse's hooves outside the house. Lay perfectly still in the quiet moments while Joe was no doubt getting Snowdrop settled for the night. She felt a rush of relief when she heard his slow, steady footsteps on the front porch. At least he had come home.

Almost immediately, she was ashamed and angry for her overwhelming sense of relief. This wasn't home to Joe; it was just a temporary stop, one of many. Her imagination had made more of their strange relationship than was really there. One day Joe would leave and he *wouldn't come back*. She had to be ready for that.

The front door opened and closed gently, as he tried to be quiet. She wondered if he'd simply sleep on the parlor floor, as he had in the past few days. It would serve him right, especially since she'd had to send the blanket and pillow he often used upstairs to the room where five of the Shorter sisters slept tonight.

But he came almost immediately to her door, a door she had neglected to lock.

She didn't close her eyes and pretend to sleep, even though it would have been the easy way—with no confrontation, no accusations. He came to the bed as if he expected her to be awake, to be waiting for him.

The odor of whiskey and cigar smoke hit her long before he reached the side of the bed.

"Good heavens," she hissed. "You stink. You smell like a . . . like a saloon."

By the light of the moon breaking through the window, she saw him smile. But it wasn't a true smile, not one of those heartfelt grins that always set her pulse to racing. "Sorry about that."

At least he didn't sound drunk. His voice sounded perfectly normal, in fact. "I hope you had an enjoyable evening," she said tightly, keeping her voice low so as not to disturb the children. "I did not, by the way," she said without waiting for him to respond. "My parents spent several hours trying to convince me to divorce you."

His smile faded. "Did you tell them that wouldn't be necessary?"

Because they weren't really married. Because one day soon the man everyone knew as Joe Shorter would ride away and disappear for good. "No."

He glanced down at the girls who slept beside her. "Looks like we're doubled up for the night to make room for company."

"You can sleep on the floor," Sarah said primly.

He didn't argue, but pulled his old bedding from beneath the bed. She watched while he took off his boots and leather vest and shirt, sniffed the offensive shirt and tossed it aside, then lay down without another word.

She couldn't stand it. Moving very cautiously, she slipped from beneath the quilt, twisted about gently, lay on her stomach and peered over the end of the bed. Wearing his denims and nothing else, Joe reclined on the floor with his hands behind his head.

"I can't believe you just . . . just *left* me here," she hissed.

Instead of an argument, Joe muttered a soft "I'm sorry." Oddly enough, by the tone of his voice, she'd say the apology was sincere.

It was impossible to stay angry with a man who apologized in that way. Sarah rested her chin on her hands and relaxed. "They won't be here long. As soon as I convince them that I'm not going back to New York under any circumstances, they'll leave. Mother already hates it here, and Father has business to attend to. I can't imagine why Hugh is still here, considering the circumstances."

"Don't let them rattle you, Miss Priss," Joe said with a touch of humor. "That's my job."

She smiled down at him. In moments like this she could fool herself into thinking he really would stay.

"About this afternoon . . ." he began.

Sarah's smile faded. "Oh, I don't think we should talk about that," she said quickly and softly.

Even though his face was in shadow, she could tell Joe was looking up at her. He was unsmiling, thoughtful. "You're probably right about that," he whispered. "But maybe you could climb down here and sleep with me tonight."

"I shouldn't—"

"Just to sleep, Sarah," he said softly. "I could stand to have someone to hold on to tonight."

Moving carefully, she slipped from the bed. Glory and Faith immediately readjusted themselves to take up the middle as well as the sides, spreading out, sighing in satisfaction. There would be no going back.

She lay down beside Joe, resting her head on his shoulder, and took a deep, stilling breath. "I wish you'd stayed home tonight," she whispered as she settled in.

"So do I," he muttered so softly she barely heard him.

They lay there, together, for a few quiet minutes. Joe seemed to hold her tighter than was necessary, but she liked it. She felt at home, here; by his side, in his arms.

"You know," he finally whispered. "I've risked my life plenty of times and never thought anything of it. It's part of the job."

Sarah shifted her head so she could see his face. He sounded so serious. "What happened?" Suddenly she knew he hadn't left the house simply to escape the confrontation with her parents. Something else had called him out tonight.

"I think maybe I'm in over my head," he whispered. "For the first time in my life. . . ." The arm that circled her tightened.

She lifted her head to look him in the eye. "Sounds serious. Want to tell me about it?"

He hesitated, as if he was thinking it over. "No," he finally answered.

Sarah gave him a quick kiss on his stubbled cheek. "Get some sleep. Maybe whatever is bothering you will look better in the morning."

She settled against Joe again, held on to him as tightly as he held her.

"I don't think so," he whispered.

Alice peered into the parlor before entering. Oh, she did not want to run into Sarah's family, if she could help it! They'd been here two days, and already they'd taken over. Mr. Prince and Mr. Towerson, in particular, always acted as if having children in the house was a nuisance, looking down their noses, demanding silence even from the little ones who were *never* silent.

From outside of the house, the occasional sound of gunfire broke the unnatural silence. Joe had demanded that Sarah spend more time practicing her marksmanship, that she become comfortable and proficient with both the six-shooter and the rifle. Alice did not take this as a good sign. Obviously, he still planned to leave.

Mrs. Prince sat alone in the parlor, perched on the edge of the settee, flinching with every muffled gunshot. She was a striking-looking woman, the kind of lady who could still turn a man's head, Alice supposed. But beautiful as Katherine Prince was, she had none of Sarah's warmth.

As if she knew she was being watched, Mrs. Prince turned her head and looked directly at Alice. There was no escaping now, not without being incredibly rude.

"Would you care for some tea?" Alice asked politely.

One Day, My Prince

"Perhaps later," Mrs. Prince said, in a distant voice that reminded Alice, a little, of the way Sarah had been when she'd come here. As if there was a wall between her and everyone else, as if she never laughed or cried or screamed. With a nod of her finely coiffed head, Mrs. Prince invited Alice into the room.

"You're Alicia, isn't that correct?" Mrs. Prince asked as she waved a slender hand to indicate the chair at her right.

"Alice," she said as she took her seat.

"Oh, yes," Mrs. Prince said with a touch of distress. "Alice." Another gunshot rang out, and the woman closed her eyes for a moment and visibly twitched, as if the sound was painful to her.

"So, tell me, Alice," Mrs. Prince continued when she'd regained her composure. "Can you shed some light on this situation for me? Can you explain to me why my daughter would give up a fine home and a wonderful man who adores her and all the luxury a woman could ask for . . . for *this*?"

Alice knew there was no way she could tell Sarah's family anything. If they knew Joe was not their father, that the marriage was a farce, they'd use the knowledge to steal Sarah away. The very thought gave her chills.

"Love, I suppose," she said softly.

Even though there was not another gunshot, Mrs. Prince closed her eyes in what appeared to be pain. "I thought I'd taught her better than

311

that," she murmured. "I certainly tried. To throw away a wonderful life for a *man* is the worst kind of folly." She opened her eyes and stared toward the window. "I can see why she might be attracted to that . . . that husband of hers, but *really*. He's handsome, if you like the type, and charming, when he chooses to be. But he's so vulgar. So common. Years from now Sarah will know I'm right about this, but by then it will be too late."

Alice decided to open her heart, just a little, in defense of Sarah. "I believe he loves her very much."

A low sound of disgust formed and died in Mrs. Prince's throat. "I've seen the way he looks at her. Trust me, my dear, it's not *love* that man feels for my daughter."

"What is it, then?" Alice asked quietly. Immediately, she wished she'd left her mouth closed, her question unasked.

Mrs. Prince turned the full force of those oddly cold eyes on her. "You're too young for this conversation, Alicia."

Alice didn't even bother to correct the woman. "Well, I love Sarah." She didn't want to cry, she really didn't, but she felt the sting of tears. "I don't know what we would've done without her these past few months."

Mrs. Prince seemed to harden. "There will be no tears in my presence," she said coldly. "Tears are a waste of energy, unproductive, and they make you look very unattractive."

She tried not to cry, she really did, but a few fat tears slipped out. "My sisters love her, too, especially Faith and Glory. They need a mother, and Sarah—"

"Sarah is not their mother," Mrs. Prince said sternly, but Alice imagined a softening of her eyes. "Once this unbearable situation is rectified, I'm sure your father will find another woman. *She* can be your new mother."

"It's not that simple," Alice said, her chin trembling.

"It will have to be," Mrs. Prince countered. "Now go wash your face and regain your composure, and once you've calmed yourself we'll have that tea."

A loud bang made the woman jump. Joe and Sarah were apparently working with the rifle, now.

Joe watched in satisfaction as yet another bottle exploded. Sarah wasn't a bad shot, especially considering that she hadn't touched a firearm until just a few weeks ago.

She lowered the rifle carefully, and he smiled at her back. Not only had her aim become good, she had proper respect for the power of the weapons she wielded.

"Not bad, Miss Priss," he said softly. "Not bad at all."

She turned slowly to face him, no smile on her face, no words of thanks for his praise. "Can we call it a day? My arms and my shoulder ache."

He reached out and took the rifle from her. "It is a little heavy, isn't it."

"A *little* heavy?" She lifted an expressive eyebrow. "I guess you could say that. And I must confess," she said, reaching up to rub her right shoulder gently. "I didn't expect it to strike me quite so vigorously."

"I warned you this rifle had a kick," he said.

"Yes, you did."

Hell, if only she wouldn't look at him this way. How could a woman be innocent and tempting at the same time? Prim and seductive. Regal and sexy.

And he, damned and determined to bring in Lockhart as well as Butler, had put her in danger. He couldn't tell her about Tristan Butler's damned plan. What if she saw Butler in town and gave away her knowledge with something so simple as the expression on her face? She would really be in danger then, wouldn't she?

"What you need is a derringer," he said, thinking of sensible solutions. "Something small and light enough to keep in your skirt pocket when the six-shooter and the rifle aren't close at hand. Maybe Garland has an over-and-under model for sale at his place. That way you'll have two shots instead of just one. I don't remember seeing an over-and-under when I bought the other weapons, but he can always special-order one."

She smiled at him, a wide, clear smile. "My goodness, you'd think I was going to war the

way you have me armed. Really, Joe, I don't
think it will be necessary for me to be armed at
all times."

"It can't hurt," he said quietly, unable to
return her smile.

"I never knew," she said teasingly, "that you
had such a suspicious nature."

"I'll check the general store tonight when I go
to town."

Her smile faded. "Back to the saloon?"

He nodded once. It was enough.

"I wish you would stay home," she said, her
voice soft and low. It was intimate here in the
middle of a deserted field that had once been
filled with Willem Sheridan's cattle. "Every
time my parents get me alone, they start in
with their blasted plans for a quiet divorce and
my return to New York. They seem to be more
well-behaved when you're around."

That was a scary thought, considering their
treatment of him. "I'll try not to be gone long,
but I have to go."

"Can I ask why?"

"No." Stealing and delivering Katherine
Prince's diamond brooch would buy him a few
more days, but he could hardly explain that to
her. Webb would be here soon with at least a
few men, and together they would take Butler
and the sheriff into custody—and maybe even
Charlie Lockhart.

Sarah didn't ask "why" again.

Joe reached out, gently grabbed her wrist,

and pulled her close. "Maybe you should kiss me, in case any of our guests are watching."

"We do want to maintain a certain appearance," she whispered, reaching up to grasp the edge of the vest he wore, Willem Sheridan's soft, well-worn leather garment, with gentle fingers.

"Yes, we do."

She came up on her toes, and he leaned down to meet her. Her mouth on his was soft and sweet, tender and exciting.

Sarah released her hold on the vest and slipped her arms around his waist as the kiss quickly became something more than a simple, innocent meeting of their mouths. It was as if he had grown ravenously hungry for her, as if he couldn't ever get enough.

He had to wonder what she'd think of a detour to the barn before they returned to the house.

"Oh, for pity's sake," a miserly, citified voice interrupted. "Do control yourselves."

Joe released Sarah and turned to face Hugh Towerson; the man who would be Sarah's husband right now if she hadn't run away on the day of their wedding.

He despised the man almost as much as he despised Butler and Lockhart and the crooked Sheriff Potter. For different reasons, of course. More personal, gut-wrenching reasons.

Hellfire, he was jealous.

"What do you want, Hughie?"

The man bristled. "It's Hugh, you barbarian," he said primly. "Mr. Towerson to you."

Joe smiled tightly at the man. "What the hell do you want? Can't a man kiss his wife in peace?"

It was Towerson's turn to bristle. "Mrs. Prince's diamond brooch is missing. She's quite sure she left it on the dresser in her room." He lifted his nose superciliously into the air. "I suspect one of your ragamuffins has pilfered it."

Joe took a single step toward the shorter, slighter man. "None of my girls are thieves, Hughie."

"The fact remains that the brooch is missing," Towerson said with a wrinkle of his pert nose. "It belonged to Mrs. Prince's mother, and she's quite distraught over the disappearance."

"I'm sure it will turn up," Sarah said, stepping to Joe's side. "Mother's misplaced jewelry before, many times. She can be careless, you know."

"She's quite sure—" Towerson began.

"Joe's right," Sarah interrupted, a touch of fire in her voice. "None of our girls are thieves."

He wanted that detour to the barn more than ever. Damn, but Sarah had gumption. She stared Towerson straight in the eye and defied him without a single tremor. He wanted to make sure that she and everyone else knew she was his . . . even though she wasn't. Not really. Not completely.

"I'd better go help Mother look for her

317

brooch," Sarah said, looking up at him and delivering a small, secret smile.

And he let her go, to search for a diamond brooch that rested safe and snug in the inside pocket of the leather vest he wore.

Chapter Twenty-two

These days Sarah took any opportunity to get away from the house, and this morning was no exception. Her mother was still abed, but her father and Hugh were up and dressed and assaulting her with the full force of their indignity. Mother's brooch was still missing, and according to them she was a complete fool for marrying a man with seven children, one of whom apparently was a thief. In fact, they made it quite clear that they questioned her sanity. Any woman in the world would be grateful to be in the position she had run away from, in their estimation.

She couldn't think of the proper words to make them understand. Even if she could come up with just the right explanation, they likely wouldn't bother to listen.

When they stopped to take a deep breath, she excused herself to head to the kitchen to make coffee—and then slipped out the back door.

It was a glorious morning, clear and still cool, not a cloud in the sky. All was wondrously quiet outside the crowded house; there was no arguing, no badgering, and there were no accusations. Three horses grazed in the large enclosed corral, Joe's beloved Snowdrop and the two more ordinary horses who so faithfully pulled the wagon. In a separate enclosure the two milk cows grazed. The animals and the beauty of the morning made such a peaceful, enchanting picture.

"Hiding?" a soft voice asked.

She spun around to find Joe so close that she could reach out and touch him, if she had a mind to. Gorgeous as always, he wore one of his charmingly devilish half-smiles.

"I suppose I am," she confessed.

"Me, too," he said, taking her hand and leading her away from the house.

She knew this wouldn't last much longer, that Joe's time here was not indefinite. But as they walked hand in hand away from the house she felt a fresh wave of love, as if this moment were perfect and the future held endless, wonderful possibilities.

"They do have their good qualities, you know. My parents," she added as they walked to the other side of the barn where they'd be hidden from prying eyes in any window of the house. "Hugh, too, I imagine."

"Maybe they left those good qualities back in New York," Joe muttered.

Sarah smiled as they came to a halt in the shade of the barn. "Perhaps. I know my mother and father are overly protective, and that they only want what's best for me. I understand that better now, since I've taken on the children. I want to protect the girls, and make sure they have a good life—the best I can give them. So I do understand, I just think it's time my parents allowed me to decide what's best for myself."

"What is best for you, Sarah?"

She bit her tongue to keep from blurting out, *You, Stumpy. You're what's best for me.*

For the past several nights they'd shared a room, but not a bed. She had joined him on the floor, twice, but with the children so close it was impossible to allow their passions rein. Just as well, she supposed. It was going to be difficult enough to let Joe go when the time came.

But being close to him, having him right *here,* was a difficulty all its own.

She wondered if she'd ever fall out of love with this Joe White. If she'd ever forget the way he made her feel.

He hadn't mentioned being in over his head again, not since that first night he'd come home from the saloon smelling of cigars and whiskey. Looking up at him now, at the strength and conviction on his face, she couldn't imagine anything on this earth that would unnerve him.

"Are you still . . ." she hesitated before continuing. Maybe he didn't want her to know, maybe he liked to keep all his fears locked deep inside. Well, he could always tell her to mind her own business, couldn't he? "Are you still worried about being in over your head?"

He hesitated himself, as if he really would rather not answer. But finally he did, with a softly spoken, "Yes."

"What are you afraid of?"

I'm afraid of losing you. The thought came from nowhere, startling him, making his heart race. Ah, he couldn't say that out loud, could he? Still, at the moment he couldn't imagine riding away from here, leaving Sarah and not so much as looking back.

"I've been thinking about something you said, the other day in the barn," he confessed.

He saw the slight tremor that worked its way through Sarah's body. Maybe she remembered that afternoon as vividly and fondly as he did.

"What's that?" she asked, trying for calm and failing.

"Remember what you said about making your life different? About not blindly accepting the life that falls to you?"

She nodded softly.

"I've spent my entire life moving from one

place to another. As a kid, before my father died, we were never in one town for very long before we moved on, and I've spent all my adult life chasing outlaws. It was like I wasn't meant to settle down. Any time I ended up in one place for a while I'd always get antsy, like inside I knew it was time to move on."

"Are you getting antsy now?" she asked softly, dark eyes wide and waiting.

"No," he whispered. "Isn't that odd?"

She nodded once and dropped her gaze to the ground. "I guess it is."

He took her chin in his hand and lifted her face so she was forced to look him in the eye again. "I don't want to leave you, Sarah. I know I have to, I know I don't belong here . . . but dammit, I don't want to go."

A spark of hope and love lit her eyes; he cherished and despised that spark at the same time. What if he couldn't give Sarah all she needed? All she wanted?

"You don't have to go," she whispered. "You do belong here. I need you. I love you."

He couldn't answer, so he kissed her; long and hard and as if he'd never kissed her before. In the instant their lips met, he knew she was right. He could stay here, with her, for the rest of his life and never be restless. He could make a real home here, his first and only real home. He could love her.

He broke the kiss suddenly, took her hand, and pulled her around the corner and through the open barn doors. Trailing along behind him, she laughed. Ah, it was a wonderful sound, so free and real. He wanted to make her laugh again and again. Most of all, he wanted to ruffle her feathers, here and now.

"Up you go," he said, pushing Sarah before him.

She placed one hand on the rail of the ladder that led to the loft, and looked over her shoulder. "Up there?" she asked incredulously, lifting her eyes briefly to the hay-filled loft above their heads.

"Yes, up there," he said impatiently. "The house is much too crowded at the moment. By God, if we're going to hide from the people in that house, let's hide together and make the best of it."

Her smile was bright and heartwarming, seductive and trusting. "I like the sound of that," she said as she climbed the ladder efficiently. Shapely legs flashed enticingly in his face as he followed close behind.

Sarah sat in a flattened pile of hay, her back resting against a supporting post. "I've never, not in my entire life, hidden in the hay loft."

"Never?" He sat beside her, stretching his legs out, relaxing for the first time in days.

She shook her head. "Never. The stables were for the servants, you know," she said primly, a touch of humor in her voice as she mocked herself and the world she came from. "And I never so much as stepped inside a barn until I came here."

She'd pulled her hair back and up this morning, securing it in a tight bun. Without a single second thought, Joe reached out and removed the pins that held her hair in place. Cinnamon-red strands fell softly, waving across her shoulders and down her back. He speared impatient fingers through the silky strands, cupped the back of Sarah's head and leaned across to kiss her again.

The way she came to him, the way she kissed him back so easily and deeply and without question, grabbed his heart and held on tight. He'd never known a woman like Sarah before, had never even known such a creature existed. She was a fine lady with a tender heart and a selfless spirit. She was full of love and goodness, yet she knew exactly how to touch him to make him want her more than he'd ever wanted any woman. The thought that she was in danger because of him caused him grief, even now.

Morning light shot through cracks in the old barn, marking its path across a hay-strewn floor. Shards of light, sharp and warm, sliced across Sarah's skirt and the plain white blouse she wore. As long as he was here with her, no one would threaten Sarah. No one would harm her.

His finger followed the path of one stream of

light, barely touching the fine linen and soft skin beneath. He flicked open one button and then another at her neck, then leaned into her to lay his mouth against the soft, sweet skin at the base of her throat. She shivered and arched her back slightly so she pressed close against him. Other buttons followed, flicking easily open, falling back to expose lovely freckled skin. He kissed each and every freckle.

Not content to lay back and allow him to kiss her freckles away, Sarah undid his own buttons then slipped her hands beneath his shirt and worked it upward an inch at a time. Her hands on his skin were his undoing.

She lifted the shirt over his head and tossed it aside. God, he'd never seen such a sinful smile on a lady's face.

He laid her blouse open to reveal a lacy chemise and the swell of her breasts. Sunlight shot across her skin, warm and tempting. She trembled when he laid his mouth over her breast and gently sucked a linen-covered nipple into his mouth, pulling Sarah to him and lowering her to the floor.

His body told him to hurry, but his mind whispered to move slowly. He didn't want this moment to end, didn't want to let Sarah go. Not ever. *Slowly*. He didn't want to take her fast and hard, not this time. He wanted to savor every second that passed, every new sensation. Every freckle.

He peeled her blouse off and tossed it over

his shoulder, slipping the chemise down so that he could taste her when he took her into his mouth again, so he could feel her flesh against his tongue.

He loved the feel of her restless hands on him, the way they touched his skin and moved on, the way they caressed and searched and stroked. He loved the way she held him, as if she'd never let go.

When he pushed her skirt to her knees she spread her legs as if she were ready for him, as if she craved the joining to come as much as he did. She wasn't prepared, as she had been on the last time they'd met in the barn. Today she wore drawers beneath her skirt. He was tempted to rip the knee-length monstrosities off, but instead he found the tapes and released them, then slid the undergarment slowly down and off, trailing his fingers across her bare legs with every downward move.

She trembled low and deep, closed her eyes and lay back with complete trust. And love. He'd denied her love before, reasoned it away, but he couldn't do that anymore. She loved him. That knowledge was scary as hell.

His fingers climbed back up her legs, lingering on the sensitive skin behind her knees and then on the soft flesh of her inner thighs. Her eyes closed and head back, she licked her lips and arched slightly toward him. He touched her intimately, stroked her wet, waiting flesh. And when he slipped a finger inside her she moaned and rocked against his hand. She was close, so close, and he wanted to watch her come apart in his hands, wanted to make her scream.

She opened her eyes and reached down to unbuckle his belt. The buttons of his denims followed, one by one, and with every heartbeat that passed he grew harder and more impatient to be inside her. Her thighs spread wider as she wrapped her fingers around his shaft, as she began to torment him as he'd been tormenting her. She stroked until he couldn't stand it any longer.

They came together at last with power and passion and maybe even a sense of relief that the waiting was done. And they came together with love. He knew that now, couldn't escape it no matter how hard he tried.

Sarah wrapped her legs around him and pulled him closer, held on tight and met him stroke for stroke, rocking against him in a slow, potent rhythm. Their bodies connected, hearts pounding, and they relished every long, deep stroke, every tremor of promise.

He felt her begin to crumble, and he quickened his pace, drove deeper and deeper inside her. His wish came true as he watched her come apart beneath him, felt her body convulsing around him, heard her sweet, low cry as she came undone.

Her response pushed him over the edge. He drove deep as the last telling quivers of her release eased, burying himself deep, losing himself inside her. Heart and soul and body, he was giving her everything he had. *Everything*.

Depleted, he let himself move down to cover her body with his. She rested her hand in his hair, stroked softly there.

"I do love you, Stumpy," she whispered. "More than I ever thought possible."

He lifted his head to look down at her, and smiled at the picture she made. Sweat on her face, hay in her hair, a telling blush in her cheeks, she was the most beautiful sight he'd ever seen. It was on his tongue to say the words himself, to whisper *I love you, too, Miss Priss*, when a voice from below interrupted.

"How am *I* to know where miscreant children hide their stolen goods? We've searched the house top to bottom and it's not there." He recognized Hugh Towerson's prissy voice, as the man angrily spoke to himself. "I suppose they might hide such a treasure in the hayloft."

"Damn," Joe whispered as he hurried to right his clothes. "What timing."

"It could've been worse," Sarah said softly, unconcerned as she slowly righted her clothes. "He might've shown up a few minutes ago." She gave him a gentle, loving smile, then began to look around at the clothes they'd strewn about. His shirt and her drawers were not too far afield, but her blouse had gone missing. She began to look beneath small tufts of hay here and there, but the blouse was nowhere to be seen.

"Who's up there?" a prim voice called out. "Come down, you thieving ragamuffins."

Joe pulled on his shirt, and then peered over the edge of the hayloft. "Well, good morning, Hughie." Sarah's blouse had made it all the way over the edge and was presently hanging from a ladder rung about halfway down. "Would you do me a favor and toss up that blouse?"

The man turned red and sputtered, but did as Joe asked, very delicately taking the man-handled feminine garment from the rung and doing his best to toss it upward. It took three tries, but eventually the blouse drifted high enough for Joe to catch it.

"Thanks, partner," he said as he turned to Sarah, handing her the wrinkled blouse.

She appeared to be a little embarrassed, but the smile on her face was heartwarming and satisfied. As she slipped the blouse on and did her best to straighten her mussed hair, hay and all, he was sure he'd never seen such a breath-taking sight.

No guts, no glory.

"I love you," he said, not bothering to lower his voice to a whisper. "I love you, Sarah."

She leapt from her seat on the floor and seized him with all her might, laughed as she feathered kisses across his face.

A voice from below drifted upward. "What in God's name are you two doing up there?"

Joe leaned over so he could see the prim Hugh Towerson looking upward in disapproval. He gave the man a wide, true smile. "Go away, Hughie. We're busy."

Deacon wiped down the last of the tables in Rosie's Café. This wasn't the way he normally spent his days—washing dirty dishes and pouring coffee and cleaning up after other folks—but he kinda liked it. It wasn't the actual washing of the dishes or the waiting tables he enjoyed, but Rosie was always close by and he sure enough liked that just fine.

She smiled a lot these days. Not a practiced, seductive grin like the one he remembered from Silver Creek, but a true, spontaneous smile that touched her eyes. He liked that smile, too.

In the days since he'd started helping her here, Rosie had kissed him a few times, but he still hadn't made it to her bed. He couldn't help but wonder if that damn Joe White had anything to do with her newfound chastity. The very thought of that man made his blood boil, but he didn't let his jealousy show. Rosie wouldn't like it.

She came into the dining room as he finished up, wiping her hands on her apron. "Looks good in here. Thanks, Deacon. You can leave whenever you like. I'm going to be here a while longer this evening. I want to make a few apple pies for the church social tomorrow."

Deacon dropped the cloth he'd washed the tables with to the nearest tabletop. "A church social? *I* don't have to go, do I?"

She flashed one of her new, real smiles his way. "Of course not. Why, I'm sure I can find another gentleman to accompany me, if you'd rather not attend."

Blackmail, pure and simple. "A church social," he said in a low voice. "Dammit, Rosie—"

"I said you don't have to go."

Rosie looked innocent enough, but he knew damn well what she was up to. She knew he would never allow her to go to that picnic with another *gentleman*. "If I take you to church and the social after, and I dress up nice and behave myself," he said softly. "What kind of reward am I gonna get?"

Her smile didn't fade at all. "A slice of the best apple pie you've ever tasted."

"I don't want apple pie," he whispered. "I want you."

Her smile disappeared. "Deacon, I told you—"

"I know, I know," he interrupted. "You're not that kind of girl anymore, you're a lady now. But this isn't just anybody asking, Rosie. It's me. It's not like . . . it's not like it was before."

"I can't," she whispered. "I won't lie with a man again until I take a husband."

Deacon shook his head slowly. "Hell sug-arplum, you don't want a *husband*. You're your own woman, free as a bird. You don't want to tie yourself down by getting *married*."

He must've said something wrong, because she got that haughty "I'm a lady" look in her eye. Her chin came up, and her spine straight-ened. "You're free as a bird yourself, Deacon Moss, so why don't you just . . . just fly away?" With that she spun on her heel and marched, without a hint of a wiggle in her hips, to the kitchen to make her apple pies.

What had he said to make her so mad? Hell, he couldn't do anything right these days.

He blamed Joe White for this. He didn't know how or why, exactly, but it was all White's fault that he was having so much trouble with Rosie.

As he left the café, slamming the door behind him, he wondered how pretty boy Joe White would like a good dose of poison with his apple pie. The thought almost brought a smile to Deacon's face.

Chapter Twenty-three

Joe didn't want to be here; milling about behind the church, making small-talk, staying close to Sarah just in case Butler got any ideas. He'd feel much safer at the farm, even if it meant active warfare with Sarah's folks.

Sarah was certain this outing would be good for them all. A chance to get out of the crowded house appealed to her, as did the welcome opportunity to convince her family and her ex-fiancé that they were a family and could not easily be separated.

He didn't really expect Butler to try anything, not today. The outlaw had come to services with his mother on his arm, the black-clad, sour-looking Mrs. Handy hanging on and occasionally giving a tight smile, shifting and clutching her black lace shawl as if she felt a chill. The two stayed close even now, as the church picnic got underway. Surely the man wouldn't pull his planned kidnapping stunt with his mother on his arm!

The girls had spread to the four winds as soon as the church service was dismissed. Every now and then he caught sight of one or more of them playing, running and laughing. He kept a close eye on Alice, who was deep in conversation with that pip-squeak Quincy Thomas.

Sarah's family stayed close, unfortunately, as if they were afraid they'd get lost in the small crowd of countrified townspeople. Not likely. The three of them stood out like a trio of pearls floating on top of a bowl of beans.

Joe would take a bowl of beans over pearls any day.

Everyone attended the social, even Rosie and some fella who obviously was smitten with her. Joe caught her eye once and nodded. The man who was with her gave him a long, menacing glare in return, before Rosie grabbed his arm and forced him to turn about.

Sarah was so obviously content, so happy. Every now and then she smiled for no reason, staring dreamily off into the distance as if she saw a pretty picture painted for her eyes alone. He liked that smile; he'd put it there.

Still, maybe he'd been hasty in telling Sarah how he felt. Hell, he didn't know what he'd do here, how they'd get by. For the life of him, he couldn't figure out how they'd make this work. He wasn't a farmer and never would be. He dismissed the nagging doubts. First things first. They'd have to be married again, using his real name this time so everything would be nice and legal.

He looked over his shoulder to see the three New Yorkers trailing in his wake. He couldn't quite contain a sneer as his eyes fell on Hughie. If Towerson had any pride at all, he'd back off agreeably and high-tail it back North where he belonged. Hughie's continued pursuit of Sarah rang false, raised the hairs on the back of Joe's neck. Something was wrong here. After yesterday he surely knew that there was no way Sarah would ever go back with him. She was here to stay. And so was he.

"Sarah," Mrs. Prince said, stepping quickly to pull up alongside her daughter. "You should've worn a wider-brimmed hat. You know how easily you freckle."

"I love freckles," Joe said before Sarah could answer. "The more the merrier." He grinned down at the content woman on his arm. "Should I tell her why?" he asked softly.

"I think not," Sarah answered with a wicked smile.

Mrs. Prince flicked open her fan and pretended she hadn't heard. Behind them Towerson snorted beneath his breath. With any luck, by the time this day was over Hughie would be disgusted enough to get his scrawny butt out of Jacob's Crossing for good.

As the day wore on he found himself relaxing. No way would Butler try anything here. With their picnic dinner disposed of, he and Sarah sat on an old quilt beneath a shade tree. Her parents came and went, and Towerson kept a reasonable distance. Once the folks found out he was a lawyer they took turns cornering him and asking all kinds of legal questions. The girls came and went, too, and Joe kept a close eye on Alice and her little friend. Everyone was well-behaved and happy. What more could any man ask for?

He and Sarah weren't often alone, but in one such rare moment he leaned over and kissed her soundly.

She kissed him back, but as soon as he pulled away she admonished him. "Joe! People are looking." If she wasn't smiling so sweetly he might have worried.

"Let 'em look." He kissed her again for good measure.

Their time alone didn't last nearly long enough. Faith and Glory came running to the blanket together, laughing but tired from the long day. They collapsed onto the quilt and spread out. Glory even laid her head on Sarah's lap and closed her eyes.

Well, he'd have to get used to this, wouldn't he? He'd have to make time to be alone with Sarah, find moments here and there when all the kids were asleep or at school or doing their chores. Oddly enough, he found he didn't mind the prospect.

Mrs. Prince decided to rest in the shade herself, for a while, so when Evie and Dory pulled Joe away from the quilt to settle some minor dispute, he went willingly. Sarah was settled on the blanket with Glory in her lap and Faith at her side and her disapproving mother close at hand.

He was gone longer than he'd anticipated. Evie and Dory had gotten into another argument over who owned a particular blue ribbon, and it had somehow ended up out of Evie's hair and up in a tree, out of reach for anyone but Joe. After trying and failing to reason with them, he'd settled the problem by promising to buy them each a new hair ribbon if they'd stop fighting over that one. It was cowardly, and probably not the right thing to do, but they immediately quit arguing.

Mayor Drake had to have a snide word, and Towerson tried to use Joe's passing by as an excuse to dismiss a chatty woman who was pumping him for legal advice. But Joe stopped, clapped Towerson on the back, and told him to take all the time he needed, since they were in no hurry to get home.

The preacher even waylaid Joe to ask how he and the missus were enjoying married life. He assured the man that all was well, and wondered how the preacher would react when they asked for yet another wedding.

He made his way through the crowd, toward the blanket where Sarah waited. He'd just been gone a few minutes, and already he was impatient to see her. At last the crowd parted and he had a clear view of the shade tree. He saw Mrs. Prince, and Faith, and a sleeping Glory. He increased his pace. His heart stopped. Sarah wasn't there.

"Where's Sarah?" he asked as he reached the shade of the tree.

"Good heavens," Mrs. Prince said primly. "She merely stepped away for a moment to have a word with a lady."

He relaxed, but not much. "What lady?"

Faith looked up. "It was Mrs. Handy."

"The schoolteacher Mrs. Handy?"

Faith nodded. "She said she wanted to speak with Sarah. *Privately*," she added with a mock air of great importance.

Joe looked all around, searching the crowd and beyond. He had a terrible, sick feeling in his gut. Sarah had walked off with Mrs. Handy—Tristan Butler's mother. He stepped through the herd of sociable folks, looking for a head of red hair. But Sarah and Mrs. Handy had gone missing.

The more he looked the less he liked it. Not so long ago he'd caught a glimpse of Butler, sipping lemonade like any normal person on a warm afternoon. But at the moment, Butler was nowhere to be seen. Neither was Sheriff Potter.

His attention far beyond the crowd, he ran smack dab into Mayor Drake. The man teetered and then sputtered in indignation.

Joe looked down at the man he disliked so much. "Have you seen Sarah in the last few minutes?"

The mayor shook his head. "No. Have you *lost* her?"

Joe wanted to pound the man, but he restrained himself. "What about Mrs. Handy?"

Drake seemed to finally comprehend the seriousness of the inquiry. His smug smile disappeared. "Lottie Handy?"

Joe felt like the earth was spinning out of control beneath his feet. "Lottie. Is that by chance short for Charlotte?"

"I believe it is."

Lottie Handy pulled Sarah further and further away from the church grounds, into a stand of trees and down a short path. More than once Sarah looked over her shoulder, watching as the picnicking townspeople got smaller and smaller through the trees. She looked for Joe, but didn't see him in the crowd.

Finally she stopped, planting her feet firmly and resisting Mrs. Handy's tug on her arm. "Surely this is far enough," she said breathlessly. "I can't imagine what you have to tell me that requires such secrecy."

The widow turned slowly, annoyance flitting across her face. Without delay, she lifted the black lace shawl that was draped around her shoulders and revealed a familiar diamond brooch pinned to her black bombazine dress. "One of your girls gave this to me," she said in a lowered voice. "At first I thought perhaps it was a piece of costume jewelry that had belonged to their mother, but the more I look at the brooch the more I suspect that isn't the case."

Sarah's heart sank. She'd been so sure that none of the girls would steal! They'd all denied responsibility with such honest faces, such innocent, wide eyes. "Which one?"

Mrs. Handy looked over Sarah's shoulder, toward the church yard and the faraway crowd. "I would prefer to discuss this at my house. We can have privacy there, and take all the time we need to sort this situation out."

"I really should tell Joe," Sarah protested. "He'll wonder where I am."

Mrs. Handy smiled. It was obvious the facial expression did not come easily to her. "My son Tristan should be home by now. I'll send him back to the church to tell your husband that you and I are having a chat about the children's schooling."

"I suppose—"

"My house isn't far. It's just past this bend in

the path." The new schoolteacher managed to conjure up a disapproving expression that did seem to come naturally. "I think you'll agree that this is a serious matter and deserves our immediate attention."

Well, Sarah thought with a sigh of dismay, she'd have to learn to take the good and the bad with the Shorter sisters, wouldn't she? This would likely not be her last unpleasant experience as a parent. "Lead the way."

There was no one in Jacob's Crossing he could trust; not a single person. If the sheriff was in with Tristan Butler and his mother, who else? The mayor? The man who ran the general store? The drunken doctor?

"Up you go," he said impatiently, hoisting Glory into the bed of the wagon. Since Tristan had threatened the girls as well as Sarah, he had to get them out of town.

"Where is Sarah?" Mrs. Prince asked, not for the first time. "Don't tell me she's run away again."

"She hasn't run away," Joe said brusquely.

"Well, then—"

"Let me handle this," he interrupted.

Hugh Towerson and Sarah's father were more annoyed than concerned. They stood a few feet away, whispering disapprovingly to one another and shaking their heads in dismay. Perhaps they were remembering the last time Sarah had run away. When they got a ransom note from Butler they'd be worried, but until then he wasn't going to fill them in on any of the details. There wasn't time.

Joe concentrated on Mrs. Prince and ignored the two men. "I want you to take care of the girls," he said calmly. "Until I come home with Sarah."

"I am not a nursemaid," she said indignantly. "I will not be—"

"You're Sarah's mother," Joe interrupted softly. "There must be some of her goodness, some of her gumption inside you somewhere. She needs it now. These girls need you now."

The woman's face softened, almost imperceptibly. "She's in some kind of serious trouble, isn't she?"

"Yes," Joe whispered.

Mrs. Prince turned on her heel and snapped at her husband. "James, would you kindly assist me into the wagon? And let's get moving. Surely it will take hours to get seven children fed and ready for bed."

Joe watched the full wagon pull away. When he could no longer see the children staring over the back and waving at him, he opened Snowdrop's saddlebag and reached deep inside. Sarah had refused to allow him to wear his weapon to church, but he hadn't been foolish enough to come to town unarmed. He pulled out the holster and six-shooter and strapped them on.

Christ, he might likely be taking on an entire

town, and all he had was one six-shooter and a belt full of bullets.

"Dammit Webb. Where the hell are you?" he muttered beneath his breath.

Footsteps, soft and stealthy, alerted Joe that he was no longer alone. He spun, his hand hovering over the six-shooter. He relaxed when he saw Rosie and her friend approaching.

"Something's wrong," Rosie said without preamble. "I can tell just by looking at your face. Where's Sarah?"

He was looking at the one person in town he could trust; fat lot of good it would do him when things got ugly. "They took her," he said simply. "I'm going to get her back."

"Who took her?" Rosie asked, her whisper sounding as frantic as Joe felt.

Joe shook his head. "Tristan Butler. The sheriff." He looked her in the eye. "Charlie Lockhart."

Rosie didn't react outwardly to the name, but the man standing beside her did. A low whistle made it clear he was familiar with the outlaw's reputation.

"Deacon can help," Rosie said, taking the man's arm and looking up at him in muted adoration. "Can't you, Deacon?"

"Deacon Moss?" Joe asked softly. "The man who tried to have me killed?"

Moss took a single threatening step forward, but Rosie held him back, hanging onto his arm. "Yeah, that's me."

"I think I'll pass on your offer," Joe said, feeling more comfortable with his hand over the butt of his weapon.

Rosie was insistent. "But you need help, and Deacon is real good with a gun. And he's promised not to try to kill you again, haven't you, Deacon?"

"Yep," Moss answered diffidently, as if he'd made the promise with great reluctance.

Joe's pride demanded that he refuse, but thoughts of Sarah made him reconsider. Dammit, he did need help; even if it was this upstart outlaw who gave it. "I don't even know how many we'll be up against."

Deacon shrugged nonchalantly. "I'm willing to give it a try."

Joe nodded once in acceptance.

"One thing, White," Deacon said as he stepped away from Rosie. "I'm not helping you because your wife is in danger. I'm helping because *Rosie's friend* is in trouble, you got that? When this is all over I might just try to kill you again. I'll do it myself this time so there won't be any mistakes."

"Fine," Joe muttered. As the three of them walked toward the hotel and Moss's weapons, Joe wondered what the hell he was getting into.

Not that it mattered. Getting Sarah back safe and sound, that was all he cared about.

"Wait just a minute here," Moss said softly.

Frustrated at the delay, Joe spun on the man. "What? I don't have time to twiddle my thumbs

345

while you ponder any second thoughts you might have."

Moss balled his fists. "I promised Rosie I wouldn't kill you, but I didn't say anything about hurting you."

"Deacon," Rosie hissed, laying a hand on his arm. "There's no time for this."

"Won't take but a minute," he said swinging up one tight fist and taking Joe by surprise with the shot to the jaw.

Joe's head reeled back, but he didn't go down. He did have to take one steadying step back, though.

"That's for her," Moss whispered, meaning Rosie.

Joe didn't hesitate, but quickly returned the favor with a shot to the gut that doubled Moss over. "That's for having me bushwhacked," he said as the man slowly righted himself.

Moss narrowed one eye as Joe stared him down. "Are we done?" Joe asked softly. "Because I don't have any more time for this nonsense. Tristan Butler and Charlie Lockhart have my wife. I'm going to get her back, with or without your help."

"We're done," Moss said, casting a glance to a fidgeting Rosie. "Let's go get her."

Sarah struggled against the ropes at her wrists while Tristan Butler had his back turned. She had been such a trusting fool to simply walk away with Mrs. Handy and right into this trap!

She'd never dreamed that the woman might be lying, that she might have motives other than the best interests of the children.

"Be still," the woman in question snapped as she reentered the small room. Sarah obeyed, settling back in her uncomfortable chair.

Sarah didn't know exactly where she was, but since Butler had dragged her through an alley to a creaking side door, she suspected she was being held in a deserted building right on the main street of Jacob's Crossing. The windows were boarded up, the air was stale and musty, the floor was gritty with dirt.

"It would be in your best interest to release me this instant," she said haughtily. "My husband will be looking for me by now."

Tristan turned to her and smiled. "Oh, I think Joe knows exactly what happened to you, Mrs. Shorter. I must confess, I let him in on our little plan days ago. He didn't like it much, but he knows better than to go against me."

She felt her face drain of blood, and for a moment, a split second, she thought she might faint. The room swam, the chair seemed to tilt slightly. "I don't believe you," she whispered.

"Of course you do," he said confidently. "Hell, Joe came to me looking for work. Said he needed the money. When a man *asks* for work he can't be too choosy."

These were the outlaws Joe had come to Jacob's Crossing looking for, Sarah was sure of it. He'd found them, and he'd come up with a way to trap them; using her as bait. That's what all his trips to the saloon had been about. That's why he was scared.

But not scared enough to *warn* her of the danger, evidently, or to take Butler into custody.

Looking at Tristan Butler, she remembered the first time she'd seen him with his mother. They'd passed on the boardwalk shortly after the judge had made his ruling on the custody of the girls.

And soon after Joe had decided to stay a while longer. Foolishly, she'd thought he'd stayed for her. How wrong she'd been. She was looking at the reason Joe had stayed in Jacob's Crossing this long. An outlaw.

"I suppose you're going to ask my father for money in exchange for my safe return," she said, her voice calm and cool.

"That's the plan," Butler said with a wide smile.

"And will you let me go when you have what you want? I have seen your faces, after all. I know who you are."

Tristan shrugged. "You can't send us to jail without sending your husband right along with us. I don't think you want to do that." He placed his hands on the arm of her chair and leaned so close she could smell his fetid breath. "Who would watch over all those little girls?"

She couldn't dismiss the warning in his voice. That threat to the children, more than her own present circumstances, gave her a deep chill.

"Before we let you go we'll give you a good story to tell your folks and anyone else who asks."

If they knew who Joe really was, that he was a lawman on their trail, she and her *"husband"* were both as good as dead. And then what would happen to the girls? As furious as she was with Joe and his deceptions at the moment, she had no choice but to play along.

She turned her head to escape Butler's piercing glare and heated breath, and saw Mrs. Handy sitting in her own chair, admiring the diamond brooch she now held in her hand.

"You never did tell me," Sarah asked calmly. "How did you get my mother's brooch?" She could almost imagine Tristan Butler sneaking into the house in the middle of the night and making off with the valuable piece.

Lottie Handy smiled and flashed the brooch toward Sarah. The diamonds caught the light of the single lamp that illuminated the small room. "Your always-cooperative husband swiped it for us."

Sarah's heart sank. So, she could add thievery and lying to the list of Joe's transgressions. "That belonged to my grandmother," she said softly.

Mrs. Handy's fingers closed around the brooch, and the look that came over her face was as menacing and chilling as her son's darkest glare. "Now it belongs to me."

349

Chapter Twenty-four

He went to the sheriff's office first; no one was there. The side-by-side cells were deserted, and Sheriff Potter's chair behind his desk was empty. The place was ominously quiet.

Moss had the good sense to trail along silently, as Joe checked Lottie Handy's little house a block off the main street. The place was closed up tight.

Charlotte Handy. Hell, no one had ever even offered the possibility that Charlie Lockhart was a woman. Joe didn't know if Lockhart was a maiden name or an alias. It didn't matter, not now.

No wonder so many lawmen had disappeared looking for Lockhart. If they made it this far they probably went to the sheriff, who would lead them into a trap. Who would suspect that sour old woman of being one of Texas's meanest, deadliest robbers?

The town had cleared out as those who'd attended the social went home and closed their doors. Night was coming. The sky was already gray. Where the hell was Sarah?

As they walked down the boardwalk, their booted footsteps echoing ominously in the quiet dusk, Deacon Moss finally spoke up. "You ever touch Rosie again and I will kill you," he said in a low voice.

Joe unconsciously rubbed his jaw. He had no intention of ever touching Rosie, or any woman other than Sarah, again. Still, he didn't think Moss would believe him if he said so. "You get that proprietary about a woman, you might as well go ahead and marry her," he said as he looked past a dirty window into the deserted general store.

"Marry her?" Moss's voice raised slightly. "I ain't never gonna get married."

If he wasn't so damn scared at the moment, he might have actually smiled. A few weeks ago, hadn't he harbored the same thoughts? No ties for him, by golly, no promises to make and keep. "It's not so bad," Joe said softly. "Hell, you might even like it."

Behind him, Moss snorted.

"Forget it, then," Joe said. "Let Rosie marry somebody else."

Before Moss had a chance to respond, Joe

stepped from the boardwalk and into the deserted street. Not so much as a breath of wind stirred. By God, Sarah was not going to be out there all night. Alone. In the dark. With Tristan Butler and his hellish mother.

He raised his six-shooter in the air and fired once. The sound echoed through the town, reverberating off the empty businesses and the darkening sky.

"Tristan Butler, you sorry son of a bitch!" He shouted at the top of his lungs, circling all the while to keep an eye out for movement, his gun ready, his heart pumping. "Only a lily-livered coward hides out like this. Show your ugly face!" He was answered by complete, deep silence.

"They're not buying it," Moss muttered.

Out of the corner of his eye, Joe saw movement. In response to the same motion, Moss spun around and drew his weapon. Mayor Drake, disturbed by the commotion and carrying a weapon of his own, stepped onto the street. "What the hell are you doing, Shorter?"

Joe waved the idiot back. "Stay out of this, Drake," he ordered softly. "Go find yourself a nice, safe hole to hide in."

Drake backed away.

Once again, the street was deserted. People had to know what was going on, they had to be watching.

Joe fired into the air again. "Goddammit, Butler! Show yourself!"

The man who stepped into the street, a good five buildings down, was not Tristan Butler. No matter. Sheriff Morris Potter would do just fine, for the moment.

"Where is she?" Joe asked as he stalked down the middle of the street.

"Don't make trouble, Shorter," Potter warned. He held his own unholstered six-shooter, ready to do battle if necessary.

"I want my wife," Joe said as he drew near. "Now."

Without warning, the sheriff drew his weapon and positioned himself to fire. As if on automatic, Joe's arm popped up, he aimed and squeezed the trigger. The sheriff's shot went wide. Joe's didn't.

"Behind you!" At the sound of Moss's shout, Joe spun. He was too late. Tristan Butler had crept up to the rear while he'd been engaged with the sheriff. Butler's gun was raised and steady, and Joe found himself smack dab in the man's sights. He held his breath as gunfire split the air again.

Tristan Butler fell, his unfired gun in his hand, and Deacon Moss lowered his smoking weapon. For a split second all was silent again. He still didn't know where Sarah was, or what had become of her.

Before Joe could thank Moss for saving his skin, a screaming Lottie Handy ran into the street, appearing without warning from between two buildings. Joe's heart thudded much too hard and fast. The screaming woman practically dragged a bound Sarah with her. Distraught over her son's shooting, she still had the sense to keep Sarah close and use her as a shield. No one was getting off a clean shot.

Lottie Handy knelt in the dirt beside her son, dragging Sarah down with her so that she was on her knees in the street. One strong hand tightly restrained Sarah, the other picked up Butler's weapon. Sarah set her eyes on Joe, and he felt that gaze to his toes. Dammit, she was scared. She was hurting. And he didn't have a shot.

"You killed him," Lottie said, softly, but loud enough for Joe to hear on the quiet street at the end of this long, long day.

He had to do something. The sight of Sarah in that woman's hands, the knowledge that at any moment the unthinkable could happen . . . "It's over," he said, taking a step toward Lottie Handy—Charlie Lockhart—and Sarah. "Let Sarah go."

The widow came to her feet quickly, Butler's gun steady in her hand. Sarah was yanked to her feet and held before Lottie like a shield. "You killed my baby, my only child." There were no tears for Charlotte Handy; just venom. "You shot him," she said as she raised Butler's weapon. Joe watched in horror as the widow turned the gun on Sarah.

"Hold it!" Deacon Moss leapt between Joe and the advancing Mrs. Handy. He gave the woman a big smile, as if he thought his charm might somehow save this situation. "He didn't shoot your boy. I did. And it was self-defense, you can't blame a man for that. There's no reason to threaten the pretty lady. . . ."

Because Moss stood between Joe and Mrs. Handy, Joe didn't see the gun change direction. It fired, his heart stopped, and Moss went perfectly still for a long moment. He crumpled to the ground.

From somewhere, Joe heard Rosie scream.

"What a fool," Mrs. Handy muttered. As she turned the barrel of the gun toward Sarah again, Mayor Drake stepped quietly from the shadows.

Would this never end? Hell, the mayor was in on the whole thing, too? He should've known. He'd never liked the bastard, not from the first time he'd seen his fat, red face. A crooked sheriff *and* a crooked mayor. What else could an outlaw ask for?

Moss was down, Rosie was crying, and Lottie Handy looked as if she were a split second away from pulling the trigger again.

Drake lifted his rifle as if he knew how to use it, pointing the barrel steadily at Mrs. Handy. From his angle he had a clear shot. "Let her go, Lottie," he demanded.

When Lottie turned her attention to Drake, Joe made his move, leaping past a prone and motionless Deacon Moss to grab the gun from the widow's hand and pull Sarah away. At two against one, and disarmed, Charlotte Handy raised her hands in surrender.

Through her tears, Rosie stared at the blood-stain high on Deacon's chest. He was still breathing, so the bullet must've missed his heart. But the injury was bad. Oh, it was very, very bad.

"Deacon?" she whispered, afraid that even though he was breathing he would never open his eyes again.

Joe bound the hands of the woman who had shot Deacon, and then handed her over to the mayor. Drake, with the help of a few citizens who'd made belated appearances, led her toward the jail.

She forgot them all when Deacon's eyes fluttered open. "Rosie?"

"I'm here," she answered.

"I sure didn't mean to get myself shot, sugarplum, but I couldn't let that awful woman shoot your friend." His voice was weak, but stronger than she'd expected. That strength gave her hope. "I know how much she means to you."

"You'll be okay," she said, not quite believing her own words. "It doesn't look too bad."

He didn't try to look at the wound or feel for it. Instead he took her hand and looked her in the eye. "Marry me, Rosie."

She sniffled, and the tears began to fall in

earnest. "You're only asking because you think you're going to die. That's not fair."

"I'm not gonna die! And even if I was, that's not why I'm asking you to marry me." His voice was too weak and soft, and the hand that held hers trembled.

"Why now?" she whispered.

Impossibly, he smiled. "It just all kinda came together, you know? That bullet hit me, and all I could think about was you. It was like everything stopped, and I was just hanging there with nothing on my mind but your face. Your smile." He stopped talking to take an easy, shallow breath. "And I remembered what that Joe White fella said right before all hell broke loose, about how if I didn't marry you someone else likely would. I didn't like that idea much."

"We can talk about this later," Rosie said, afraid he'd hurt himself if he kept talking.

Deacon shook his head, gently and slowly. "No, I've got to say this now."

Rosie laid a hand in his hair and leaned close. "All right."

"I'm not jealous anymore, not of Joe White or anyone else," he whispered. "None of that matters. I don't care about the past. I don't care that I wasn't your first and only man."

She started to pull away from him, afraid of what he'd say next.

"I just wanna be the *last* man," he whispered as he closed his eyes again. "That's all I want."

Sarah and Joe were headed this way, stepping quickly. Rosie leaned forward and gave Deacon a soft kiss. "Deacon Moss," she whispered. "You're the best."

Tristan Butler was dead, Sheriff Potter and Deacon Moss were both severely injured, and Lottie Handy was locked up in the Jacob's Crossing jail.

Along with the incompetent doctor and Rosie, Sarah saw to the two wounded men in the doctor's less-than-sterile office. She turned her back on Joe when he tried to talk to her, using the two injured men as an excuse. She wasn't ready to talk to him, not yet. Maybe not ever.

He'd used her. Why was she surprised? Hadn't he told her how important his job was? How dangerous the outlaws he chased were? Perhaps he didn't think it at all wrong that he'd used her as cover and then as bait for his trap, that he'd stolen and lied and made her fall in love with him so everyone would think he was truly Joe Shorter.

He wasn't Joe Shorter. There was no Joe Shorter. The man who kept trailing along behind her asking if she was all right was Deputy U.S. Marshal Joe White, and she didn't know him. She didn't know him at all.

When the doctor pronounced the sheriff dead, tears sprang to Sarah's eyes, though not for the sheriff, not for Rosie and for the man she hovered over. They weren't even tears of sorrow, but tears of absolute rage.

When the doctor stepped up to examine Moss, Joe stepped around Sarah and shoved the doctor aside. "You're drunk," he said as he ripped away Moss's shirt and began to poke at the wound himself. "I'll cut this bullet out myself."

Rosie wanted to help but couldn't bear to watch, so she left Deacon's side and came to stand beside Sarah. Exhausted, she draped an arm over Sarah's shoulder. A moment later she was holding on for dear life and sobbing quietly. Sarah, who had rarely been touched before coming to Jacob's Crossing, put her arms around Rosie and let the woman cry on her shoulder.

Joe worked quietly and quickly, once Deacon had passed out. Only once did he lift his eyes to her, to deliver a cutting, questioning glance. Outside it was fully night, now. Black. Dark as pitch. Only the light of a few brightly burning lamps lit the room.

What would she do when Joe left? And she was quite sure, watching him remove the bullet from Deacon Moss's body, that he would leave. She couldn't see him living a quiet life, farming, raising seven children. Loving her. Oh, he might like to come through and visit on occasion, as he'd mentioned once before, but she knew her heart couldn't bear watching him come and go. Wondering when he might knock on her door. Agonizing over how long he'd stay. It would be torture.

He quietly declared Deacon's surgery a success. The bullet was removed, and according to Joe the damage was not as bad as it might've been. Deacon had lost a lot of blood, he warned, and anything could happen . . . but the kid was alive and strong, and the outlook was good. Rosie took up a hopeful post at his side.

Joe washed his hands, but his shirt was stained with Moss's blood. Sarah shivered as he came to her and placed his hands on her face, forcing her to look up at him.

"Are you all right?" he whispered.

Sarah stiffened and tried her best to be cool, distant, precise. "My wrists are chafed," she answered. "And I had a nasty scare. Other than that, I'm quite well, thank you."

He frowned at her. "What the hell is wrong with you? Dammit, I was scared out of my wits."

"Why is that? Did some part of your master plan go awry?" She took his hands in hers and removed them from her face. "All's well that end's well, isn't that what they say in your business? I'd say that as long as Rosie's beau recovers, this fiasco ends quite well."

"I never wanted them to touch you, to drag you into this," he whispered.

Sarah wanted to believe him, but she didn't. She'd been a fool to think he could truly love her.

The door to the doctor's office swung open, and four armed strangers strode into the room. The one in the lead, an older, tough-looking man, spoke up.

"The mayor said I'd find you here," he said, looking at and speaking to Joe. "Looks like we missed all the fun."

Sarah turned her back to Joe and smiled too sweetly at the man. "How do you do?" she said with a smile. "I'm so sorry you missed all the fun, Mr. . . ."

"Marshal Webb," he said, obviously annoyed by the pleasantries.

"Yes," she said. "I've heard all about you. I'm Sarah Sh—Sarah Prince. I've been assisting Deputy White in his duties here, pretending to be his wife so no one would suspect that he was anything other than a lowly farmer. It made perfect sense, for who would suspect a man with a clinging wife and seven children?"

"Sarah . . ." Joe said, a warning in his voice.

"And I did so well at that charade," she said, her voice growing only slightly angry, "that he decided I might do double duty and serve as a *decoy*. It worked quite well, as you can see."

He touched her shoulder and she stepped away so his hand fell. She couldn't bear to turn and look at him. "Since the bad men are dead or behind bars and the world is a safer place tonight, I will assume I'm finished with my duties and can get on with my life."

Marshal Webb looked more confused than anything else. "I thank you, Mrs.—"

"Miss Prince," she corrected.

"Miss Prince," he said, and then he looked over her shoulder to Joe. "Your telegram was cryptic, but I had no idea you'd gone so deeply undercover. Brilliant, White."

Sarah's snort was so soft she doubted anyone would hear her, as she brushed past Webb. The three men behind the U.S. marshal, deputies like Joe she assumed, moved aside to let her pass. She heard Joe curse and call her name, but she didn't slow her step or look back.

Once she was on the safety of the dark boardwalk, she let the tears she hadn't wanted Joe to see fall freely. With every step fresh tears flowed. She had been such an idiot to believe his lies! He'd never intended to stay. He'd never loved her. It had all been part of his plan.

"Sarah!"

She increased her step when she heard Joe call her name, hurrying away from him.

"Dammit, Sarah." He ran now, his big booted feet noisy on the boardwalk behind her.

"I have nothing to say to you," she said when he was close enough to hear her soft words.

"Well, I sure as hell have plenty to say to you," he said, grabbing her arm and spinning her about. "Dammit, do you really think I'd purposely put you in danger?"

"To catch Charlie Lockhart?" she asked.

There were tears in her eyes, she knew, but her voice was calm and clear. "Yes, I do."

He shook his head. *"No."*

She stared up at him, anger chasing her tears away. "Answer one question for me, Stumpy. Why did you stay? When the judge made his ruling, and the girls were safe, why did you stay?"

He hesitated.

"Was it perhaps because you saw Tristan Butler on the street?" she asked crisply. "Was it perhaps because you found yourself smack-dab in the middle of a nest of thieves, and decided it would be prudent to remain Joe Shorter for a while longer?" She lowered her voice, in case there were curious ears nearby. "Did you think it would be smart to have an adoring wife as cover? Make her love you and no one will ever suspect that the marriage isn't real, that you're not precisely who you claim to be." Her lower lip trembled. "Pretend to love her, and no one will ever suspect—"

"No," Joe said, shaking his head slowly. "I never intended—"

"You never intended anything at all, did you?" she whispered. "You certainly never intended to stay here any longer than it took to catch your outlaws."

How could he possibly defend himself? She knew him too well.

"It's what I do," he said softly.

Sarah turned her back on him and walked away.

"Where are you going?" he called as he joined her.

"Home."

"What are you going to do," he snapped. "Walk?"

"I suppose."

He mumbled, probably something horribly obscene, and shoved his hands in his pockets. "Well, hell, I'll give you a ride."

"No, thank you," she said crisply. "I'd prefer to walk."

This time she heard his curse quite clearly, as he reached out, grabbed her, and flung her over his shoulder. "You are not walking home, Miss Priss," he said angrily. "I don't care if I have to hog-tie you, you're riding home with me."

"Unhand me, Stumpy," she said primly.

"I don't think so," he muttered.

Chapter Twenty-five

Once he had Sarah on Snowdrop, she didn't try to escape. She did glance down once, though, as if judging the distance of the fall she'd have to take if she jumped.

Joe wanted to argue with all her rash suppositions. The only problem with that was . . . she was right, in a way. He had used her, and the kids, too. He *had* decided to stay after seeing Butler on the street, falling into the role of husband and father Joe Shorter much too easily. Okay, so he'd liked it. He'd liked it a lot. That didn't mean he was Joe Shorter.

Hell, Joe Shorter didn't exist. He never had.

The hour was late, but Sarah's father waited on the front porch of the Shorter house, pacing as he watched the road. Maybe the man was a jerk, but he obviously loved and cared about Sarah. Of course he did; she was his daughter, his only child. Joe felt like a genuine ass. What had ever made him think he knew better what was right for her?

He dismounted first, and then helped Sarah down. As soon as her feet touched solid ground, she was quick to step away from him and turn to her father.

"Where were you? We were getting worried," Prince said, her father's worry evident despite his demand.

"I'm fine," Sarah said, her voice making it clear she was anything but. She sounded, in fact, an awful lot like the woman he'd first met here; in control, distant, condescending.

Once they were inside the house, they were bombarded with questions by the Princes and Hugh. The girls were in bed, long asleep, he hoped. The questions were fired faster than he and Sarah could answer. After a few minutes of total chaos, Sarah raised her hand to silence the room.

"I think I can settle this quickly," she said. "I'm very tired, and the rest of your questions will have to wait until morning." She looked at him for the first time since they'd left Jacob's Crossing. In that instant, when their eyes met, he knew she wasn't as tough as she appeared to be, as she tried so hard to be. "This is Deputy U.S. Marshal Joe White," she said calmly. "He's been chasing some nefarious characters, and this . . . this ruse was his cover. Now that the outlaws have been captured or killed, I imagine he'll move on."

"Oh, thank God," Katherine Prince said, fanning herself with her hand. "You're not really married to this . . . this . . ." she glared at him. "This deputy U.S. marshal."

"No," Sarah said primly.

James Prince's only response was a wide smile.

Towerson, however, did not smile at all. "I believe I heard one of the girls mention a wedding," he said softly.

"Well, yes," Sarah explained sensibly. "But since Deputy White used the name Shorter rather than his real name, the marriage isn't valid." Towerson remained ominously quiet. "How can it be when there *is* no Joe Shorter!"

"Were you aware of this deception when the wedding took place?" Towerson asked Sarah icily.

"Yes," Sarah said softly.

"Then we can't claim fraud," he said, shooting a sharp glance Joe's way. "And even if we could, the two of you cohabitated after the marriage. You lived together as man and wife."

Well, Joe couldn't argue with that one.

"What are you saying?" Sarah asked calmly.

"I'm saying," Towerson snapped, "that like it or not, you two are legally married."

"We are *not*!" Sarah snapped.

"I don't think so," Joe muttered at the same time.

She spun around and did her best to stare him down. God, the look in her eyes cut to the bone. Poor, prim Sarah was horrified and angry at the prospect of really being his wife. She'd been playing all along, just as he had, all for a damned adventure, knowing all along that their time together would be short and unbinding. She had played at wanting him to stay; she had never really expected or desired the real thing.

"While I would dearly love to blame you for this, too," she asserted, proving his fears correct, "I know it is your greatest wish *not* to be married. As it is mine."

Well, if she was trying to pay him pack by hurting him, she was doing a damned fine job. "You got that right, Miss Priss," he said softly.

"So what do we do now, Stumpy?" she snapped.

"Ask your friend the lawyer," he suggested. "I'm sure he has a plan."

Together, they faced Towerson and waited.

"It won't be simple," Towerson said, his voice calm and professional. "But I believe I can still arrange for a divorce, given the circumstances. You two will have to separate immediately."

"Fine," Sarah whispered.

"Works for me," Joe said beneath his breath.

"As soon as the divorce is finalized—which

might take months, I warn you—then, I will marry Sarah and we'll return to New York."

There followed a moment of dead silence.

Finally, Sarah whispered, "I can't leave the girls."

Towerson gave her a tight smile. "Then we'll take them to New York with us, if it's important to you. They'll receive a much better education there, and when it comes time for them to marry we'll be able to arrange suitable matches for them all."

"They could take dancing and music lessons," Mrs. Prince said, almost energetically.

"That oldest young lady seems to be very intelligent," Mr. Prince said softly. "She needs to be attending a better school than you'll find out here in the middle of nowhere."

Still, Sarah said nothing.

"Alice," Mrs. Prince whispered to her husband. "The oldest girl's name is Alice."

Joe knew they were right. If he had the best interest of the Shorter sisters at heart he'd jump into this conversation and tell them it was a grand idea. Shoot, Alice might even go to college, and he knew Faith and Glory would love dancing lessons. Becky could ride fine horses to her heart's content, and Clara would never have to cook another meal, unless the notion suited her. Dory might become a *real* actress and shock them all, and Evie could sleep in a big feather bed all her own.

But he didn't say a word.

"I don't know. . . ." Sarah whispered.

"It's a perfectly sensible solution," Mr. Prince said soundly, as if it were a done deal.

"There are a lot of things to consider—" Joe began.

"You have nothing to say about this," Towerson interrupted. "You're not even their real father, are you?"

"No, I'm not," Joe snapped. "But that doesn't mean I don't have any say in this."

A low sniffle drew his attention to the parlor doorway. The door to his room, the room he and Sarah had shared for a while, was open, and Faith and Glory stood side by side in their white nightdresses. They stared at him with wide, accusing eyes.

"He said you're not our real father," Glory said softly. "Tell him you *are* our real father. Tell him, Poppy."

Dammit, not like this. He'd known all along he was going to have to tell them the truth sooner or later. Later had always seemed better.

Sarah reacted before he could, going to the girls, kneeling down before them. "You know Joe cares about you very much," she whispered. "He's always wanted only what's best for you."

Glory's lower lip trembled. "But . . . but Clara said . . ." Her soft voice faded away as she lifted her head and stared up at him, confused and reproachful as only a five-year-old beauty can be.

Faith looked up at him, too, with accusing eyes. "You're *not* our father, are you?"

Joe joined Sarah, kneeling before the girls. "I love you as much as if you really were mine. All seven of you. For the rest of my life I'll carry a little piece of each one of you in my heart." He swallowed hard. Damn, this was tough. "Maybe I'm not your real father, but I'll always be your Poppy."

Glory sniffled. "You're leaving, aren't you? Becky was right. I heard her one time whispering that to Alice. She said you wouldn't stay, no matter what."

Joe looked at Sarah, waiting for her to jump in and save him. She comforted the girls and ignored him completely.

"Yes," he said quietly. "I'm going to have to leave."

"He has *important* work to do," Sarah said, and Joe was sure only he could hear the hint of sarcasm in her voice.

Faith looked at Sarah, her eyes wide and scared. "Are you going to leave, too?"

Sarah smiled at the girls, put her arms around them, and gave them a big hug. "I will never leave you," she whispered. "We're a family now, and families stick together."

"How would you girls like to come to New York?" Mrs. Prince asked, her voice falsely cheery.

"No!" Faith and Glory said in unison.

"Off to bed with you," Sarah said, turning the

girls about and giving them a gentle shove toward the bedroom. "We'll discuss all this in the morning."

They took a couple of short steps, then did a quick turnabout and came back to Joe. "Good-bye, Poppy," Glory said as she looked up at him.

"Yeah, 'bye," Faith added.

They both had forlorn expressions on their angelic faces. Tears in their eyes.

As they turned away, Faith looked at her sister and whispered loudly, "I wish *I* was important."

Glory put an arm around her sister, comforting Faith with a hug of her chubby short arm. "Don't cry. Sarah thinks we're important."

When the door was closed, Joe turned to the waiting ambush in the parlor. He was angry—because Sarah hadn't trusted him, because he didn't want to feel guilty. . . . "I think New York sounds like a fine place for the girls." He grinned at Towerson. Funny, but a smile had never *hurt* before. "You have my blessing."

"So I should proceed with the divorce?" Towerson asked, a touch of hope in his voice.

"Yes," Joe and Sarah said at the same time.

The light of dawn lit the room, and still Sarah stared dry-eyed at the ceiling. With Faith sleeping soundly to her left, and Glory deep asleep on her right, she was warm and snug in this bed. And yet she felt so alone, so lost.

How was it possible for her life to change so drastically in one single day? Joe was gone, riding off last night to join Marshal Webb. They were probably already gone from Jacob's Crossing, with their prisoner in tow, and Sarah was quite sure he wasn't mooning over her at the moment. He wouldn't lose a moment's sleep over his deception.

But she'd been so sure she'd seen . . . something in his eyes. Maybe it hadn't been the love she'd wanted, but the affection she'd seen couldn't have been entirely false. Could it have been?

Everything was going to be all right. She didn't know exactly how, yet, but yes . . . everything would be fine.

A soft knock on the door startled her so that her heart skipped a beat. Her first thought was *Joe*, but it was a fanciful idea she quickly dismissed.

As she sat up, the door opened slowly and quietly. Katherine Prince stuck a surprisingly unkempt head through the opening.

"You *are* awake," she whispered. "I thought you might be."

Sarah scooted, gingerly so as not to disturb the girls, to the end of the bed. Something must be very wrong to drag her mother out of her room in her wrapper, her hair undressed. "What is it?"

Sarah watched as her mother very gently closed the door behind her and walked to the window to stare out at the new morning. The view from this window was vast and plain.

There was beauty there, but you had to *look* for it, Sarah had discovered.

"I'm worried about you," her mother whispered as Sarah joined her at the window.

"I'm fine," Sarah began, her voice low as well.

Her mother stopped her with a cutting glance. "You are most certainly not fine," she said. Something in her face softened. "I didn't tell you at the time, of course, but you appeared to be *quite* fine when we arrived. Happy, smiling, a bloom in your cheeks." She smiled softly. "You have grown into a lovely young woman, but I don't believe I've ever seen you quite as attractive as you were when we arrived. Your attire was entirely inappropriate," she added, as if it were required, "and there was hay in your hair, but . . . but you were stunningly beautiful."

"I have never been stunningly beautiful, Mother," Sarah said. "I look too much like Grandmother Prince, remember?" Hadn't she been reminded of that fact often enough in her lifetime?

Katherine Prince smiled again. "Ah, yes, your Grandmother Prince. You have more than her hair and her chin, Sarah. You have her adventuresome spirit. I must admit, I tried to squelch it. I wanted your life to be easy. Quiet." Her smile faded. "Safe. I wanted you to be safe, always. Your grandmother was never satisfied with what society or her husband had to offer. She was always getting herself into trouble.

And the men! You were much too young to remember, but after your grandfather died, your father practically had to beat them off with a stick!"

"I've seen her portrait," Sarah said. "She was not a beautiful woman."

"Some women can't be captured properly on canvas, and your grandmother was one of those women. There was a light in her, a spirit, and when she smiled . . . when she smiled the world lay at her feet."

Sarah almost flinched when her mother placed an arm around her shoulder. "I saw that spirit in you, when we first arrived. But, last night . . ."

"Mother, I really don't want to talk about last night."

Katherine stared out at the land before her, and she did not drop her arm. "Do you want to return to New York with us?"

Sarah stiffened. "Well, it would be a wonderful opportunity for the girls."

"I'm not asking about those girls. I'm asking about you." She sighed, as if this were a difficult conversation. "What do *you* want, Sarah."

Sarah took a deep breath. "I will do whatever is best for the girls. New York will offer wonderful opportunities they could never have here." She lifted her chin, trying to be strong. "It's really quite generous of Hugh to offer to take them on." The very idea of being married to Hugh made her skin crawl, still. He wasn't a bad person, he wasn't a monster . . . but she didn't love him and never would.

She wondered, not for the first time, why Hugh had remained so persistent when he knew about her relationship with Joe.

"Generous?" Katherine asked, her voice less than gentle. "*Generous* is not the word that comes to mind."

Sarah stared at Katherine's profile. At forty-five she was still a stunning woman, but there were a few lines around her eyes, a new wrinkle on her throat. They'd never talked this way before, open and honest, dressed in their nightclothes and watching the sun come up.

For the first time, she felt like she could open her heart to her mother. "I don't think I can do this alone," she whispered. "I don't think I can raise seven little girls all by myself. I thought I could, at first, but . . . it's harder than I ever imagined."

"I don't think you'll have to raise them alone."

"I know Hugh will be a great help to me," Sarah said stoically.

"Hugh is a ninny, and so is your father—on occasion. They think they know everything, that they can manipulate the world to accommodate their wishes."

Sarah shook her head. "I don't understand." She held her breath as her mother faced her and placed two warm hands on her cheeks.

"I haven't always been a good mother to you," she whispered. "I tried, but . . . but you're so different from me, so hard-headed and bright and curious. I wanted you to be like me, to be quiet and demure and easily satisfied. It would've made your life so much . . . simpler. That's another matter. You are who you are, I suppose. Yes, you were often a difficult child, but you've grown into a lovely woman." Her fingers caressed Sarah's cheeks. "I've gotten entirely off the subject. Sarah, your Aunt Mabel left you an inheritance."

"That's very sweet," Sarah muttered.

Katherine shook her head. "No, you don't understand. She left you *everything*. You're rich. Your father and Hugh were afraid that if you knew that, you'd never return to New York and marry. They decided to wait a while to share this bit of news. A long while," she added.

"Everything?" Sarah asked, stunned.

"Everything. If you don't want to return to New York, don't. If you're afraid raising seven children alone will be too difficult, hire an army of governesses." She sighed, deeply. "If you must be like your grandmother Prince and search out adventure, do it in style."

Sarah threw her arms around her mother and held on tight. "Thank you for telling me," she whispered. "This changes everything."

Her mother tried her own hug, gentle and a little awkward.

Oh, no *wonder* Hugh had been so determined to marry her! He wanted her money.

When Sarah backed away, she only had one

other question. "Why did *you* tell me? Last night you seemed as determined as Father and Hugh to get me back to New York."

Katherine pushed back a strand of hair that had fallen into Sarah's face. "I couldn't sleep. I kept seeing you the way you were when we arrived, and then again as you were last night. Last night you looked . . . much as you did the night before your planned wedding to Hugh. The night before you ran away. Scared. Uncertain. Unhappy. I haven't been a particularly good mother," she confessed, "but you are my daughter and I want what's best for you. If you want to come back to New York with us, seven children in tow, then come. I will help you all I can. But if you want to stay here on your own . . . well, you should have all the pertinent information before you make that decision."

"Thank you," Sarah whispered. "I love you, Mother."

"I love you, too. Very much."

A small voice from the bed whispered. "I love you, Sarah. I love you, too, Granny."

Katherine Prince, regal once again, strode to the bed and stared down at Glory. "Did you call me *Granny*?"

Glory answered with a sleepy giggle.

"That's *Grandmother*, young lady, not Granny." She shuddered. "Can you imagine? *Granny*." And then, after only a moment's hesitation, she bent down carefully to give Glory a quick kiss on the cheek.

Chapter Twenty-six

The capture of Lockhart was a feather in any lawman's cap, and Joe was no exception. Charlie Lockhart, alias Charlotte Wylie Butler Lockhart Handy, made him an instant legend. There were already stories about Lockhart's capture, most of them false, hitting the Eastern newspapers. Some of them had almost gotten the story right.

With her only child dead, Lottie had confessed to everything; including shooting her third husband, Sheriff Frank Handy, when he found out who she really was. No wonder so many lawmen had disappeared in the search for Lockhart! They'd probably gone straight to the sheriff, and then, within hours perhaps, they were dead.

Joe should've spent the last month floating on a cloud, but instead he'd felt like something on the bottom of a farmer's shoe. He didn't sleep well, he snapped at the folks who congratulated him on his victory, and everything he ate and drank tasted like . . . something from the bottom of a farmer's shoe.

The only respite had been the two days at Tess's home in Tennessee. He finally allowed himself to see that she truly was happy now. She wasn't sixteen anymore, her dreams had changed, but she was happy. That's all he wanted for her.

She'd named her fourth child Joseph, and everyone called him Joey. The poor kid looked just like his uncle.

Joe pulled the reins and brought Snowdrop to a halt as soon as the Shorter house came into view. This was one of the most foolish things he'd ever done. He was surely wasting his time. Sarah and the girls probably already had gone to New York. Maybe the divorce wasn't yet final, though, since Towerson had said it would take months.

Towerson had made it clear that he was to stay away from Sarah. They couldn't claim desertion if he kept coming around, the lawyer had pointed out as Joe had left the house for the last time.

Too bad, he thought, as he kicked Snowdrop into a trot. Maybe he didn't *want* a goddamn divorce. Maybe, once her head had cleared,

Sarah had decided she didn't want one either. There was only one way to find out.

Sarah was in the kitchen when Dory came running into the house, slamming the door behind her. "Someone's coming!" she screamed.

Sarah was trying to decide if she should slip the derringer into her skirt pocket, just in case, when Dory reached her and grabbed onto her skirt. "On a white horse," she added dramatically. Within a minute all the girls were gathered around, all of them asking questions and some of them jumping up and down.

With great effort, Sarah remained calm. "I'm sure your Poppy doesn't have the only white horse in all of Texas. Clara, you take over here, and the rest of you . . ." Oh, what if it *was* Joe? "Wait here and help her."

"But Sarah. . . ." Faith whined.

"Please," Sarah said softly, and with a smile. All the girls agreed.

He was still a good ways off when she stepped onto the porch, wiping her hands on her apron. When he was so close she could tell it was, indeed, Joe, she reached behind her to untie the apron and take it off. It was stained, after all. Not that she was worried about making a good impression.

She smoothed her hair, which was loose and beyond redemption at the moment, and wiped her sweaty palms on her calico skirt. By the time Joe was close enough so she could see his face, she stood on the steps. Waiting.

Somehow she would have to be strong. Joe could *not* come riding in and out of her life whenever it suited him! She would not pine and cry for a man who did not love her, waste away wondering where he was and what he was doing, as she had for the past month.

She shaded her eyes with her hand as he came closer. "What do you want?" she asked.

It was difficult to read his expression beneath the shadow of that black hat, but she could see very well that his lips hardened. "Well, hello to you, too."

It was not exactly an auspicious start.

Joe dismounted and removed his hat, and Sarah lowered her hand. "Where are your folks?" he asked.

"They've been back in New York for three weeks now."

"You didn't go with them?"

She shook her head. "I decided to stay here." She didn't want him to think she'd been sitting around waiting for his return. "It's best for the girls."

He nodded his head. "I'm glad."

"You are?"

He looked her straight in the eye, and her heart skipped a beat. "I kept thinking about what you said, about feeling like you were living in a box that got smaller and smaller every day. I don't want you to live like that, and I don't want it for the girls, either."

"You remember that?"

"I think I remember every word you ever said," he whispered.

Like *I love you*? Sarah thought with a shudder. Surely he knew he'd just reminded her of every confession she'd ever made, of all those nights they'd whispered in the dark. He was going to try to charm his way back into her life and her bed, and then, when there was important work to be done, he'd disappear. For a month? A year?

"Why are you here?" she asked, lifting her chin and steeling her spine.

"I'm here for you, Miss Priss."

"I don't know what you mean," she said, solid as a rock on the outside, shuddering on the inside.

He smiled, blast him. "You need me, so here I am."

In love with him or not, she was insulted. "I do not *need* you, Stumpy. I know it must pain you greatly to know that there's a person in the world who doesn't *need* you, but I'm afraid it's true."

He glanced up and around. "So you can run this place and raise seven kids all by yourself."

"I won't have to," she said. "It seems my Aunt Mabel left me . . . some money. I'm building a private school in town, and in just a few months the girls and I will move there. I'm selling the farm to Jake Halberg, and he was quite generous, even though I don't need the money."

"A private school," Joe muttered.

"Yes. I've already inquired as to teachers, and in less than a year the Elizabeth Shorter Academy for Girls will be in operation."

His smile faded. "Sounds like an expensive operation."

"My Aunt Mabel left me a lot of money."

Joe shuffled his feet slightly, as if he was suddenly nervous. "And you're going to blow it building a school."

"The town needs to be rebuilt," she said angrily. "This is my home now, and I can help. Rosie and Deacon were married last week, and they're going to buy the hotel and fix it up."

"They're going to buy it? With what?"

"With money I loaned them."

Joe spread his hands wide. His eyebrows shot up. "You loaned money to the man who had me bushwhacked?"

"I loaned money to the man who saved my life," she corrected softly.

Joe shook his head slowly, no longer so confident. "Well, maybe you don't need me to take care of you, but we did live together as man and wife, and if there's a baby on the way—"

"There's no baby," she interrupted. "So you see, you're off the hook. I really don't *need* you. I have enough money for the girls and me to live well the rest of our lives. You didn't leave me with any . . . extra responsibilities." He looked almost angry at that. "You're free, Joe White, free to do whatever you like and go wherever you like. Isn't that what you wanted all along?"

"Maybe," he muttered.

They stared at one another for a long moment. If she turned her back and walked away he'd likely ride off without another word and she'd never seen him again. She faced him bravely.

"So," she said softly, "don't stay because you think I need you. Don't give up your dreams and your important work because you've convinced yourself that I can't get along without you. Don't sacrifice anything for me. If you're going to stay, stay because . . . because. . . ." She took a deep breath. "Because you love me as much as I love you."

Joe grinned as he walked slowly toward her. Her heart skipped a beat when he reached out and grabbed her, and when he kissed her . . . all of a sudden everything was all right again.

"You *do* need me," he insisted when he pulled his mouth from hers. "Who else is going to dance with you in the moonlight, and keep you up all night, and make you laugh? Who else is going to ruffle your feathers, Miss Priss?"

"Only you, Stumpy," she whispered with a smile.

"I love you, Sarah," he whispered. "I wasn't

pretending when I said that, it wasn't a part of any plan. I love you and I need you. Marry me."

"We're already married, remember?" she teased.

He shook his head. "I want to do it again. Right, this time. I want Joe *White* to marry Sarah Prince, and by God I want the whole town to watch their new sheriff take the woman he loves as his wife."

She backed away a little bit. "Their *what*?"

"You're looking at the new sheriff of Jacob's Crossing, darlin'. I told you I was no farmer." He kissed her again, quickly. "But it didn't take me long to figure out that I couldn't live away from you. So . . . I asked about Potter's vacated job and I got it."

"What if I hadn't been here?" Sarah asked, horrified. "What if I'd returned to New York with my parents?"

"You think I couldn't *find* New York if I had to? I hear it's a big place, and I do have a little experience tracking people down."

Sarah smiled and melted against his chest. "You would've come after me?"

"Yep."

"I love you," she whispered against his chest. "And you're right, I need you, too. After you left, I had no one to talk to when I couldn't sleep. No one to kiss until I felt lightheaded. My life is not an adventure without you."

He let her go so quickly her head began to swim, rushing back to Snowdrop and opening a fat saddlebag. "Speaking of adventure," he said. "When we get married, I want you to wear this."

He whipped a long length of something red from the saddlebag, something that caught the sunlight and billowed in the wind. When he turned to face her he held the dress before him. The gown was shockingly red, and much lower cut than anything she owned.

Sarah grinned widely. "I can't possibly wear that in public."

He looked down, studying the gown carefully. "It's a little wrinkled," he said as he stepped forward, "but I'll bet you can iron the wrinkles out in no time."

"But it's—"

"And if you don't want to get married in it, the least you can do is wear it for me," he said as he climbed the steps. "There's going to be a full moon in a couple of days. We can dance right out there," he said, nodding his head toward the barn.

"With no music?" she asked.

He grinned and tossed the gown over his shoulder as he reached out for her once again. "I'll provide the music. There's this bawdy song I want to teach you . . ."

"What are you up to, Joe White?" she whispered. "Are you trying to make all my dreams come true?"

"Each and every one," he said seriously. He glanced over her shoulder, briefly. "I'd love to pick you up right this minute and carry you to the bed or the barn or a soft patch of grass, but there are seven little faces in the window, watching. I guess it'll have to wait." He kissed her, soft and deep and much too fleetingly. "I have a feeling finding time to be alone will be an adventure all its own for the next few years."

"They love you, too," she whispered with a smile.

Without taking his eyes from her face, he lifted his hand and waved the girls outside. They came, laughing and jumping, grappling at Joe's legs and her skirt and the red dress. Seven different voices asked the same question, over and over; soft and loud, hopeful and excited.

"Are you going to stay?"

Joe got down on one knee and took Sarah's hand in his. One by one, he took seven little hands and placed them on top of his own, until there was a pile of waiting hands before her.

"Marry me?" he whispered.

"You already asked."

"You didn't say yes."

A symphony of soft voices urged her to accept.

"Yes," she whispered. "A hundred times, *yes*."

Epilogue

Joe tried to shake off the nervousness as he walked down the aisle with a beautiful bride on his arm. Dammit, this never got any easier.

Who'd have ever thought that the little girl who'd nursed him back to health would defy convention and become a doctor herself? It had meant a long time away from home, years of study and training, but apparently Quincy had cared enough to wait.

"Sure you want to marry that pip-squeak, Doc?" he whispered as they approached the altar.

Alice didn't look at him, but she did smile. "Absolutely, Poppy."

He delivered his daughter to Quincy, squelching his usual paternal glare in deference to the occasion. When he sat beside Sarah, she took his hand in hers and squeezed lightly. There were already tears in her eyes.

He shook his head. His sentimental wife had bawled like a baby when Becky married that horse farmer, and again when Clara had married the new preacher—the man who was performing the ceremony for Alice and Quincy today. Maybe she wouldn't make a spectacle of herself today. After all, Alice was twenty-six years old. It was about time she married and settled down . . . even if she was going to be the first lady doctor in these parts.

He looked over his shoulder to make sure the rest of the brood were behaving themselves. Dory was sitting, much too chummy, with the new headmaster of the boys' school, that damned Englishman. Joe gave him the glare he usually reserved for Quincy, for good measure. Evie wisely sat alone, though he couldn't help notice how she occasionally cast a quick glance across the aisle to where the rest of Quincy's family, including his younger brother Zack, sat.

Faith and Glory quite properly had their eyes on the ceremony that had just begun. Joe smiled. He'd thought he'd be so glad to see them grow up, so relieved. He wasn't. Faith and Glory were still his little girls, though likely not for much longer.

Hank, a typical nine-year-old boy, already was bored with the wedding. He poked seven-year-old Ian in the side, and then played innocent as the redhead turned about. Joe caught his eye and he settled right down. For now. Sarah said Hank was too much like his father . . . and the little rascal already had his eye on Rosie and Deacon's oldest daughter, Millie. He pulled on her pigtails every chance he got.

Sarah and Rosie thought the two kids were adorable. Joe was distressed by the fact that one day, in the far off future, his eldest son might end up married to the daughter of the man who'd had him bushwhacked. What was the world coming to?

Jacob, barely five years old, already had fallen asleep at the end of the pew. His dark head rested easily against the hard, wooden arm.

They were all growing up so fast. He kinda missed having babies around. Who'd have ever thought. . . .

Sarah tugged on his arm. "Pay attention," she whispered. "For goodness' sake, you're as bad as Hank."

He held her hand tightly, and leaned forward to see the tears in her eyes. "Don't cry," he whispered. "Quincy is a good enough kid."

She looked at him like he was crazy. Well, living with a houseful of women and a passel of baby boys would do that to a man.

"I'm not crying because Alice is getting married," she whispered softly. "Quincy is a wonderful man and they love one another very much."

"So stop crying," he ordered softly.

From across the aisle, Quincy's mother delivered a pointed glare of her own.

"I'm not crying because Alice is getting married," Sarah whispered. "I'm crying because Becky is going to have a baby."

Joe felt like someone had kicked him in the gut. That damn horse farmer. . . .

"And so is Clara," Sarah added. Hanging onto his arm tightly.

Joe glared at the preacher.

Sarah held on even tighter. "And so am I."

Joe rotated his head slowly to watch a single tear fall down Sarah's cheek. Another baby? "We were careful. . . ."

"Except that one time when it rained and we got caught in the stables. Remember?"

Remember? Brother, did he.

"I knew you would be angry," she said softly. "We'll talk about it later. Pay attention to the ceremony."

Well, he had told her more than once that he'd be glad when he could have her alone more often. And they had decided together that seven girls and three boys was enough for any family. But like Sarah always said, life was an adventure.

He wiped the tear from her cheek and leaned over to whisper in her ear. "Angry? How could I possibly be angry? I love babies." He moved in closer. "I love you."

Her tears didn't completely dry, but she did smile. God, he adored her smile.

And when the preacher told Quincy to kiss the bride, Sheriff White gave in to an improper impulse, taking Sarah's face in his hands and leaning forward to kiss the woman who would always be *his* bride.

The Seduction of Roxanne

Linda Jones

Roxanne Robinette has decided to marry, and Calvin Newberry—the sheriff's new deputy—has a face to die for. True, he isn't the sheriff: It was Cyrus Bergeron whose nose for justice and lightning-fast draw earned the tin star after he returned from the War Between the States, a conflict that scarred more than just the country. Still, with his quick wit and his smoldering eyes, Cyrus seems an unfair comparison. And it is Calvin who writes the letters she receives, isn't it? Those passion-filled missives leave her aching with desire long into the torrid Texas nights. Whoever penned those notes seduces her as thoroughly as with a kiss, and it is to that man she'll give her heart.

___52357-4 $5.99 US/$6.99 CAN

Dorchester Publishing Co., Inc.
P.O. Box 6640
Wayne, PA 19087-8640

Please add $1.75 for shipping and handling for the first book and $.50 for each book thereafter. NY, NYC, and PA residents, please add appropriate sales tax. No cash, stamps, or C.O.D.s. All orders shipped within 6 weeks via postal service book rate. Canadian orders require $2.00 extra postage and must be paid in U.S. dollars through a U.S. banking facility.

Name_____
Address_____
City_____State_____Zip_____
I have enclosed $_____ in payment for the checked book(s).
Payment <u>must</u> accompany all orders. ❑ Please send a free catalog.
CHECK OUT OUR WEBSITE! www.dorchesterpub.com

Jackie & The Giant

LindaJones

It isn't a castle, but Cloudmont is close: The enormous estate houses everything Jacqueline Beresford needs to quit her life of crime. But climbing up to the window, Jackie gets a shock. The gorgeous giant of an owner is awake—and he is a greater treasure than she ever imagined. It hardly surprises Rory Donovan that the beautiful burglar is not what she claims, but capturing the feisty felon offers an excellent opportunity. He was searching for a governess for his son, and against all logic, he feels Jackie is perfect for the role—and for many others. But he knows that she broke into his home to rob him of his wealth—for what reason did she steal his heart?

___52333-7 $5.99 US/$6.99 CAN

Dorchester Publishing Co., Inc.
P.O. Box 6640
Wayne, PA 19087-8640

Please add $1.75 for shipping and handling for the first book and $.50 for each book thereafter. NY, NYC, and PA residents, please add appropriate sales tax. No cash, stamps, or C.O.D.s. All orders shipped within 6 weeks via postal service book rate. Canadian orders require $2.00 extra postage and must be paid in U.S. dollars through a U.S. banking facility.

Name_____
Address_____
City_____ State_____ Zip_____
I have enclosed $_____ in payment for the checked book(s).
Payment <u>must</u> accompany all orders. ☐ Please send a free catalog.
CHECK OUT OUR WEBSITE! www.dorchesterpub.com

The Indigo Blade

Linda Jones

Penelope Seton has heard the stories of the Indigo Blade, so when an ex-suitor asks her to help betray and capture the infamous rogue, she has to admit that she is intrigued. Her new husband, Maximillian Broderick, is handsome and rich, but the man who once made her blood race has become an apathetic popinjay after the wedding. Still, something lurks behind Max's languid smile, and she swears she sees glimpses of the passionate husband he seemed to be. Soon Penelope is involved in a game that threatens to claim her husband, her head, and her heart. But she finds herself wondering, if her love is to be the prize, who will win it—her husband or the Indigo Blade.

___52303-5 $5.99 US/$6.99 CAN

Cinderfella

Linda Jones

The daughter of a Kansas cattle tycoon, Charmaine Haley is given a royal welcome on her return from Boston: a masquerade. But the spirited beauty is aware of her father's matchmaking schemes, and she feels sure there will be no shoe-ins for her affection. At the dance, Charmaine is swept off her feet by a masked stranger, but suddenly she finds herself in a compromising position that has her father on a manhunt with a shotgun and the only clue the stranger left—one black boot.

___52275-6 $5.99 US/$6.99 CAN

Dorchester Publishing Co., Inc.
P.O. Box 6640
Wayne, PA 19087-8640

Please add $1.75 for shipping and handling for the first book and $.50 for each book thereafter. NY, NYC, and PA residents, please add appropriate sales tax. No cash, stamps, or C.O.D.s. All orders shipped within 6 weeks via postal service book rate. Canadian orders require $2.00 extra postage and must be paid in U.S. dollars through a U.S. banking facility.

Name_____

Address_____

City_____State_____Zip_____

I have enclosed $_____ in payment for the checked book(s).

Payment <u>must</u> accompany all orders. ❑ Please send a free catalog.

CHECK OUT OUR WEBSITE! www.dorchesterpub.com

Linda Jones
On A Wicked Wind

Hurled into the Caribbean and swept back in time, Sabrina Steele finds herself abruptly aroused in the arms of the dashing pirate captain Antonio Rafael de Zamora. There, on his tropical island, Rafael teaches her to crest the waves of passion and sail the seas of ecstasy. But the handsome rogue has a tortured past, and in order to consummate a love that called her through time, the headstrong beauty seeks to uncover the pirate's true buried treasure—his heart.

___52251-9 $5.99 US/$6.99 CAN

Dorchester Publishing Co., Inc.
P.O. Box 6640
Wayne, PA 19087-8640

Please add $1.75 for shipping and handling for the first book and $.50 for each book thereafter. NY, NYC, and PA residents, please add appropriate sales tax. No cash, stamps, or C.O.D.s. All orders shipped within 6 weeks via postal service book rate. Canadian orders require $2.00 extra postage and must be paid in U.S. dollars through a U.S. banking facility.

Name_____
Address_____
City_____State_____Zip_____
I have enclosed $_____ in payment for the checked book(s).
Payment <u>must</u> accompany all orders. ❑ Please send a free catalog.

NO ANGEL'S GRACE

LINDA WINSTEAD

From the moment Dillon feasts his eyes on the raven-haired beauty, Grace Cavanaugh, he knows she is trouble. Sharp-tongued and stubborn, with a flawless complexion and a priceless wardrobe, Grace certainly doesn't belong on a Western ranch. But that's what Dillon calls home, and as long as the lovely orphan is his charge, that's where they'll stay.

But Grace Cavanaugh has learned the hard way that men can't be trusted. Not for all the diamonds and rubies in England will she give herself to any man. But when Dillon walks into her life he changes all the rules. Suddenly the unapproachable ice princess finds herself melting at his simplest touch, and wondering what she'll have to do to convince him that their love is the most precious gem of all.

_4223-1 $5.50 US/$6.50 CAN